Lizard Blue

a novel by Robert Wintner

Twice-Baked Books

Wintner, Robert
Lizard Blue / by Robert Wintner
ISBN: 978-1-7366222-2-3
1. Middle-age men—Fiction. 2. Americans—Europe—Fiction. Midlife crisis—Fiction I. Title Printed in the United States of America

Layout & design by Keith Christie
Cover photo, *Single Male Lizard Seeks STR*, by Robert Wintner

Twice-Baked Books

$9.00
ISBN 978-1-7366222-2-3
50900>

9 781736 622223

Also by Robert Wintner

Fiction:

Whirlaway

Reefdog

A California Closing

Homunculus

The Prophet Pasqual

Hagan's Trial & Other Stories

Memoir:

Brainstorm

1969 and Then Some

The Ice King

Reef Politic in narrative and photo/video:

Dragon Walk

Neptune Speaks

Reef Libre, An In-Depth Look at Cuban Exceptionalism
    & the Last, Best Reefs in the World

Every Fish Tells a Story

Some Fishes I Have Known

Lizard Blue

1

Hattie

Hattie was hungry. "*J'ai faim.*"

"Meat, fish or fowl?"

She ignored me.

"Italian, Mexican, Chinese? Or French?"

She gazed off, on a dramatic exhale. She hated my acid wit and seemed to resent me too, like I'd tricked her into this charade far from home and wouldn't play along.

Day two of our first week in Paris felt like long time passing. Curtains would fall on the second millennium in hardly a decade, and third millennium beckoned as all new, as a future innately different, by nature improved, stronger, smarter and certainly more chic. The delusional matrix in Paris, *La Bastille*, became a gravitational hub for *les plongeurs*. *Plonge* means plug, as in electrical. *Les plongeurs* were plugged in, as in hip, a cut above the cutting edge and at least a cut ahead. Shabby chic and existential elite knew what few people could know—that was the delusion. Days of caffeine and nicotine led mostly to poses struck in clay. Like Gumby disgusted with life, a plongeur could find refuge in Paris, a safe place to think. Hattie's hunger was mental, fitting in.

We began the day wide-eyed and nauseated, because cigarettes and coffee take getting used to those first few days. Ecstasy transcended Hattie's discomfort, with such potential and new tastes untried. She would harvest experience in all forms, like a squirrel on acorns, kind of.

Paris also disappointed. I'd gone back to a place that had disappeared, as they do now, like changing channels. It's the airlines, the cheap fares and hoards of kids having a pull on life, as seen on TV. Besides the world going away, another loss formed up in the difference between her and me. I admired her as ever, and she held up at close range, where some people attempting allure can't hide the truth. Hattie needed no cover. Good teeth, clear skin, big eyes with a fun-time sparkle; she had the spirit and youth. But we'd arrived at our dream destination and our waking dilemma. *Nous sommes ici*, she striving for a vague process, me realizing that a right woman is mythical; she drifts, in and out of range, a continuing approximation requiring tolerance, bitter sweetness and compensation.

She came so close, knowing the world far more than girls did when I was twenty-two. Sure, the girls were willing then too, and free love was the release valve on generations of pent-up demand. Experimental all the time, with strong demand, intimacy could be casual as lunch, often a lovely, leisurely lunch.

Hattie wanted more and less. Her stupid show was a vogue behavior, or so she thought. Was she putting me on? I wondered. Could she mix insight and original ideas with remedial talk and reach an elevated plane? Did she mean to be street smarter, or something? She knew things intuitively, like where to go and what to say or not say. She had an instinct for me, I thought. I moved her mind, and she liked it. And vice versa. It was plain to see. We shared a wonder, pleasantly inebriated on the low-odds reality of our union.

That morning was the beginning of the end. The bubbles churned, and our simmer came to a boil. I stewed uncertainly, old, cynical and resolute. That was the worst of it, her awful skill at showing my age. Feeling old or young: the feeling was hers to bestow. She told me early on, "You really talk neat sometimes." Gee, she noticed but sounded stupid. She said, "God, we could blaze with all those credit cards." I thought her stupid yet again, but then realized what she meant, in a good way, I think.

I took the compliment on talking neat, knowing I would love spending foolishly with Hattie; so beautiful and spritely. I allowed for inexperience, thinking her speech patterns would evolve, and in the meantime, we'd have fun. And we did, and she seemed more circumspect in her choices. I thought it was chemistry and the seasoning I brought to bear. But she was merely myopic; I was overbearing. No man wants to love like a lizard, cold-blooded and quick, but that's what romance looks like in the rearview mirror.

The smoke cleared on her mood when I suggested a trip to the money exchange for more moolah to squander on whatever came our way. We would walk the *Bois de Bologne*, you know, where Henry Miller walked with the hookers. We might swim at *Les Halles Piscine*. She let the mood go and cheered up. Old guys need exercise.

Alas, the park was scrub weeds and stunted trees on a few acres of greenbelt gone brown, riddled with streets now like heartworms in a good dog. Bad breath and exhaust fumes wheezed a hoarse bark and signaled death close at hand. Little French cars infested the has-been park and made it ugly.

The *piscine* was underground, under a sci-fi shopping mall also underground and packed with people. It had no windows. The swimming pool felt stagnant, and reverberated with the nearby subway. Does Paris have earthquakes? The outing felt dirty, and by early evening in another café, the mood thickened again in smoke. I asked why *les plongeurs*—the café elite—looked so disappointed.

"They also feel the hunger," she said, explaining what I apparently couldn't see.

"I hope they feel something," I said. "They look tired. Too much free time, and their adrenal glands must be fried. If they were busier, they might shake the funk."

"You miss the point," she said.

"I love it when you say that."

"Their contribution is their critique on society, and if they had jobs there would be no critique. Don't you see? As long as they exist, something is wrong."

"Ah."

She called them an advance group with time to consider the human condition, time to speculate on human development. "People with jobs don't do that. They don't have time. And they're too tired."

"Caffeine and nicotine never led to development. Maybe some vegetables and exercise…"

The unspoken question congealed: Why are we here together? I felt our bind constrictive. She sounded stupid as ever. And there I was, defending jobs as a concept, when even now the thought of an eight-hour shift gives rise to mild angina.

She said, "Try something new. It's not too late." She lit a smoke, like I was meant to follow. Fine, I lit one, too. She'd picked up a French inhale only two days in. She pulled on it, held the smoke in her mouth and eased it out, into flared nostrils. She relaxed, exhaling through pursed lips, with smoke rings at the end.

That was all. She wanted me to shut up and make smoke rings. If I couldn't do it right, then I should practice until I could, because we'd come a long way to get up next to this hip/chic Bastille scene. It felt fundamental, a challenge to crotchety old me: Adapt or perish for prospects on our continuing companionship. I champed the bit and French-inhaled a few and went to a teeth clench, cowboy-style. She looked unsure; was I cooperating or mocking? I got dizzy and turned pale. She said, "Let's walk." I followed. I always thought it a sign of good health, getting dizzy and sick on French smokes and espresso.

Like most dirty cities, Paris felt better at night.

In the second block we approached an ashen man with gray skin that hung like a cheap suit. His lanky stride stuttering from a life overflowing with wine and smoke, he staggered our way, tipsy tall and off his mark. He stopped, quivering in the chest and stomach, on a cataclysmic verge. I steered us clear, in case he wanted to puke, convulse or drop dead. As a *plongeur* in the antique-clothing vogue, his old but elegant suit was less threadbare than him and matched his blue-gray hue. As he neared, his chest and stomach tremors heaved together on a reverse pump, spittle spewing, jowls to collar, like a volcano at first burp. He stopped, ten paces out, to tilt forward, open and wait like an espresso machine to finish brewing and give up the bitter black stuff. His spigot spewed, a quart or so. This man had gone too far but stood stoic in his endurance and acceptance of what might come next.

I stepped off the curb and crossed the street. Hattie stayed on course. Did she want a closer look? Would she wipe his chin? No. She only avoided reaction, as a good, hip person would do.

Once past the wobble man, I came back across. She looked disappointed. "You're so intolerant," she said. I pumped my stomach and chest and made puke noises. A couple approaching veered off. Why couldn't she be like them? But she walked ahead of my little dance, ignoring my effort to play along, stupid as the next youth.

It was a night for tolerating, with so many derelicts and mutants in need, so much glaring intention. She let me catch up for the next little stretch that had no lights. In deep shadow, identity seekers and lost thinkers reverted to the undead desperadoes they were. Like reef nocturnals, street people cruised for feeding. Garish souls fluttered and scurried, at once alluring and defensive.

Hardly a hot buffet, it felt more feverish and frenzied. Cooled to alley temperature, it failed to arouse a hungry man. She laid a hand on my arm. "I never want to keep you from anything," she said. "I'd feel terrible."

That's what I meant by uncanny instinct. Of course, I'd looked and looked again, just as any tourist sees the sites. "Yeah, thanks," I said, because a low murmur seemed best. She was too smart for a denial, so I saved it for a better time.

"I'm serious." She turned from the waist, stretching her sheer, clingy blouse across her breasts, translucent as a denial. She understood sexual manipulation; rational men default to hormones.

She had big, tough feet like a tomboy and knew her broad shoulders turned on the homos—her word, as if mocking them for what they did.

I assured her that her square chin and high cheeks didn't hurt with the soft boys. "Yes," she said. "They love the combo. It's like feminine lumberjack, or rugged bitch, you know."

"Maybe they think you used to be a guy."

She laughed; such a ridiculous idea. "Maybe they envy me," she said. "I got the power. They don't." She made her point: I could look and want. She could look and have.

"Why are you with me?"

"Don't sell yourself short, Mister. You got some power too. It's one of those things. Don't worry about it. This won't last forever." Maybe I liked her honesty, or loved it, making the moment viable with no hint of an old fart who ought to get lost. I'd worried that she'd want me indefinitely. I suspected she was in love and afraid I'd get bored of the silly pirouette and two-step.

She pranced ahead, turned with a flourish and announced, "I'll be your slave tonight. Anything you want." On again, she swirled in eddies of doubt and wonder.

People stared. She didn't care, or maybe she did. I didn't know about tomorrow. These kids. I figured she wanted me tonight to scratch the itch and loved the uncertainty as well. She knew my weakness, my strength and limitation. Call me a pup; I followed along through Paris until way late. She flitted and flirted, smoked and drank with tireless energy, like my youth passing before my eyes.

11

High Café

Waking just past noon was a dull jolt, a shot to the surface and sudden pain. Too much fun in the vast little village made for a concave chest, a bowling ball where the head used to be, heavy bones, creaky joints, raspy lungs. I breathed short. I reeked of liquor and smoke. This far round the bend, a person should not confuse optimism with delusion. She slumped in the shower, a wet blur, likely in a mood, pissed off at being so young and hung over. I checked my noodle for wear and couldn't be sure. It felt better rested than the rest of me. But why did I care?

We'd hit a funky little North African place like hundreds of funky little North African places or Indian, Indonesian, Egyptian, Albanian or Brazilian places. The global array lives in Paris, each cultural flavor neatly boxed and smoked. Hattie flitted from one to the next, as if sampling would lead to knowing, as if darkest Africa could be just what we came for. We couldn't stay in stuffiest, hottest Africa. I left. She followed, and to the next funk she went, as if with purpose.

I waited outside when lungs cringed, craving oxygen, and scanning the little room showed only people lost in thought or chattering like chipmunks, smoking. I watched her push through the little room that felt like a soiled pillow with no linen, like you get in jail. She came back disappointed, finding no vacancy in that vault of souls. I shrugged, "Bummer." I got the cruel glance as she moved to the next place, a seemingly local smoked box, went in and slid into a booth halfway back. I took the outside seat for better air or a quicker exit or something.

A German fellow sat across, smoking, gazing at his butt, clamping it softly in his teeth, as his lips enwrapped it. Maybe he'd waited for us to see the show, lungs pulling, the little ember glowing. He half smiled, held the thought and exhaled half and inhaled the rest again. Some went up through his nose. He exhaled half and inhaled the balance again and again.

His waxy yellow hair, dull blue eyes and perfectly straight nose seemed secondary to his ashen, ocher skin, his crude, blurry tattoos, his greasy, ragged denims and his girlfriend. She too devoured her cigarette. With tattoos like his, she'd upped the ante with two nose rings in one nostril and a stickpin in the other, making her *haute vogue* among *Deutchlander plongeurs*. Unsettled kids in a revolting phase, they inspired discomfort and disgust, as intended. They'd called me out. I imagined Hattie wanting to chat them up. I imagine the *fraulein* in a February nose blow, snagging woolly *oogies* on her through bolts, frozen in place.

Hattie slipped into café mode. It begins in the brain, the only meaningful organ. Great thought occurs there by spontaneous generation. The obstacle was me, a vacuum with no flies. I felt chronic. I stared.

Staring is judgmental, *une faux pas.*

How could I not stare? The German guy had a tattoo spanning his shoulder and biceps. A line drawing of a woman kneeling with her hands tied behind her and three dots and a dash for eyes, nose and mouth and more lines and dots for breasts with nipples and a small squiggle, like Hitler's mustache, for a pussy. Hattie didn't like the word, pussy, and could hardly be blamed for not knowing it would come into vogue, bye and bye. So the little squiggle got reframed as her vagina, or cooch. Sideways sloppy Joe went up the flagpole later but got shot down. Back in the moment, the guy talked German to his girlfriend and glanced at us, grateful, I think, for the stares.

I turned to Hattie, as if to share thoughts like a thoughtful companion. Too bad about stodgy old me, who had no more insight than, "He has a pussy on his arm. I mean a vagina."

"He has a woman on his arm. You think it's the same thing?"

"A woman is sitting across from us. But she's not tied up, and her twat's not showing."

"That's disgusting."

"Yes. We agree."

"It's a statement," she said.

"What?"

"It's art."

"A tattoo of a woman with a squiggly pussy?"

"You're so judgmental."

"Hmm…. Yes." So we poised again for conflict. Two guys at a near table smoked competitively. Like kids whitewashing a wall, they huffed and puffed in feverish effort to get the job done. Deep, long draughts of life itself filled the room with their view of things. I stared again and asked, "How can anyone feel good about that?"

A light rain fell from the inversion layer outside, so someone closed the door and fixed the latch, and the little box shrank, secure from the torrents of nature. The waiter arrived.

I stood up for a situation report. "I can't stay here." I left quickly and judgmentally, like a man leaving a building on fire, because breathing is required for life. Maybe that's where it ended or reached midway in the ending process. My exit underscored my limitation and left her alone, at a new low of disappointment. Worse yet, she was weak for a strong lead.

She sat, breathing smoke as thick as sludge, looking casual, showing comfort in ultimate pollution and independence. She split too in a minute and double-timed to catch up.

She took my arm. We were on again. She led me to the next bar up, another hole in the wall or rather near the wall, more of a bar running parallel to the sidewalk with a back wall, no door. Traffic wheezed by, three lanes of little cars hurrying to next cafés. She lit a smoke and got a *cafe noir* that looked like blackjack roofing caulk in a demitasse. I had one too. It coated my tongue with bitterness, put my nerves on the rack and made me yen for a smoke to cut the edge. And we settled in to try again, from the top, with feeling.

But the fat frog next to us had something else in mind. He took a break from his butter-and-ham sandwich with a giant ooze of *Bel Paise* on the side. He looked at us on a slow turn and kept turning till he faced the gutter, to which he hocked up the cheese ball from the back of his throat and flipped it nearly to the curb. Dangling hardly any snot on his greasy, smelly shirt, he ordered another carafe of rosé, to cleanse the palate, as it were. I said not one word. None was necessary. Even Hattie got the picture; the guy was that good.

So I ordered a carafe as well. It was tart and cold, and I put my arm around my date. "This is living," I said, but we'd reached the point where anything I said was one more cynical quip. So when she shot me the snake eyes I said, "Really. This is much better. Thanks."

She bought it and snuggled in, to my amazement. She said she wanted to get drunk, really drunk.

III

Inner Meaning

 Yamaoka Tesshu said, "Hear the soundless sound, see the formless form. At a glance, control your opponent and attain victory without contention. This is...inner meaning."

He described a sorting process of the social food chain. I think he identified the phase in which beings stop fighting physically and come to know intuitively who is dominant or submissive, like some species do, to spare themselves the fight and injury.

Tesshu taught passive dominance. His prime weapon: the sword of no sword, by which ultimate victory is bloodless, still and calm. In all his hundred duels he never lost and never killed.

A hundred years after he wrote that passage, when I was eleven, scuffling seemed the way to sort things out. I found Tesshu on Uncle Roland's bookshelf. Uncle Roland was considered strange, but that profile appeals to boys, and he had books about invisible swords, magical power and old samurai.

Hattie, at first glimpse, was far away and long ago, a sudden new reality. She transcended hormonal response, galloping directly to that ache in the chest of man. Desire can annihilate rationale, thereby requiring rebirth for as many lives as necessary to let it go.

Driving one day on Beach Road by the bluff, watching waves, considering their height, the depth beneath them, seeing the inverse relation between hazard and thrill, I looked down at the narrow beach below the bluff just as Hattie pulled her pants off, shimmying, aiming her ass up at passing cars, mindless, maybe. Bent over, she fumbled with her bikini bottom. I followed into the rough, steering up that other sunlit avenue, headed for the shoulder and drop off. I hit the brakes in time but stayed stuck in the tawny haze. She seemed immortal, or was it eternal? She stopped fumbling, stood up and closed the show.

I nodded a friendly hello.

She grabbed a towel and wrapped herself.

My heart pounded. Within calling distance, I wanted to speak, but a breaking wave pinned me to the bottom, where I could only blow bubbles. It wasn't love from the start with Hattie Summer and me. I got fooled at first sight of the Magic Kingdom. She felt serendipitous, a gift of chance. Seeing her again the same day in a health food store affirmed something or other. Sure, it was a small town, but men past the hustling age know that chance meetings twice are synchronous. I stared again, shameful as a pup who pisses on the floor. I wanted to tell her: I am different. But she knew otherwise, so I couldn't.

So I turned away to ask a health food clerk about of basmati. But among the subtleties—shorter cooking time, softer husks, more delicate flavor—I turned back. She waited.

"I have a feeling…" I said and ran off the road again, as she pulled me into the vacuum. I scanned once briefly until her eyes pulled me to safe haven. Women don't mind eye contact so much. Surely she saw my sincerity. Later, she told me it was the opening line, *I have a feeling….*

She said I looked tongue-tied and confused.

I said yes, I was, and I asked if that surprised her.

She said yes, old guys never came onto her before. She offered her hand. "I'm Hattie," she said.

We took two days. I dropped everything. Nothing else mattered. We got some wine and hit the bluff over the beach. We walked the beach. We had drinks in town and watched passing people. She sensed my uncertainty, my excitement and…gratitude. She kept dialogue minimal. I would have told her who I was, where I'd been and for how long and why, because men on the move are often compelled to talk, because silence can belie the thumping truth. They ramble inanely, and so would I, but she shushed me like a spirit guide, "Ssh. Osmosis."

"Is that like Tantric?" I asked.

"Yes. Can you feel it?"

I shifted to a new angle.

"Can you let go?" she asked.

"Not yet."

But then I could. What was only physical made room for something more. We held hands. I walked her home. At her door she looked into my eyes. "I like you."

"Are you free tomorrow?"

"Don't worry about that stuff," she said.

I couldn't have imagined that we would travel to Paris. I couldn't imagine tomorrow, or that we would share another proximity. So I worried all night until rolling around casually just after noon. A note on her door said, *Same place.* I was catching on. I sat down quietly beside her. We didn't speak for an hour, which made the game easy for me, until she said, "That was beautiful."

"Mm," I went along.

"People talk to the point where they can't be together."

"You mean together like this?"

"Yes. They can't be quiet and still touch."

"Did we touch?"

Stupid question. She didn't answer stupid questions. I went along like a pup for a milk bone. In a while she said she had to work at six. I said nothing. I was getting good. She said she'd be off at two. She waitressed.

"Mm…. Late. You'll be tired." We knew I would be tired, or sleeping sound as an old guy.

"Yes." We strolled toward her place. She was fairly impressed that I, adult male of reasonable means, could learn so quickly to shut my mouth and stay calm. I played along and looked safe enough.

And that was how it went; seeking the sweet reward, whatever form it might take. How long would the stifle be required? How much handheld silence and posing in earthly communion would such a reward require?

Forever and all of it, if a man has love in his heart. He must give his all before the sex. That way he has a chance of giving after as well, a chance for love to survive the immersion. If a man wants something so badly it thumps in his chest, he should take time up front to see her faults. In that kindest light, he will forgive her imperfection and iffy syntax, because he wants her. Before the fact is best for establishing love, so later he can recall his easy transcendence of her human frailty with the same zest.

It was easy, and Hattie was good company, with a bit of blissful idiocy in the mix. I only longed for the other so we could relax and get to know each other. Isn't that how it goes? I was clear on the right thing to do, but slowing the action was hard as stopping a stampede on the lone prairie.

I stayed mum and alert and followed her inside where she took off her top casually but not sexually, or at least that was the presentation, as if a woman could be oblivious to a man so moved. Maybe she was well practiced. Big and firm with feminine curvature all over her, she seemed confident and knowing.

She sensed thirst among her window plants and proceeded to give them a little drink, filling her water can and pouring just so. She shimmied from her bottoms, bending over like she did roadside in traffic, like that was random too, and natural and relative to her free spirit. Or maybe she meant this display as a pointed response to the fucked-up constraints ruling our society. I could only speculate but took it on the chin as my legs went weak. Her cat came in and cried, so she was all over him next, until I tried the same line, "Meow!"

She laughed. I'd caught on, which gave rise to more affection in the animal realm and to romance. An intimacy deferred gave way at last. She was twenty-two. A man past forty understands the meaning of the end, and loves all things more. A man who comprehends slowing down can smell more roses and touch the details of daily life. Here was life in grand detail, stretched in time and crashing on the far shore like waves never ending. Afterward was not a small mourning but a lovely awakening, relaxed, revived, and like a rock-concert crowd, wanting for more.

"That's not true," she said. "That's not what happened at all." We were drunk in Paris, in a café at night, telling a sleazy Pierre how we became lovers, because he wanted to know—*How you become loffers...* He wanted to know how her personal essence might just slip itself over his stiff self. "It wasn't romantic like that," she said. "We...we just fucked."

"Zuss like dat?" Pierre was on to something, most likely a conclusive route to the contents of her underpants.

"Okay, okay," I said. "It wasn't like that. I'm a sentimental fool. She didn't offer me her hand. We didn't walk on the beach or spend hours not talking. I made that up, like in *Incident at Owl Creek Bridge*, when the guy blinked and the rope broke and he hit the river that swept him to freedom, except that in the next blink he dangled dead."

"What bridge?" she asked.

"I have read of this book," Pierre said. I liked him better, but not by much.

"Then you get the point, Pierre. I made it up. It was fantasy, you know, for masturbating. You know?"

Pierre was French and sanguine, such as it was, "Ah, oui. Tonight I will myself fuck Mademoiselle just as you did."

Hattie and I joined in a disgusted glance at Pierre, who shrugged and held it while jutting his lower lip. *Tant pis?* What can you do? So I told the story again, to clear the air or maybe for Hattie and me and love. "She made me work. It was true up to the health food store, but when I tried to talk to her, she got defensive, like I'd attacked her."

"You did attack me."

I smiled at Pierre. He understood. "She read me is all. She knows what a man wants."

Pierre showed his teeth, black and yellow. "Yes. She must know by now." It was easy to know Pierre. Would she dislike him for that? Would she remain open-minded to the free French way of things?

"I asked her if she wanted to get a beer or something. That was all. She turned away and told me to have a nice day. She walked over to a guy with a ponytail. He stunk, and she hugged him. She meant to discourage me."

"Yes, but you would drive off the cliff for her."

"That's right. I nearly drove off the cliff, in my foolish distraction."

She drank. Pierre said, "So, you never got to fuck her?"

"No. She wouldn't talk to me. Wouldn't see me."

"But surely you fuck her now!"

"It's a long story, Pierre. We don't fuck as much as we used to because of our disease, you know?" Pierre glommed onto his wine like he did know. "I thought about her day and night. Some women love the goat smell on a man. I couldn't imagine liking it or wearing it. But I was messed up. In love."

She looked up.

"I took a huge dump the next morning and got in the shower. I'm soaping my butthole and wondering if I shouldn't leave some shit in there, you know, for the smell, and go back down to the health food store."

He drank.

"Give it a shot, Pierre. You got a head start."

"That's disgusting," she said. "And mean."

"It's not meant to be mean," I said. "It's true. If you don't think it's true, just say so."

"If you don't want to tell me, it is okay. My name is Étienne, not Pierre."

I finished my wine and asked, "If I don't want to tell you what?"

Hattie turned to Pierre. "Yeah. Tell you what?"

IV

Synchronicity

Letting go was easy, unless I saw her. I saw her every week or so after failing at the health food store. I'd look and nod, but she'd have none of it. I took it as assurance, that when we finally got tight, she wouldn't flirt with other men. But how assuring can body language be, speaking rejection with precise articulation? I got the message. She didn't like me. Maybe I'd failed to like her, to demonstrate peaceful intentions. She needed more dynamic contact, and I think about that now. Back then, I wanted to hop in the saddle and ride; I was only forty-two. And isn't that what the male of the species does?

I could romance her to the horizon, and she would love me in return, once we dispensed with formalities. We could only reach potential by putting a first foot forward. Was I too forward? She'd been around guys who made me look shy. Good riddance, I thought, in my grasp of acceptance and real love, which was love for him who loved me most. She was beneath me, inferior and immature, unseasoned and lacking insight to a worldly man. And she had a boyfriend. Don't they all?

I knew it was nothing, a juvenile pursuit. It would pass as things do with these kids today. The boyfriend was a galoot, a simpleton surfer about her age or younger, who profiled good for repetition and staying power. I saw them around town. He didn't drink and couldn't dance, except for two steps forward and two back.

Muscular and stiff, he was on her like a security blanket. I thought he rang her bell by *force majeure* but had to be a dud on the soft touch, the finesse and flourish. I recognized the slam-bang phase of these, his glory years. A young man counts women in quota, by the year or the month, so laziness won't set in and boredom is avoided. I learned about love by learning what it is not. How can a man know without learning? Or a woman? And illumination follows immersion for a lucky few.

Order and goodness can prevail. I would not facilitate the hostile vibration between us. She was a breaking wave. I had no choice but to stay calm and enjoy the ride as a matter of policy, key to surviving middle age. No policy, however, can preclude a closeout to the bottom for a pounding. You make love where you find it, which is nearly everywhere, because love can't be contained. I let her go over and over again.

I woke nights from dreaming of contact, knowing we'd made it. But it was like bringing money home from a dream. I lay awake, thinking her a bimbo, repeating my mantra of no chemistry, manning the barricades.

She penetrated easily because it didn't matter how moody or remedial she might be, because the chemistry sat in my chest as an ache. I lost weight and couldn't pay attention, which, I have read, can indicate love or pancreatic cancer. I laughed, opting for love; it seemed so much easier.

As an old cowpoke on the lone prairie I felt another ache, which is nature's blessed fatigue that lets a man slow down. If we were to find communion, it must occur, unforced. We would arrive, or we would not. I forgot about her to improve our chances. Yet I woke at night and fell back to sleep near sunrise.

Business was good for me then. I'd bought a small apartment building and the house next to it and cut both into tiny cubicles, like in Hong Kong. I rented my cubicles to surfers and windsurfers and let them camp six to a box, if they wanted. Most came for a week or two, for waves and wind. Income was regular, work easy, life stable. It evolved, and my days became free, until leisure time led to distraction and then preoccupation.

I fended off, but there she was. Plenty of other women came through, young, fit women whose eyes trolled for potential for a day and a night. I could get laid, if I spoke simply, preferably in the monosyllabic. It's not easy to ape the surfers. I thought Hattie was different but didn't know why. I wanted stimulation on a few levels. She seemed like more of the local sameness but with a niggling difference.

I planned a trip to get away, to get refreshed. Reservations and tickets felt like a commitment, a step toward independence and growth. On a clear afternoon I drove along a country road a few miles out. She walked on the shoulder with a heavy bag. Dark clouds overhead rained in the cool breeze. The bag was stuffed with clothing. I pulled up. She looked in. I smiled. She sighed and got in. We rode in silence but questions resounded; *Who are you? Where are you from? What are you and why? Do you have any ideas? Anything to say? What's in the bag? Can I see it again, just once more?*

I wanted her past and future. I was obvious and unconstrained in spite of myself. Tediously tolerant, she offered the same silence. I focused on the road, and we soon cruised in a beautiful spring rain, as oblivious to each other as the moo cows roadside were unaware of hamburger.

I asked Hattie sometime later what she'd felt. She said, "I didn't feel anything. You gave me a ride. I was glad I didn't have to walk it. In the rain, too. Bummers."

Unfolding events were just as simple, unencumbered by introspection. At the edge of town she said, "I'll get out here," which she did, looking back in. "Thanks."

I shrugged, "Sorry." The oblique apology caught her off guard, making her squint at a hazy recollection. Did I hear the ice crack? She smiled and walked away. I let her go again, so she could find me again, theoretically at least.

I saw her two nights later in a bar—two nights after two days of living two steps ahead of thoughts spinning in a shrinking radius. I walked in for a drink. She sat at the bar, crying. I sat beside her, ordered a brandy instead of a beer and played it light, sipping before asking, "Hard day?"

She nodded. We were on, I thought. I finished my drink and ordered another and please, one for my friend. She sipped it and said thanks. We sat. We drank. She said thanks again when I ordered another round. Oh, we were making time, except that every time I thought of something to say, I squelched it; small talk wouldn't get it. In a while she turned to me and said, "You're probably a good guy."

It sounded lukewarm. "I don't know about that," I said. "What are the symptoms?"

"I don't know," she said. "Call it intuition."

"Where are you from?"

"Wisconsin."

"You're a long way from home."

She stared, until a tear rolled. She wiped it away and said, "Sorry." I wanted to hug her and banish her loneliness forever or until tomorrow. But a hug could reveal the awful truth of me. This, we feared. But the drink was taking hold, and once past initial emotion, she relaxed, easing into background, thoughts and opinions, until she looked up and asked,

"Will you take me home?"

Would I? Well, she meant a ride to her place, didn't she? I hoped our love wouldn't be based on convenience in transportation or rebound vengeance. How attractive is anyone who can't stand solitude, not even for a week or a day or an hour? I could be the old guy with the car, good for a mercy fuck. That was not my first choice, but, given other prospects...

We gathered ourselves out of the bar and into the car and headed down the street to the stoplight, when I looked over for direction, and she smiled, little stars twinkling in the remnant tears.

My God raced through my brain and beat my chest. I knew she could see and regretted comprehension of taking her home, to my home. Well, convenience can take many forms. Perhaps we pursued a cure for what ailed us.

I opened a medium fine wine and poured it into wine glasses. She ogled this orgy of sophistication, and at first sip, missing the customary cringe of the jug on the beach, she said, "Oh, boy." I think she'd never tasted wine from a small bottle, one with a cork.

Refreshing as an excellent pinot in cool weather, she assured me of a comfort between us. I laughed, shrugged and topped her off. She opened up and gained momentum. Soon she rambled, until she cried. Then she rambled again, until I had a headache, which was good, I thought, underscoring the fault lines in my incessant drive. Still I drove, plotting to the sweet spot.

I regretted the ease of our indiscretions. She was out for revenge. Few men aspire to service stud, but I rationalized it to break the ice and get us going. Of course this sophistry was backdrop to the drive of man. Honesty is the best policy, and on we drove, slowly, leaving the navigation to her. This prerequisite allowed the vulnerability to resolve. She cried like a child with a skinned knee who needed to tell the whole, sad story. Then we could move on to womanhood.

She'd been abused and rejected that afternoon. And here she was, on the rebound by sundown. Getting me was a function of wanting, however briefly or vengefully. She ruled our world and knew it. The woman I longed for had coupled with the first guy she met in a bar, who happened to be me. But I helped her scratch the itch and deferred judgment for later, once distractions were absolved.

Big Surfer had chosen another beach bunny. "She's got huge tits and a string bikini, I mean, really." BS had transferred his affection shamefully, in public, beginning with a hug, going to a writhe and, oh, God, the smooch. Hattie did not feel open-minded or tolerant of the playful spirit. She felt wronged and foolish. I shook my head and stifled a laugh—at what I'd craved and at myself. She sobbed and rambled. I listened.

I required nothing, even as sympathy included a gentle embrace. I felt her sorrow, yet there between us was my joy. I think she too was sympathetic and sensed the tool of vengeance. Maybe she needed affirmation as a woman, or her daily dose. I cared for her self-esteem, but empathy paled in comparison to the presence between us. Later, I would think she would learn to like me in time, because simple affection takes a while longer.

She relaxed into me. We touched. I moved. She moved back. That was all, soft and sensual, briefly, until she became deliberate, practiced and methodical in short order, shushing the verbal drudgery and me. Who needs it? It surfaces soon enough when the mystique starts to fade. She stepped back, peeled off her shirt, dropped her shorts and shucked her skivvies with her foot. She smiled sweetly as a fairy godmother and pushed me to the bed. "Come on," she said. "Let's get this over with."

"You're using me for sex," I said.

"Yeah, well, I didn't think you'd mind."

"But I do mind." She stopped. "I'll let it go this time, you know, so we can break the ice." She laughed, and there you go, and there I was, man on a stick, meeting the woman of his dreams, until she stopped laughing and burst into tears. It ruined my rhythm and cast a shadow. Happiness is transitory by nature. It comes and goes. Sure, I was on the come, feeling the curvature of the earth as it spun on my axis, knowing this world was flat, and the fall off the far edge would be endless. Yet she displaced concern when she cried, ending my fantasy of recent days and nights. I wanted her back in the moment, with me, so I ventured, "You must not do this very often."

Like magic and poof, tears be gone. She laughed again, raucously now until a dainty grunt made her blush and rise for a shirt from my closet. I loved her; it fit so well. She shagged another bottle from the high end, giggling that she loved this stuff, she really did. We talked and drank slowly.

"I didn't think you liked me," I said.

"I didn't."

"Hm. You do now?"

"I don't know. Too soon to tell. Why don't you give it a chance?"

So I sat like a bump on a log, drinking an exquisite merlot, knowing I could not yet make love with Hattie but could have sex with her if she allowed it. Moody and uncertain again, I became a bump on a log with a log on the bump. I pulled a blanket over.

"Jesus," she said. "You're an animal."

"Is it that bad?" I asked.

"I'll let it go this time," she said, catching on.

V

Getting Acquainted

 Either she tolerated me or was equally driven. I changed her assessment of old guys, and she went along. Her heartbreak over Big Surfer seemed shallow and weak. She could have the pick of the litter, yet she cried over a mangy mutt. Big Surfer was a dolt, a stand-in boy. I didn't share this with Hattie but assured her that she'd suffered no loss. The guy was generic, a nice fellow, maybe, easily replaceable, if that was what she wanted. It was the rejection that hurt, I advised, not the loss. She remained forlorn. Never fear, I counseled; we had the cure.

She said, "You're an asshole. Sometimes."

"How often could it be? We've been together five hours. I'm only realistic, I mean, about the cure. Beyond that, maybe it's time to look beyond that scene."

"You mean I should talk like a smoothie?" She turned on a dime, on me or to me.

"That's better than being an asshole. Sometimes. You judge so quickly. We never shared complete sentences before tonight."

She blushed. "I didn't know you were so, you know."

"No. I don't know. So you do like me?"

She laughed. "See. Like that." Humor brought her around, even a simple display of wit. She assured me that I wasn't invisible to the nubile women at the beach. She and her friends discussed men who cruised the beach. I wasn't exactly the old guy with the rentals on the hill, but I was known for big eyes on a slow drift. That hurt. I didn't think it showed. At my turn to blush, she said, "Your eyes are beautiful."

She soothed self-consciousness with a stroke to vanity. I was discussed but not for social potential. "Look," she said. "You're different than I would have guessed. Okay?"

"You mean if you thought about it at all?"

"I like it with you. It's different."

"You should see my ten-minute version."

"And you're funny. But the girls I know…." She shrugged.

"You mean the young girls."

"Yeah. They don't want to…. I mean, the main thing is your hair." She looked stern but sympathetic, delivering the difficult news.

"You mean they're not attracted to a man who's thin on top?"

She filled my denial with truth. "Man, you're gone on top."

Maybe I was in denial on top, but there she was, fantasy fulfilled. "So why are you attracted? And why tonight?"

She poured more wine. "Don't you think it's a mistake to question stuff like that?"

"Yes. You're right." She censored my weakness and left me dangling with no place to think to. I liked that, I thought.

Maybe she thought I talked too much, that my compulsive mentality was a hurdle to be cleared, and silence would do me good. She led the way into a lull until we could hear the fronds growing in the listless air. Then she led the way in youthful movement, blithely toward zero inhibition, toward what she called natural in the natural world. I loved how she talked sometimes. In the ephemeral yet eternal communion, she stopped and asked, "Do you think I'm too big?"

"Yes," I said. She laughed again; I was such a kick, and she continued with the gift. She didn't mind. Life changed. I'd fantasized a kiss with the woman of my dreams. But she seized the bull by the horn and took him whimpering to the dust. Like a dogie roper going for nine seconds flat, she finished and towered overhead, perky as a teen champ. "There you go," she said.

She shut me up but left me hungry as a third-worlder after whole milk and burgers. I couldn't digest this fare, because I wanted what the other guys on the beach wanted and then some. Spelling it out would have scared us both.

I wanted hot, young sex all the time and a woman like Hattie to share the time. In her promiscuous, naïve, ill-advised and tasteless ways, I saw salvation.

She took me back in a tearing-down process that precedes growth. The fantasy was more than realized and less. I wanted something more, but she held out.

She altered reality like a psychedelic drug. After ignition and lift-off and sub-orbital convulsions threatening delamination on our primary heat shield, I could only hold on. She changed, faded away and came back. From a distance she was perfect in form and movement and the air about her. She had the stimulators that draw men near. Up close, she faltered. Her feet were tough and big as a Samoan's. She could walk to town with no shoes. Her hands matched, strong and masculine and rougher than mine. An angular face with a strong chin and prominent jaw profiled rigidly. Too much sun had left her face coarse and turned her hair white. Yet her flawless skin with no tan lines felt warm and, to me, like an elixir. I took it in. She basked. I loved her for the wrong reason. Yet I loved her spirit and foolishness and sense of discovery too.

She propped her head on a hand. The line from her torso to her hips arced and descended to her thighs and drew me in. Her scent drew me closer. She sensed her power and played it. Oh, those old guys can fool you, with their hunger and appreciation.

Then she told me the basis of her preference for surfers, and why windsurfers where so bogus. I bolstered myself for nature's cruel truth and listened to my perfect mountain, as it crumbled.

"I mean, really, the windsurfers…. I mean…those guys are sooo fucked."

VI

Old Friends

Who can fault a child for being childish? Not that she was a child. She played at the beach at twenty-two, going on twenty-three, for the same reason I drank good wine at forty-two, to experience the best of what was available. Morning, noon or sundown didn't matter; it was the access and the going that counted. The beach was her world. I listened for an hour with no interruption or nodding off because she needed a listener. She found her rhythm and opened up.

"The guy I work for now won't pay me what I want," she said. "He gives me $35 a shift. I tell him I'm worth fifty, and he says go get it. I should. I really should. Do you know what he did? He had me driving all the way to the other side for a banquet setup. That's fifty miles round trip. He gives me five bucks extra for gas. Then he has me drive all the way down there again the next day for cleanup. He gives me another five bucks. So he gets a banquet down here, and I still charge him ten bucks extra for setup and cleanup. He says no, no. I'm not paying you that. He gave me five bucks less. He says he can't pay me more. He doesn't have any money because he's building a house for him and his wife."

"Don't you get tips?"

"From surfers? Right." She stared off.

"Why not work in a better place?"

"I like my job. He has the most beautiful lips, the sexiest lips in the world."

"Who?"

"The guy I work for. Sometimes, when I'm around him, it's very difficult. I'll be in the middle of something, and he'll look at me, and I just can't stand it. Those lips. I imagine them between my legs and can't do anything. And it's all bullshit because it'll never happen. He's married, and they're between his wife's legs. So all I get is fucked over."

"Sounds bitter." She sighed. I did too; how quickly the characters in a dream can change. I reached again for something higher. "What did you feel when I looked at you?" But I knew at the crack of the bat it was a dumb question—a pop fly to center and out.

"Same thing you felt," she said. "You got what you wanted. Let it rest. This guy I'm talking to now about working at his place, he'll probably fuck me over too. I don't know. All these worthless fuckers can't even read one lousy sex manual to know what to do. I can't believe what these guys' mommies didn't tell them. I get so frustrated, trying to guide them. One guy rolls over and says: Oh, do it yourself. Then he falls asleep. But not for long. I do it myself and tell him: Get out."

"Wait a minute. We were talking about your work, and now we're talking about your social life. Right? Or were you intimate with your employers?"

"Not really. Except for once. We were drunk. He ate me till I pulled him off. He fell asleep too…. It was terrible. It didn't count."

"Ah! No good," I commiserated, taking a long pull on the pricey sauce.

"I had this one guy down there like he's sucking eggs, and I'm thinking, oh, God. I don't even care anymore. It feels okay sometimes, and sometimes I like the guys, so it's a favor. But they all think they're great. I knew this one guy, says he likes to let a woman get her pleasure first. He's got a beautiful body and walks around naked all the time, like it's supposed to turn me on. It does. But then it all gets down to him. I've never, ever, ever been fucked right. I might as well charge for it. What else can I get out of it?"

She took a breather. We drank more wine, because it displaced the angst. It covered my wince and helped me keep quiet. *Never, ever, ever been fucked right?* That was three tries in one sentence. I was flattered and flabbergasted; she'd made me confidant and confessor. And I'd had my blowjob. On she rambled, distancing us from images of perfection.

"The worst of all was this guy who practically moved in, a real heavy hand. What a billy goat. You saw him. But I like him. I don't know why. I finally got him to the point where he could get me going a little bit. Then one day we woke up and fucked and I left, but the job was canceled so I came back home and he's jacking off. That's the most perverted thing I've ever been through. Using my hand lotion. God, I let him have it… And then, once he let me know he liked jacking off, it was like that was okay. He'd get cocaine—the guy never had any money, and he'd get cocaine—and he'd hang around the house all day snorting cocaine and jacking off. Five, six times a day! Perverted! I told him

45

to leave, so he swore he'd stop, but I busted him good. I came home, and the laundry was ready for the wash. He'd never done that before. I checked it out. Pecker juice in the dishtowels! Shit!

"I kicked him out that minute. I told him we could stay friends, but I won't fuck him again. I swear I won't, but I don't like bad feelings." She tilted the bottle up and swilled. A while ago I'd counseled personal development, calling her former date a lug. She was the nut.

I finished the bottle, but we didn't need another. I'd died, and this was purgatory—anguish with a young woman and vintage wine. The dream melted. Reality can fool you from a distance. I'd known women to confess unpleasantry, but a sexual cavalcade of disappointment was something new.

I was moved, and so was the romance. The bed beneath us felt like a bus terminal, where her past continued, on schedule, coming and going from all directions.

"What about you?" she asked. "What's on your mind? Where you been all my life? Ha, ha. I love to talk to smart guys."

"My past is different from yours."

"Yeah. You're like all guys. You just like to fuck."

"Yes. I'm easy. A little squish, and I'm a happy man."

"That's so simple. It must be great."

"You were great."

She blushed again. "You make me shy." What a laugh.

"Work is different for me," I said. "It feels urgent and important at the time. But every money hustle either falls apart or I make a few bucks, and they seem forgettable as the rest."

"I know how you feel." She snuggled up as if to a wise old teddy bear. "Tell me what you were doing twenty years ago; no, twenty-two years ago, when I was born." How quaint. I appealed to her sense of history.

"I was in college. It was Viet Nam time. I would have quit otherwise. It was smoking joints and plowing fields, mostly."

"Plowing fields?"

"Sex with coeds. It was fun. Everyone was stoned or tripping. Free sex wasn't new, but it was freer than ever. It was an act of rebellion. We questioned everything and threw most of it out. It was great for the guys. All we had to do was be there, and the girls would do us up."

"Yeah, we still do that." She laughed a far away laugh. "It's great for us too. Gee, you could have plowed my field if I was around then."

"I just plowed your field. Didn't I?"

"That was different."

"How was it different? I'm trying to see you on equal footing, but it's not easy. You sound like you've had more sex than I have. And I have twenty years on you."

She thought it over. "Equal footing. I love that. The guys I know talk about goofy footing."

"I got twenty years on you."

"I did some guys, but most of them only once or twice. You were married. You fuck every day when you're married. I go sometimes a week, sometimes three weeks without."

"You go longer than that when you're married, especially when it's winding down. Besides, you don't know I was married."

"Yes, I do. I can tell."

"No, you can't. All you can tell is that I speak in sentences. And I wash my clothes before I dry them."

"You're not crazy. So you were married."

"Oh?"

"Guys I hang around with got nothing to lose. They drop into fifteen footers and stuff. You're not like that. That's all I meant. Maybe you weren't married. But you should have been."

"I think you're a fifteen footer. And you hang around a big crowd of guys. That's all I meant."

She shrugged. "I try them out. Besides, I'm old for my age. Don't you think so?"

Old for her age or showing higher mileage than average? I didn't ask.

We lay back. We slept.

She stirred in the night, snuggling in. I moved with the movement. "Boy," she whispered. "We came a long way in a short time."

VII

Letting Go

 A media-culture man often trades his sensible sedan for an expensive roadster. I did that. I went faster, like time. But something loomed ahead with troublesome certainty. I could face it, or not.

Brahmin men leave family and home and go on the road with a beggar's bowl. The road becomes home, a place of faith, in which to meet the world, to give and receive. What good is life, if it can't follow a poetic notion from time to time?

Clarity is a gift. Signs said the time is now. Bare-assed Hattie bending over, showing the way to Kingdom Come, could lead any man astray. She was the Promised Land, the End of the Rainbow. Yet her steady denial of my foolish notions was a clear memo from the Scheme of Things. *You are not here,* it said.

So I planned a trip.

I bought a globe with a light inside and spun it slowly in the dark, scanning the world for where to go to become nobody. I passed over Paris and came back to it, recalling a man in the Metro with no legs, whose horn fugue played down the years. I would find him again, I thought, because I longed for what I'd missed since then. I regretted what I'd missed, drunk in the Metro and late again, so I'd hurried past with the hurrying minions.

A street bum with no legs on a filthy rug with a beat up saxophone and a death squint in florescent light seemed an unlikely backdrop for the lovely sound he made. But pure music is clean and concise and beyond market value. I stopped again and again over the years to watch this still life with sound track in truth and beauty. Set in a godless world, it revealed God in the beggar's fingers. As I wondered what happened to him, I fancied a return to a moment, a buzz, an oblivious crowd, a tiled tunnel harshly lit, some magical notes and me.

With enough kneading, a memory rises, as if an event is a place you can go back to. I thought it real and available to a man of mobility in middle age.

I set a date and called it a deadline. All before the line was past, even before the line was crossed. Daily life became relaxed as a dream. This was good. Unlike many deceased people, I had time to settle my affairs. I didn't plan to die but to go away for a rebirth in a world of wonder. But something happened before the line, a gift of sorts that couldn't be denied. I took it as a blessing, the kind that comes to those who can let go at last. She came to me. The line got moved.

She was a novelty, an entertainment, a great adventure and a dream come true. She was warm, instinctive, instructive and fresh. She became a habit and, in a short while, an addiction. She was game for anything, anytime, anywhere. And though she never came on to my money, she loved the special kind of fun money can buy. She tired quickly of fancy restaurants and seemed relieved to get that out of her system. Indifference carried over to good hotels too, except for room service. She said they must have room service in Heaven. She invited bellhops to stay for a drink and tipped them thirty-percent, or a hundred if they had something to say. I allowed everything, and so did she. I told her I wasn't rich. She assured me I had more than enough.

She asked if I thought her greedy. No, I said, only hungry, and besides, immersion often precedes resolution. "God," she said. "I love the way you talk." I loved her certain attributes as well, and we moved ahead with further immersion.

Sexual relations were exquisite and moreover enhanced by early recollection. A man past forty may see beauty more easily. I saw Hattie naked and saw the innocence of no clothing. She retained that with which she came into the world. I enjoyed hanging out with her, naked. I asked if casual nakedness would lead to casual love. She took me to the mat, saying she surely hoped so, taking care to keep things fresh and adventurous.

I recalled her beach scene during intimacy, when the little piston would chug up the mountain of love. Her look of defiance way back then had told the score; she knew about one more hustle. Yet here we were, her eyes sparkling in the thrill of upset victory, hers and mine.

She liked the change of pace, I thought, until she told me about women faking orgasm. She thought most women did, for acceptance, to get things done with, or something. She became oppressive with lines like, "I fucked some worthless assholes over the years. Maybe I'm getting old."

"That kind of talk is getting old," I said.

"What kind?"

"You like it when I share insight."

She nodded.

"I like that you like it."

She nodded again. "It's not just your language. It's the imagery. We may not go anywhere, you and me, but for the time being, let's behave as if it's only you and me. I'm very fond of you."

I thought she understood, but she laughed. "Imagery. Very fond of you. What do you want me to do, lie?"

She made me want to be alone. Who knew where such strange communion could lead? Maybe it was the best contact we could manage between generations; at least it was continual. I think she liked it. I wanted a reset. Like players of different technique, we volleyed. We brought each other up or down to the way of the other. We forced each other let see what was rubbish in the other.

We had fun in spite of us. Cruising along Beach Road one day without speaking, I had a feeling. "Hattie?"

She waited.

"If you had a sexual fantasy, would you share it with me?"

She blushed. Was she putting me on? "Maybe."

"Can I share one with you?"

"Maybe."

I unzipped and wiggled my pants to my knees, which can kill you behind the wheel, if you need to clutch or brake in a hurry. My other self bonged the steering wheel, fantasy revealed. "It might be fun, you know. Beach road, you know, where we first met."

She shrugged, "Easy," and she rendered my fantasy mundane. Near the apex, eyes on the road, I asked her to tell her new boyfriend about this, if we ever broke up. She stopped and sat up. "Break up? Are we going together?"

"You're right. Sorry. We're not." I watched the road and moved in that way men move to urge resumption.

She got her far away look and said, "God. My old boyfriend, what he made me do. He was so weird." She made her point. She watched me fidget. "Boy. You really look funny. I wish we had the camera. That would be great, wouldn't it?" She rummaged the glove box.

"It's not in there," I said.

"Sure it is. I know it is. That's your problem. No faith."

"Hattie. Do you mind?"

"Oh! That! Sure." She helped me down the road, icing me on a fantasy delivered, helping me leave the old school behind.

I sought to return the favor and told her, "I'm leaving."

She watched me, turning away to look out the window. "Forever?"

"For awhile."

She turned back. "Why?"

"It's a personal trip. A trip I have to take."

"If it's personal, then you can tell me."

"It's… I have to get away."

"Away from me? You don't need to leave."

"Not away from you." She waited, verging on tears. That surprised me. "I have to go to Paris."

She lit up, bright-eyed and happy again. "Take me!" It was another view I would save, one of sublime happiness for the cafés, hotels, room service and Paris we could experience together.

And it was more. "*C'est plus beaucoup*," she said. She'd lived in France for two years, seventeen to nineteen. She'd had her heart crushed in France by the most beautiful Arab boy you could possibly imagine, who for some reason after one fuck couldn't get it up ever again. She never knew why, but she had to go back, just had to.

"You mean to try again?"

"Oh, you. No. It's just a time and place that mean so much, and you know you can't have that back, but going back seems, oh, you know."

I knew. She was old as me and in some ways as needy. And she was fluent. She said she dreamed of the place. "Oh, please!"

VIII

A Fork in the Road

She had her way with me. It was mostly sexual power, and she knew it. But it was magic too, with a dash of intrigue, a homecoming to the long lost.

I had a different power: money. I was security, no more toil, death to tedium, gone the bullshit jobs, vanished the bullshit people who ran them. I was creature comfort. She was naturally attracted. Old guys with dough have that advantage.

Yet our two wills had the interface of oil and water, or sex and money. We loved each other for what we had to give. We gave, each to the other, and enjoyed the giving, to a point.

Planning the trip was a first test. I thought carry-on bags would be best. This trip was no lark but also a quest, a pilgrimage, a test in spirit, free of gravity, weightless. I would hitchhike to the airport one morning and go, peacefully, without notice or pain, as a happy man should go.

She saw it differently. She studied maps, recalled adventures and planned itineraries and places we had to see, until my pilgrimage became a vacation adventure, not what the doctor ordered. Cutting lead-time to a month and cutting two weeks off that and a few more days off that. We leave in five days. That cured the problem, kind of. The problem lingered, like storm clouds on the horizon.

They darkened with luggage. Youthful and free-spirited, she got down to bare bones. The duffel bag bulging with essentials tipped in at seventy pounds. Her overnight case went another thirty. The thought of paring down saddened her—she needed shoes for all terrain, dresses, pants and accessories for every occasion and mood. "I got to admit though, it's good, hanging out with someone who knows how important this is to a woman." She had me, and I felt better when she called herself a woman. I carried the overnight case until it wouldn't fit in the little rack at security. Baggage check was a half-mile back. Baggage claim would take another hour on arrival.

We didn't discuss it; so potent was the airport mood, with stifling air and sweltering heat, ass to elbows. I felt the sheer poundage imposing on my life. She felt my resentment imposing on her dream vacation. "Put your mind somewhere else," she said.

"I love it when you talk like that," I said.

"Look, I'll give you a blowjob in the bathroom, okay?"

She wasn't kidding, so nobody laughed. She set us up for the hard truth. I agreed to some risky fun, to get the trip rolling. "You're on."

She said nothing but slid into the cattle-car crush of the friendly skies, fell asleep for three hours and woke up in pain, announcing to sixty passengers in a ten-foot radius. "Shit. Great time for a period. Excuse me." They say you don't know a person until you travel together. She slid heavily past me and asked, "Are you coming?"

Arrival was equally difficult. Jet lag and baggage claim were compounded by culture shock, trail fatigue and a taxi line at Orly four blocks long. The French crowd pushed and shoved like grocery hoarders before a storm. I put my mind elsewhere. We'd be in our hotel soon, and soon after that would come wine and espresso and all that. Hattie surrounded us with elbowroom, inserting herself in the crush. Swinging widely she announced, "Jesus Christ! Back the fuck off!" Even the French understood. Again, she wasn't kidding.

The hotel was small and cramped, eked out in centimeters, its essence striving for parsimony. We called it Bleak House and shared a bleak chuckle. It offered shelter and nothing but, its single window overlooking a noisy, hot street that wafted black spume up and in. Car exhaust in Paris is the rich, visible kind, with lead, because the French want to go fast and cheap as the meager franc can take them, damn the consequence. It felt like a city of lust and survival through a continuing process of decay, a city far gone from what Parisians call *Le Grandeur.*

We slept all day. I went for French groceries, baguettes, cheese, nectarines and horsemeat. I thought it was cold cuts. She said it was cold cuts. I said it used to whinny, not moo. She said we were on the road. Make do. We drank a bottle of red wine and two bottles of water and slept all night.

Dawn was foreign as a splinter. But primed on a coffee jag, the spirit returned, or at least a strong pulse resumed. That much raw caffeine calls for movement, so we moved through another day or two with no direction. Random routes felt good, but the pace felt forced. Sexual contact was her initiative, more as a palliative, I think, than a passion. Sure, it was her period. She was making nice, or making do again. I went along like a good fellow, like doing the dishes or walking the dog.

We waited like anxious family for word that the patient would survive. We waited with more coffee and more wine and some smokes, trying to arrive.

The café sitters sit, and we sit too. With the sitters in one café or another, we think: I am. Ain't I? I think I am. I think I'm stuck on this carousel for the wax museum.

At least that's what I thought. She reached for the swing of things, the delusion of that little burg by the Seine that this was the enviable place to be. What was the cure for tedium? Easy yet again: drift to another café for another entry, another cool pose, another pretense that nobody was checking us out.

We sat in rickety chairs, elbows on rickety tables, smoking the tits off cigarettes that tasted like charcoal, drinking black jack coffee at three bucks a gulp and gazing off, our brains on overdrive toward real meaning.

I have sat, have emptied the vessel and joined its inner space for hours. I have felt life ease away and come back, just like true love is supposed to do. I've traveled the path of no path, of no thought nor response, no baggage nor burden of material life. I've shed things to the point of nothing and honed it finer still, until it vanished. I've shed again and obtained again, making time to nowhere. Who knows where the road goes from there? I spin with the planets, hugely, slowly, floating free.

But this café stuff with the caffeine and nicotine and preponderance of pondering, this sub-orbital debris with eyes blazing on the verge of… insight and…conclusion…. Well, it ain't the same.

I tried but couldn't get it. I stopped trying and couldn't get it. I wanted to get it in order to please her and have the fun she'd anticipated. So I tried again and failed again and didn't know why, but then of course

I did.

It wasn't working. She didn't ask what was wrong or what I might want to do. I was grateful for that. Virtuously patient, she waited for the gap between us to stop growing. In the meantime, she got down to the work at hand with things to do and sights to see. I went along, in my way. She got tickets for a show, Ray Charles, which was a great gesture, considering her paltry funds. I was glad I went and knew I wouldn't have gone on my own.

We had wine and light fare and took the Metro to the concert hall. We had good seats but alas, one seat over was a thinker, high café. We'd seen this guy on the Bastille circuit, two p.m. to closing, sitting, thinking. Six days a week, sometimes fourteen hours a day with time off for a concert, he would sit and think, rolling his eyes, arching his beady brow, nodding, shaking, working things out, lighting now and then on a frail twig of resolution then flitting off again in cerebral gyration. He looked viably homeless but must have had a trust fund.

He'd shaved his head for the concert and pierced a dozen earrings on both sides. He wore a puffy silk blouse with no collar, buttoned to the neck in a fashion statement, something on hip asceticism. He looked like Zippy the pinhead, but I didn't say it. A beautifully painted woman with remarkable breasts remarkably revealed sat beside him and flowed over him, stroking his pinhead, his chest and thighs.

Ray Charles came on much older than he looked on his album covers. He opened with a few standards, to which Zippy hunched with intensity and rocked and soon hyperventilated with the rhythm and soon after that gasped and flopped like a soul possessed. I couldn't take it but watched him with morbid curiosity more than I watched Ray Charles. I think that's what he wanted. I didn't want it, but he left me no choice.

I scoped some empty seats a few rows back and said I wanted to move. Hattie didn't respond but aped Zippy's intensity. I moved. She came around a few songs later.

"Isn't he something?" she asked.

"Yes, he is."

Later that night was romantic as an empty cup and a full ashtray. At least I had my poke to look forward to, just like I looked forward to cool sheets and a nice snooze. A jaded man tends to group pleasure centers. Or any man. But he's often wrong again. Why would a girl want to have sex with an angry man? She doused the light and lay back. "We can't have sex," she said. "I love you too much. Something's wrong."

She had balls, cutting off her meal ticket like that. I breathed, as if to speak, to ask the embarrassingly needful questions, like *For how long must we wait?* But it was only the philistine in me, squelched in time. I exhaled with no words in a great long sigh like a café sitter considering life. Maybe she liked that. I said, "All right." She rolled away and soon softly snored. Women can do that.

She woke early, refreshed and resolute. She made a phone call and talked twenty minutes, laughing in recollection. She hung up and sighed; we would part company, she said, so we could air out, give ourselves some space and breathing room, to see if that would help, maybe, for a few days.

IX

Deadline

 They say you know a language once you dream in it. It's not true. I dreamt in French the next night and didn't understand. A few syllables lit up: *jamais, comprend pas* and so on. But the context was lost. I woke up cold, muddled in imagery and meaning, reaching in the fog. Clarity had come and gone, like happiness does from time to time. But then again my wants and suppositions were analytical, intellectual, introspective and rational—factors common to the high café, where I sat, where my path that day led and ended.

It was only a day but felt long ago that she left. We'll meet up again soon, we agreed.

"But here's your ticket, in case…," I said.

"Yes. My ticket," she said.

I think the foggy French dreams came from confusion in the midst of so much French chatter, from the strange place I slept in to this sad café in the morning, with strong black coffee and a harsh smoke.

The place was dark and old, dirty beyond funk, way into crummy, long used up. Ambient vibration was that of a junkyard too long sifted by gleaners, losers and thinkers. Nothing remained but the absolutely unusable, the grossly inapplicable, the pure trash and dregs. These scraps were so far gone the rats looked bored. Decomposition felt palpable.

The place had been new in a former lifetime but suffered a thick layer of grit and smoke. From the ashes, new life can arise, but not here. Here, ash prevailed, and the souls burrowed in to sift again for something organic. With imagination long gone, they fed on each other. I think they liked it. I think they're doing it now.

Out front, between the debris and the street, three old men sat on a bench, carousing in German, perhaps recalling those few years the world would never forget. They had more power and meaning than ever before, and people were afraid. Now the world passed by, bumper to bumper, and they could only sit and watch. Maybe they counted German cars, as they breathed cigarettes and exhaust, wagging their heads in denial. I think their heels itched for a crisp click as their haunches ached to spring: *Achtung!* I'm judgmental, but so were they.

Personifying Europe and history, these aging Nazis lived under the heap of cars and traffic. Bicyclists die young here, if not from injury then from lung disease, and the only motorcyclists I saw were racing down the highway at 200 KPH for a thrill still reachable. Speed kills, but going too slow will spring the other death from motorists in cars.
Soot will rule here until the world runs out of gas. People will die younger with less to show for it each year until they learn to use rubbers or unleaded fuel or both. The old Germans sat, recalling a past and greater madness.

Two rows of cars sat behind them, between their bench and the drab café. Two more rows of cars sat in front, between them and the street, where four lanes of cars sped in both directions and beyond that sat four more rows of cars parked near the far sidewalk. Cars and exhaust rule like the Germans once did. Both the invasion and the infusion met mild resistance. The cars too will one day sprout rust and weeds, recalling glory and dominion.

Colette worked like corrosion on my thoughts. She lived in a world gone sour. Her *joie de vivre* felt needy and perhaps failing from the inside out, like bad cells. Skeletal and looking old at barely fifty, her sockets sank hauntingly, and the jawbone of an ass jutted from the thin skin of her face. With a cigarette clamped in her horsy teeth, she became a skull enjoying a smoke. Her big, drooping breasts, loosely displayed, recalled a glorious youth. She worked her last attraction to advantage, as she pointed along her bookshelf at her small paintings, childish doodles, mostly, oil on canvas. The shelf was designed for paperbacks, perhaps predicating small format for her art. The images recalled childhood, not finger-painting but similar, when form and color are met head-on, on the floor, and everything comes out purplish brown.

Colette avoided the purple mud here and there and some of her paintings succeeded with impressionistic forms of people, houses, flowers and happy suns. The one by the door suggested self-portraiture: a supine woman with a single huge breast, a grossly detailed nipple and no head on her shoulders, all in purplish pink. She could have called it *Womansong*, or *The Goddess Within*, or *The Headless Shrew with One Big Tit*, or something creative and topical like that. She waited for my praise, expectant and past tense, like Paris.

She'd come out to greet me like a spider greeting a fly, out from her apartment in the back of the courtyard with a charming French how-do-you-do, as I stood reading her sign on the street: *Appartement à louer.* The street was Rue du Faubourg St. Antoine, built a few centuries ago for horse carts and small people, now jammed like a box canyon full of humans, cars and refuse from posterity and yesterday. Grit, junk, frogs and third-worlders log-jammed this diminutive gap in the labyrinth.

Turning to any direction led to more of the same for miles. Outward it spread.

I needed a place to stay, but this place looked dirty as the street and felt hardly changed from the last afternoon the Jacobins staggered out drunk after some satisfying beheadings. But there she was, so I followed her through the tunnel into the courtyard. Laundry lines overhead connected the four floors of apartments. Shadowy faces watched from several windows.

"You are wanting for a place," she said, leading up the steps.

Hattie was gone. I'd planned a pilgrimage and there I was, climbing the stairway to heaven.

"I wrote for years," Colette said, impervious to my strident reverie. "I was very good, but now I think I'm better at painting. I love to paint. I can feel paint. I take classes now twice a week, and I go every summer for two months to the island to paint. It's important, you know, that a painter mostly paints, that she keep a schedule and that she doesn't deviate or allow interruption…."

She droned softly as Muzac on an elevator. We labored up and soon arrived. Looking out the window, I reviewed the personal indictment leading to my recent companion's departure. *Stop sex. I love you too much. Something wrong.* She was gone, quick as a phone call and confirmation that they would take her in, these people. She'd known them before, in the south, in Arles, a lovely place. It was best.

Colette's drone found emphasis. "Any interruption at all." Back in the practical world, she sighed and said yes, I could have the apartment up in front, because art is the essence of life and must continue, so please, give me your money. The rent, in this application, would be no less than a commitment to life and art, on the island, painting with no interruptions. She turned to her little row of swirls and smurfs so I could comment on their spirit and artistic merit.

"Can I read something?" I asked. She looked puzzled. "Something you wrote."

"Ah!" She shrugged it off. I never really wrote anything. Not finished, you know, like a… a…"

"Like a story?"

"Yes. Like a story." I nodded over the French facial expression that means, *What are you going to do?* Or, *It's all bullshit, isn't it?* The chin juts as the shoulders shrug and the lips are pumped with air until they flap. She covered quickly; "I would write, for example, about a waiter, how he might move, or serve, or maybe something unusual he might say."

"You mean you would observe and record?"

"Yes."

"And you had this feeling that meaning and drama were implicit in these little sketches?"

"Yes."

"But you never made a story I could read, with a beginning, a middle and an end?"

"No."

"Ah, too bad." *Touché.* It was a clean kill; the cafés were full of writers.

She smiled a sourpuss smile and delivered the news. "I'm leaving Tuesday for the island. I've been planning it for months." She bent to an unnecessary task, unstacking the bigger paintings leaning against the wall, more of the same, silly doodles but in larger format, and lining them in display.

"We can have a look then," I said, watching her, not the paintings. I meant the apartment. She smiled again, more sanguine now, and described the apartment up front and the sacrifice required for its purchase and the further sacrifice demanded by its complete and quaint restoration. Down the steps and back across the courtyard to the flats fronting the street we slogged for art.

She lied, but I lied too. "It feels very nice here," I said. She stole a sideways glance defensively, perhaps anticipating another jab. The steep narrow stairs were dark and cold and a relief from the swelter outside, which was Paris in July.

"You see," she said. "It's much cooler here. Much, much cooler."

By the seventh landing we were hotter, much, much hotter, in a gasp and a sweat. The apartment was a box, ten by twelve with a small front window, closed, locked, shuttered and curtained with no oxygen and built-in claustrophobia. The pull-down shade had no spring. We hung limp and lifeless. I pulled and released it again and again, savoring its failure in view of such sacrifice, until Colette said, "It used to work." She brushed me aside. Sweat streamed, and our breathing was labored. "It's cooler with the shade down," she said.

I brushed her aside and rolled the shade up by hand. "You want me to live here?" I opened the big, awkward casement requiring a three-foot radius inside. I unlatched and pushed open the shutters.

The hot wheeze engulfed us. Rush hour honked and choked as if through a floodgate. "Come," she said. "This is your table." It was old and rickety, two by two. I felt like a new dog being shown his dish. With two steps to the rear she continued the tour. "This is your kitchen." It was three by three with a shallow steel sink, a cold-water spigot and a one-burner hot plate. She rhapsodized on the rigors and trials of refurbishment to this level of quality; and oh, the terrible, terrible expense. Even with costs so high, she'd planned two burners instead of just one, after all, but then, you see, there was no room for two. "It was impossible. Impossible. But, you see, it is tiled!" She twitched her nose and grinned and caressed all four of the tiles.

"I've seen bigger galleys on small boats," I said.

"What is galleys?" But I was into the closet with the munchkin door. Below the clothing rack was a toilet in a space twenty inches square, no shit. The seat, down, held the door ajar. This was for ventilation, I was told. I sat down for a test drive, uninhibited as a Frenchman. My knees were in the kitchen, my ass and shoulders squeezed tight in the closet. I sensed the only shit possible here would be of the urgently flowing variety with adequate pressure to override prevailing constrictions. Then again, the bedpan kitchen sink would always be available. I felt the sink around the edge to test its fastenings. She read me like a tasteless book and moved to the shower, designed by the same architect.

I didn't squeeze into it but surveyed the tiny, dark dungeon that was the bathroom. Unwilling to share my negative view, Colette turned her back and removed her blouse and brassiere. "Oh! It is so hot!" She lifted each breast one-handed to wipe the sweat from beneath with her bra. She put her blouse back on and turned back, pumping it like a bellows, rolling her eyes back so I could gaze freely. I suspected a sincere effort to distract from penitentiary conditions, a natural show presented as practical and quaint.

She smiled, perhaps at the cultural richness of it all, inhaling until her breasts pressed the wet blouse. I asked about the evening breeze, scanning, wondering if this was a playful offer, a bonus on top of such penthouse luxury. I returned the smile, granting her the self-esteem she seemed to need. In the heat and desperation, her formidable set was easy to gander but hung like a memorial in another sad café. Need mixed freely with grit and heat. I looked. She saw. It felt French, cool and objective and, as ever, natural. *Comme ci comme ça*, but this Parisian interlude was merely humid and blessedly brief.

The little room felt far from home and way past my deadline. I imagined Hattie watching the French countryside on a train heading south, harking back to the most beautiful Arab boy and her heart, once crushed. I reached for the small vent window in back and pulled the latch to test for cross ventilation. Colette protested, but only with her innately French aversion to fresh air. Opened, it allowed the gritty heat a place to flow through.

I stepped to the front window, around the mattress and the table. I looked out at the crummy little street and all the crummy little cars and wondered what to do. I didn't even know her. How could I? She was too young. And now she was south, where she'd once lost her heart and maybe would again, or maybe she'd find it. Colette stepped up behind me. "It's only three thousand," she said, about five hundred dollars a month. "And I'm putting in a little refrigerator. So you can cook!" I must have nodded, thinking how Hattie was open to adventure more than I was. She wanted to be in the world on a daily basis, and I was only aging.

Colette said, "Good. Well, I'm just on my way for something to eat. You know we have many excellent restaurants in this area. Many excellent restaurants. I can tell you them. Would you like to go?"

I knew it was easier for her now, out in the country where, come to think of it, I should be. "Yes," I said. "I could eat."

X

Resolution in Movement

Colette became my friend. The deal between us displaced the difficulty between us. We breathed deep to assuage what was between us, which was only her oversized need and my bad mood. Her mood improved. She lit up with prospects for three months of rental income, and she couldn't help but like a sure thing. Fifteen hundred dollars paved her way for twice the time on the island, which meant twice as many paintings. She knew her little hovel up front was more horrible than quaint. But she sensed cash, because Americans are mostly rich. So who needed a bad mood? I was mobile and intelligent, within reason and dollars to commit, to the island, for art. With terms restated, she moved quickly to service after the sale, so I might feel better too.

Easing me into my European adventure with a local guide, she took my arm to lead the way down an alley lined with cafés and tiny restaurants. Each alcove offered a different hue of music and movement, smoke and thought. Practically hidden, shadowy, nondescript, smoky but with no *plongeurs* or their mentality, the little lane seemed more charming, and I wouldn't have found it easily on my own. Welcome to the neighborhood, she seemed to say, with its incredible panache. We strolled to a soulful little eatery full of people talking and smoking in a light atmosphere with linen and crystal. *This is now yours,* she seemed to say. Open air felt alluring in simple practicality, giving the talk and smoke a place to go.

I liked Colette ordering in French, and I liked the wine she chose. I liked taking two hours over lunch, and I liked our long talk about books we both knew and our overlapping ideas. I felt humbled in my evolving perception of her and moreover loved the growth she enabled within me. Neither she nor I required sexual contact with the other, though she insisted on presenting her once-fabulous set one more time, leaning in with a dramatic shoulder hunch in an innocent, French way. They were only natural, and why shouldn't a girl let her hair down?

And I felt nothing at all about picking up the tab when she made no move for it. She worked her shoulders instead, with tireless generosity in presenting the show between us. I smiled and picked it up, allowing her the odd but endearing play. On that note, she leaned forward for a confidence, to say that I must come up for dinner tonight; I must. Geoffrey would be cooking, and though he was worthless at everything, he'd become in his way a marvelous cook. A few women they knew were coming too, so I could help balance things out and maybe make some new friends. She provided prospects as a distraction as I scanned the check. I knew that play too but begrudged her nothing; the prospects sounded good. She said, "He's not worthless at everything. Not really. He can't fix anything around the place. That's what I meant." I thought she meant that the door would remain open. Lunch and wine were only eighty bucks, and there I was, far away and making new friends, with more coming up.

Hattie was south by then, but difficulty had dissipated on a surprisingly good wine, an excellent baguette, extraordinary *fromage* and a most civilized smoked *chanterelle* salad under my belt. It was only creature comfort but facilitated a lovely first step on my journey.

Back in my hovel, I could imagine things improving. Time would come for soulful transition to simple needs. For the time being, prospects for a dinner party in Paris danced like sugar plum fairies in my head. A few women we know shaped up well, swirling happily in the exhaust that drifted up from the street. French babble mixed well with the fumes and fantasy, until a well-earned nap came on, which seemed equally propitious and natural. I could nap till seven and dress for dinner at nine. Oh, these Frenchies know how to live.

Dreamless sleep indicates repression in a troubled mind. I didn't mind because the sleep was deep, transforming my lumpy mattress and curing what ailed me. I surfaced to a big bass drum.

I didn't mind that either. Waking was sudden and loud, so I stepped to the window and saw a parade approaching, hordes of revelers marching my way in a boisterous display of banners and pennants, hats and signs. Most of the revelers wore cut-off T-shirts that said *Stand Up and Shout,* or *Stop SIDA,* or *London Boy* or *Paris Boy.*

SIDA is French for AIDS, and this demonstration called attention to the dreaded disease that raged like a brushfire. Six or eight females marched along with hundreds of males, prancing, waving pennants, shouting mottoes, holding hands or thrusting hands inside pants other than their own. Some marched alone, sincerely. Some embraced. Some kissed Frenchly, obsequiously and rebellious. Some looked up at my window. Jubilation seemed universal, fit for heroes home from a war. Proud as a conquering army, these boys marched in resolve, perhaps giddy for prospects after the parade, when a fun day of victory, glory and heroism could climax happily. I pulled my shutters and dressed for dinner. The parade was interesting but too noisy and demanding. The boys looked vindictive, having suffered losses of security and fair play, ready for changing times.

I should have forgotten the boys but left them simmering on a front burner, so after cocktails in French and seating for dinner, and table talk in French, the parade was my entrée to polite discourse. *Some women we know* were two women, both married. Sophie had three children and a husband who cleared his schedule at the last minute to join us for dinner. Alouette was called Ali. She'd left her husband in New Zealand to come see her parents in Paris. Her long, black hair mystically framed her big, dark eyes, and she could stare back with the best of them. I wanted her forever, briefly, but came to my senses on a friendly gesture to the American among us. All agreed that English would be spoken this evening. It felt like a small sacrifice, and excitable bits caused lapses into French, but I got most of it. First up were Geoffrey's prospects for new roles following his recent role as a country squire showing Inspector Poirot around the estate. Geoffrey called it nothing, really, but beamed with pride. Everyone raved. I asked if I might see the show sometime. Geoffrey nodded regally as a magnanimous king. Geoffrey was an actor, apparently, and apparently not so worthless at it.

Ali said she recently tried the new drug, Ecstasy, and wanted to know who else had tried it. She looked at me, and I said no. Sophie loved it. Her husband thought it bad. Colette said it was just all right.

Ali thought it bad; it made her so tired the next day. "But it is very good when you are coming. And I am coming much more with it." This summary came with compliments on the fish and the green beans. I asked if she had any. She said no, she didn't, "But I wish that I did. I have forgotten how…difficult Paris can be. I am so…stressed out. I wish I had some drug, for fun." She put her beautiful hand on my forearm and leaned over. "Maybe we can find some." It sounded like a wonderful idea. Nobody paid the least heed. Ah, these French and their normal, natural nature. You had to love them. I'd get laid after dinner, cognac and mints, maybe with some fun drugs. If you can let things go, I lectured myself, then things will be foregone, just like it was with what's-her-name. My God, I wanted to engage this exotic, dark-eyed beauty.

Geoffrey served salad. In his apron, swirling sauces around the kitchen, swilling wine and making merry, he played the bon vivant, as seen on TV. English and about my age, his career had begun to materialize with the BBC, bit parts in low-budget dramas when they called, and they'd been calling. The niche suited him, he said, while he was under-employed. He had the dynamic range for a lead, he said, and one day it would come. In the meantime he honed his skills. He longed for more money and felt optimistic. He'd come to Paris ten years ago on a stint and met Colette at a Jim Haynes party.

Jim Haynes, Colette explained, was an American who'd lived in Paris for years, who threw a party every Sunday. You couldn't just drop in but had to be recommended, but then you went, and you paid, but not too much, maybe ten or twenty dollars. She stopped short, and I turned to see her measure my reaction to the sound of ten or twenty dollars. She was chronic. Hadn't she seen me buy lunch with nary a wince? Had I winced?

"At these parties, you meet people. That's the purpose. And maybe you will meet someone you can click with. Maybe not. But you go. You must go. I will call for you and recommend you."

"Yes, well, anyway," Geoffrey said. "We met at Jim Haynes', and that was that."

"No, it was not," Colette said. "He took me out for the weekend. Then he left. I thought I would never see him again. But he called back. And now, we are here."

"Do you think you will marry?" The other woman, Sophie, asked. Everyone looked at me.

I smiled. "It's long odds, I think."

"What is long odds?" Colette asked.

"I would need to meet someone I could love, someone who didn't want to marry. That's long odds. At my age. The only marriages you see past forty are practical. One is rich and fears growing old alone. The other is poor and hates it."

"So, you are a romantic after all." Alouette's eyes waited.

"If that label makes things easier for you, sure, I'm a romantic. I meant that romantic love is the rare thing. Marriage is incidental."

Colette whispered to Sophie, "What is incidental?"

Alouette's eyes turned downward with her mood, her sadness and French nature commingling intimately. "He is right," she said. "When you are young you have ideas, but no grasp. So you wait, and you get distracted by your needs. You get a few years older and you get your grasp, but you get depressed, because you realize you can't really get what you want. You get to be thirty and you learn despair, thirty-five can be worse and forty is not too young to die from sheer sorrow. Fifty can be hell. I know."

"How old are you?" I asked.

"That is a very American question," she said.

"No, it isn't," I said. "It's a very normal question to a woman who claims to be fifty and sad."

She smiled sadly. "I am as old as you."

"You don't look it," I said. She let it go.

"I think you must forgive yourself," she said. "I think you must only seek the happiness of others." She stared at me. Our warm and cordial fuck felt certain and urgent.

"Yes, I've thought that myself lately," I said.

Geoffrey cleared the salad, served the beans and boiled potatoes. "The French love sadness and death," he said, playing the vibrant host again. He poured more wine. "Everything they say or do is right. It's the best. Do you remember the nuclear accident at Chernobyl? The French news said don't worry, the deadly radioactive cloud has bypassed France. Bypassed France? Do you know why it bypassed France? Because of *Le Grandeur.* Because: this is France!"

"Those fucking frogs. Right, Geoffrey?" Colette humored him sarcastically.

He replied, "The fish is served." And he served it.

Eating accelerates for the French, who keep their forks right-handed and upside down, cutting, stabbing, gobbling, frenzied on flavors, down to the last baguette torn in vengeance to vanquish the evil spirit, hunger. With the spirits subdued, everyone wiped their plates squeaky clean with bread. Then they sat back to ponder cheese.

In that digestive lull, I asked, "Did anyone see the parade today?" Yes, they had, but no one had further comment, so I told them, "Aggressive,

I thought. And too loud."

"Oh, but they have such a terrible struggle," Alouette said.

"Yes, they do," Colette said.

"They've been terribly persecuted here," Sophie's husband said. "For no reason."

"Yes, and in America too," Sophie said.

"They've done nothing wrong, have they?" Geoffrey asked.

"Are you a homophobia?" Colette asked.

"I think that's a misnomer," I said.

"What is misnomer?" Colette asked.

"It's homophobic," Geoffrey said.

"Phobic means afraid. I was never afraid. I could have been more anti-homo for a while. I didn't like them." The rest waited, aghast. "I lived in San Francisco for awhile. I didn't care what they did with each other. But it was a shame what they did there."

"A shame?"

"Who did they hurt?"

"Did they hurt you?"

"It was a charming city of neighborhoods. I moved into a neighborhood they took over."

Geoffrey smiled. "And so you did in Paris."

An awkward pall put Colette in a twitch, until she sat up straight and pointed obliquely to the left and then downward. "Norman Mailer," she said. "I want to see it." She meant the rehash movie now playing at the corner cinema, but she was way offbeat.

I shrugged. "I don't dislike them and don't care what they do. It's the scene I find obtrusive. The insistence and overbearing noise of the thing. I'm only honest." The rest agreed in French that honesty is best.

"I remember when two men having anal sex was considered unnatural. Nobody cares anymore, because it doesn't matter if the people are men or women."

"What is unnatural about it?" Alouette asked.

"You said you don't mind what they do," Geoffrey said.

"I don't. I don't know of any other species engaging in it, but humanity is unique among species on many levels," I said.

"Do you not love any man? Have you never loved a man?" Ali asked.

"Of course I have," I said. "I sailed the oceans on small boats with men I love. I rode many miles on motorcycles with men I love. I've achieved success with men I love."

"So. You are not honest," she concluded.

"I honestly never wanted to put my pecker up their butts, or wanted theirs up mine. That's honest. And it's also incidental—make that irrelevant to the point I'm making. I honestly don't care what the gay boys do, except for their insistence that I pay attention and love what they do."

She shut up, sadly disappointed with my limitation in love. She looked up slowly, smiling in coy bitterness. "I think what you call honest is simply a lack of imagination. You want to 'put your pecker' into a woman's body. Don't you?"

"Yes. You got me there, Ali. But I don't think natural or unnatural is the question on the table."

"Oh, don't you? Well, good for you. I don't either. The question is one of consent, between two adults who have every right to do anything they want to do with each other."

"The question is public or private, a pep rally or a personal matter."

"You didn't mind the homos when they lived in the closet?" Sophie asked.

"No. I didn't mind. I still don't. But it's not sexual anymore. It's political, because the politicians need the bunghole vote."

"Your language indicates hatred. Hatred indicates fear," Ali said.

"What is *bongue haute?*" Colette asked.

"Your language indicates dogma," I said. "Dogma indicates lack of freedom. Freedom of thought, in this case."

"Yes. You're right," Ali said. "We're both right, and maybe we can yet agree. But you are still not seeing something." She was frustrated by my ignorance. "The homosexuals are a political force."

"Yes, I know. But what do politics and sexual habits have in common?"

"Nothing! It has to do with money for AIDS and persecution."

"More people have breast cancer than AIDS," I said. "But breast cancer doesn't get parades or publicity. I think the people who control publicity are often powerful gay men, who control, for example, Hollywood. If you have powerful media people suffering from AIDS, and that keeps them from the star-studded sex they love to have, well then, that calls for more publicity than a cancerous breast. Doesn't it? And social persecution claims a new victim by way of neglect, in this case women with breast cancer."

"That makes no sense. I think you want the gays to stay in the closet so they won't bother you, even if they get persecuted."

"Not all gays are persecuted." I sought equal, illogical footing. "They are a movement. They seek political power and social recognition. They need attention. Maybe the attention will give them identity. I don't mind that either, though victimhood seems to be a shallow fulfillment.

Maybe it's an honest sexual preference, which I think is often the case." She pondered. I rolled on, way too fast for a safe arrival at the station. "They used to be called homosexuals. Now they're called gay. That's a misnomer too. I would speculate that many gay people are sad in the same proportion as the straight population. To put it in extreme comparison, you wouldn't think of hot turds as éclairs. Would you?"

"What is hot turds?" Colette whispered.

I felt the momentum and sped onward, like a fool, explaining hot turds, briefly, to Colette. She did not appreciate my candor. Ali fell out of the lively discourse with a final harrumph.

"Your language is hostile," Ali said. "Even if the parade was loud and public and you didn't like it, that has nothing to do with AIDS or homosexuals. You are afraid of them for some reason. I get as excited as you do, and I may sound dogmatic. But you are afraid of them, when all they do is between themselves, with consent. They don't need your consent, nor should it be required." Ali was irate. "You can get AIDS much more easily from a drug needle. But I would bet you aren't nearly as afraid of druggists."

I smiled. "You mean druggies."

"Yes. Druggies."

"I don't use needles. I would not share a needle with anyone. I don't care what people do on mutual consent, if it presents no public hazard. I've never cared, until they started yelling at me. You know it's popular now to consider all males as potential homosexuals who won't admit it. When apologists come to their logical stalemate, that's the turn they like to take. Is that what you're saying, Ali? That I'm only contentious because deep down inside I want to come out of the closet too, but I'm afraid?"

"I didn't say it. You did."

"No, I didn't. I said I was awakened by a parade that banged its drum too loud."

"There!" she said. "Why didn't you just say that in the first place, instead of letting us know how much you hate and fear the homosexuals? You make no sense. I see nothing unnatural with two people expressing their love, especially if they are adults and in agreement. And I don't think the drum woke you up at all!"

I sensed our romance was off. Her grim countenance suggested great distance from intimacy. Relieved of the need for charm, free of the lie men believe is key to a woman's interest, I enjoyed a redirected flow of blood. All surged north to the other head, home of the brain. Logic restored led to resolve, in my most effective volley in days. "I remember the late fifties when people drank red wine in jugs, and men wore sweat shirts and grew goatees, and the fringe was clearly defined. If you hung out in a coffee house listening to poetry and bongo drums and talked like a beatnik, you were a renegade. You said things like 'Daddy-O' or 'Crazy, man, like it's splitsville on this uncool scene.'"

"Those were not homosexuals," said Alouette.

"Touché!" I turned to her. "Some were not. Some were. It wasn't an issue. And it wasn't an issue when those people thought all that stuff was passé. So they ditched their bongo drums and sweatshirts and goatees and grew long hair and got some beads and smoked dope and took LSD and said things like, 'Oh, wow,' or 'Far out,' or 'What a bummer. That's not my bag. Go with the flow. Do your own thing.'"

Ali sulked. I honed in. "That stuff got old too, and the next social phenomenon to come along was homosexuality. Same gender sexuality wasn't new. Coming out of the closet was new. It was the next rebellion.

I lived in San Francisco when you could walk down a street and see thousands of men cruising for some action. It was a major cultural event."

They stared. "Where is Splitsville?" Colette asked. Geoffrey fetched the whiskey; such a good row was shaping up. I changed pace, going to soft and quiet. "The point here is that anyone can shave or change the way they talk or trade in their bongo drums for some beads. And when that's over they can move on to something else. The point here is not homosexuality. It's that a bunch of fellows are demanding compensation for something. The crux—what you accuse me of, Ali, is that I do believe that a man having sex with another man, in mutual consent, changes things. I do believe that it's difficult to move past that experience, if a man is not gay. They have organizations now in American cities for men who got caught up in the gay movement, who need therapy now. I'm not suggesting that gay men are weak. Far from it. I'm suggesting that some people are weak minded and will follow a fad or social movement as a means of identity. But same gender sex may be more difficult to forget or move beyond."

Ali's chair screeched. She had to pee. "The point here," I called after her, "is that the frequency of homosexuality in nature is severely less than it is in human society! It's often a show! A compensation. Something other than a natural predilection."

Geoffrey poured for Sophie's husband, himself and me. The women declined. A rugged, revolting cringe accompanied the cheap rye whiskey. "God, I love rye," Geoffrey announced.

"Did anyone see the *fête* today?" Colette asked. And she broke into an explanation, for me, because of me, of another grand demonstration, this one by the farmers of France, who came to the *Champs Elysée* with

83

tractors and wagons full of wheat in a display of France's formidable agriculture and *Le Grandeur.* "A million people were there."

"Yes!" Geoffrey said. "And they sold more *merguez* than crepes. It's the new national food!" He explained: *merguez* is a hot dog made from ground lamb, an Arab favorite, making for high demand in Paris and quickly accepted on the French menu. "*Merguez* is more popular than *crepes.* What do you think of that?"

Colette spoke of the island and art. Geoffrey said the national gallery was woefully depleted this year. Sophie's husband blamed the farmers. Sophie wanted to know who would clean up the mess. She meant in the Champs Elysée, but it was a cue. The women were up when Alouette returned, and so was Sophie's husband. Geoffrey said no, no, no, either resisting this early departure or help in clean up; I couldn't tell which. In three more minutes, they were gone, a withering stillness in their wake.

Alouette's farewell was three kisses cheek to cheek, her cool fingers lingering on my neck with a gentle sigh in my ear for the passing of what might have been. Another shot of rotgut rye seemed in order. I'd won. I watched her go.

And there we were, Geoffrey and I, swilling paint thinner as if it were fine cognac, and we were rich. He delved into my net worth posthaste, filling our cups, leaning forward in warmth and manly communion, elbows in crumbs and sauce. The little room was strewn with bookracks and cookbooks and low-watt light bulbs dangling here and there or hooded with cheap tin fixtures, cords clamped to the racks. Pots and pans and a sink piled with dishes settled like wet clay in half-light, congealing roughly to still life in a Paris flat, as the rotgut cringe eased off.

In another moment, guilt displaced self-consciousness. I had ended

Geoffrey's dinner party like a Philistine in a china shop. But he scoffed in the French way, pumping air behind his lips until they flapped, jutting his chin as if to say, *At least we're not homos, thank God.*

I said I didn't mind gay guys and in fact liked most I'd met and I thought they served a vital function an overpopulated world. "I was only having fun, trying to make some lively conversation."

Geoffrey waved it off. It was nothing, done and gone. His firewater rose up with renewed warmth and burn. It caused a light sweat, requiring some effort to ignore, allowing easy disregard for the other, what had been said and to whom.

It was another still from over the line and I tried to savor the low-lit, French spirit of the moment, along with the whiskey. Both were probably dear to Geoffrey. The cheap river perch sautéed in jug wine and butter, the pound of green beans with garlic and butter, the baguettes and butter, all simple and straightforward, home-cooked and served warm, and the unique dinner party would all remain memorable. I said, "This place has a good feeling."

Geoffrey said, "Yes," in a half-drawl, half-whine, wishy-washy agreement. "I suppose. You're in a place for ten years and it grows on you. I mean I've done it up as best I can, tried to make it a comfort and all that. It's fine, I suppose. I'm glad you like it. It's not for me, though. It's not how I want to live."

"And how would you live?"

"Mm… I want some… some privacy around me."

"Mm. A house."

"Yes, with a garden, I think. And more. I want some trees and open space too."

"Like the squire?"

He laughed short. "Well." He drank and repoured. "Tell me about your home. I want to know. Do you have a house?"

"Yes, I have a house and space and trees and a garden and warm weather. It's a step and a stumble to the beach." He laughed again and repoured me. And what did I do, you know, to make a go of it? "Oh, you know, this and that, business mostly."

"Yes. I suppose your business is doing quite well, if you can take a holiday like this."

"Yes, well, I've been very busy the last year or two. I don't really see this as a holiday but a...change."

"Yes, well, a change of scenery is good. And you've come to the right place. We're glad to have you. Don't think a nit about Alouette. She's always been that way, you know, difficult and all that. About everything, really."

We drank to Alouette and her blessedly forgettable difficulty. "I'm afraid I was the difficult one," I said. "The parade woke me up, and it felt aggressive. And intrusive."

Geoffrey jutted his chin, flapped his lips. We drank some more. We enjoyed the hour, weathered the bottle and agreed that tomorrow would soon be here. With a warm exchange of welcome and friendship, we bid each other good night. Geoffrey showed me out.

I crossed the courtyard in the dark, climbed the narrow steps to my tower dungeon so far from home that home was a small, warm spot in my heart. I sensed progress. I'd sought nothing for two days, and felt adjusted, further along, flat on my back in a box in Paris, drunk and falling quickly asleep.

XI

Adjustments

 Fitful sleep went deep at last to frenetic dreams of a jungle, closing in. Vines and heat crawled with predators, as water trickled and flowed nearby. The trail opened at long last to a light in the thicket, and the long slog ended at a crashing waterfall. In dream logic, the cool, fine mist settled soothingly as lace over thighs. With dream strength I pressed into the falls, and woke to dirty rain slashing through the window. Oh, and a rubber mallet banged my skull from the blind side.

A summer storm had stopped traffic, if not thinned it, so the bumper-to-bumper Frenchies below, stuck in the morning jam, did the logical French thing: honked their horns. By revving their engines as well, they could pump smoke into the deluge to express themselves naturally.

I sat up, ready for death, if this was it, but wanting reason if life was on for another day. I wanted a why for the pain and the pounding. I watched, constrained by numbness, as the rain drenched my kit and caboodle. A small stream flowed toward my mattress. Beyond the drenching, someone had stuck a bicycle pump in my ear and inflated to a hundred pounds of pressure.

I found a shirt near the mattress and wiped my face. It was mostly numb, and the drip was not all rain but included a steady leak from my nose. And about six inches of barbed wire was lodged in my throat. The smoky swirl penetrated the rain and defined life in terms of nicotine, soot, carbon monoxide and no oxygen. I laughed at Geoffrey's moonshine. We'd slammed it back like men in Paris. The coughing fit came next.

The cough eased up to make room for the shakes. Freezing in the dead of summer, I bowed my head to the big D, who grinned from above. I could feel his focus on the aches and pain, the flashing heat and searing cold. Goose bumps rose, hypothermia coming on. In America, I could jump in the shower. Here, I could stand in the wind and rain for a whore bath with a wet rag, to cleanse my few minutes remaining until certain death.

Struggling to hands and knees, I closed the window, toweled off and pulled on last night's clothing. They weren't too wet but the effort was exhausting, so I eased back down before fainting. But down was cold, and the sooty mist on my chest felt like a battered French truck. It was clearly a case of do or die; get up and go or stay forever. A hotel seemed the thing, one with five stars or seven. Rising again with the shakes and dizzies, I followed instinct down a hundred steps to street level, where the Frenchies didn't stare or smirk but ignored me, except for another wino, who nodded and smirked, with acceptance I think. I had arrived at last.

Like a bum who drinks wine until he can't and sleeps outdoors until he can't, I shuffled into the first café and back to the dark and stuffy, smoky, warm and dry of the place. I ordered a big black joe and waited with the shakes.

I liked this refuge, straightforward and blue-collar French instead of pink-collar mental. Like men adrift, clinging to the same flotsam, these guys seemed too obstinate to let go, too strong to die. A dark-skinned fellow leaned over from two tables down. He seemed regular, likely pale under his shirts but ruddy in the face from drink and dirt and whiskers. About my age, give or take, he showed more miles, off road. The dirt was on him, down his coat, on his sleeves, scarves, hair and hat. His eyes shone, clean and bright, as he leaned over with a pack of Gitanes in his burly paw. He shook a few out and instructed, "*Tien!*" I took one, feebly, and he said, "*Bonjour, mon ami.*"

It felt like communion and redemption; welcome to Paris. I lit up and breathed the heinous smoke. The barbed wire slid up and down, but suffering suffered its own death, once I moved beyond. Warmth rose in me. I loved this man and let it go at that, until lungs convulsed on the exhale, looking like a bad engine impersonation. Tears rolled, and the ruddy man ordered two hot brandies. I nodded, accepting alms from the only being in the world who cared. He said something like, *Ce n'est que mal chance.* Down on your luck is all. He seemed a man of the world. I nodded; yes, luck is all it is.

The brandy was shit but hot. It stopped the shakes, mostly, leaving only residual bone rattling that made my new friend laugh. Dropping a few smokes on the table, he slapped my back on his way out.

Alone again, I sat two hours, numb and soggy. Standing was painful, like life, and necessary. I would climb back up the tower and come back down to hike three blocks to the laundry. Dryness seemed a distant refuge and a chance for survival. Do or die.

I stopped on the way back up at the *boulangerie* for a gooey Danish with icing and raisins and nuts, because solid food with carbs, sugar and fat seemed integral to endurance as well. Yet at the summit, huffing and puffing and unwrapping the little Danish I watched grease ooze from it like a sweat. Setting it down, I opened my window and sat on my chair. I picked it up and ate, until maggots squirmed from the syrupy swirl, Bonjour, mes ami. I hocked the sweet and sour gob out the window. Below, the prune-faced *boulanger* restocked his display of maggot Danish, keeping an eye peeled for thieves. On a better day I would have taken time to explain things to him, but with resources depleted, I only lobbed the snotty dough ball. He took it on the chest and looked up. I yelled, "Fucking maggot!" I coughed and wheezed, "What ees focking magote?"

He didn't care. He pumped and flapped his lips and blew me off. A man on the corner slapped the shit out of his kid for being a bad French kid. The kid yelled a death threat, so the man swung again, but the kid ducked and ran.

I lay down two more hours and dreamt of people who visit Paris and simply love it. I woke up wet and pained and struggling out of the dream. Sick enough to worry, I gathered my clothing and went for the dryers, wondering if I could fit inside.

With glands like gum balls, swallowing tore at my throat. The daze thickened. I hobbled on, Quasimodo headed to the laundry. Inside was warm and dry, grim and luxurious, so I settled in to watch the spin.

A hard-faced, supple woman with big frizzled hair drifted in. Her denim skirt looked short enough for stand-up sex with no leaning. Falling off her shoulders, her ragged chemise hinted the oo la la, and she sought my eyes. I felt like a tom too beat to go again. Sensing my weakness, she turned to two Arab boys who looked like an old habit with enough giggling thrown in to emulate fun. With animal need, they moved through their ritual of lust and hunger. Maybe they grew up together on the same crummy street, where they learned the difference between childhood and the rest. I wanted to play too but could not.

I gathered my bundle after many spins and drifted back under clearing skies. Around the corner in the second block, into the alley of cafés with their grimy façades, just in from the endless parade of little French cars, three men swaggered my way. Young and unkempt with bad teeth and ashen skin, they swilled pink wine, drunk at noon. Life span looked short. Like the ruddy man who knew about luck, they looked intimate with hard times. Their stride matched their song, call it Singing in the Pain; swinging from lampposts, vaulting cars and missing, they laughed. They bounced off each other and floated free, arrogant to the ghastly hangover they would share by sundown. They celebrated everything. I envied them too, their life without thought. I trod on, wondering how far.

Laboring up the tower again, I felt dead. At the top was a note from Colette saying that Geoffrey was gone to London on short notice on a decent part. Should we have dinner and see a movie? The cold shower assured me of my body, and in dry sheets I slept till seven. With a big head, a dripping nose and a scarred throat, I pressed on to another night in Paris.

She whisked away my sniffles and sneezes. "That is normal," she said. A "good cold" always comes soon after arrival, what with the jet lag, the adjustment, the place. She took the lead, down the street to the movie house on the corner. At the ticket window she verified the movie and time, and she smiled. I paid, first for the movie, a slow-paced story with no subtitles. I think it was about gay men, but you can't always tell in France. Colette said it was good practice for me, but I'm sure she meant the language.

Then I paid for dinner at a new Armenian place she wanted to try. I couldn't taste it, and by eleven the place was packed. By eleven-fifteen it was jam-packed, and crammed tighter than a gnat's ass by eleven-thirty. I didn't share this imagery to spare us the certain confusion. Colette leaned near and said now is when it gets good. It buzzed with talk of this and that and talk of past talks and talks to come. The white sound of overlapping voices drowned our talk. People vied for space to shape with their hands and wave their arms in. Smoke ruled.

Colette accelerated along with the crowd when I sniffled or sneezed and especially when I blew my nose into my napkin. Expounding over the tradition of hipness in *L'arrondisement de la Bastille*, she said it actually derived from a history of chic, emanating from an age-old past of *avante guard*, and so on back to oblivion. Blah, blah, blah, she said. Atchou! I replied, struggling to breathe and keep up, with voluble wheezing through clenched teeth. When my napkin got soggy I pulled a free corner from the tablecloth and blew my nose into it. Social numbness prevailed from congestive delirium and the French segment of humanity in critical mass, engaging in worst habits. Great gobs formed in my lungs, so I discharged them as I'd seen an elderly patron in spitting distance do. I loogied the gob down to the floor, which was cement anyway, and I'd gathered that the indoor loogie must be carefully directed in a line shot with no lopside and no arc. Colette sped happily on through the history of high cool, as if it was nothing but one more oyster hatching on the floor.

She moved from high cool to medium cool, which all cool goes to in the long haul, or something. Hipness gives way to human nature, which, in the best of times is generous and giving. Magnanimity was the soul of France and, more specifically, when factored with *Le Grandeur*, defined the soul of Paris. "This is my home," she said. "I was born here. I am Parisian." She attempted pride, as people devoid of resources will do, as if her accident of birth was currency in the world. The hour seemed late, the fatigue overwhelming. I glared at her in dire wonder that she remained blind to my discomfort. I imagined a cold beer back home in front of some idiotic TV, and I smiled weakly. From deep in that dark, rank cloud of smoke, she smiled back, because, I think, I had understood.

The barbed wire swelled and moved, and when I could take no more and excused myself to call it a night and take refuge, she hunched very close and grew gravely serious and said, "You know we have a problem." I could only wait in the dank, padded cell of my head cold, knowing that beside my health, I had no problem at all. "We have a problem." She dabbed her chin, raised a hand to the waiter and ordered another round of cognac from the high end. "You need it."

She leaned in anew and said, "We spent so much. Much more than we had."

I coughed and wheezed and managed to ask, "How can you spend more than you have?"

"The linens." Two sheets. "The dishes." Two bowls—two, in case I wanted to entertain or try an exotic recipe. "The silver." A knife, a spoon, a fork, pot metal, used, perhaps from this very restaurant. "It has an excellent view of *L'Opera Bastille*." We sat then in the bowels of *L'Opera Bastille*, choking to death. "I think we need…" Ah, there was the rub. "A thousand francs per week." The ante was up from five hundred dollars a month to eight or nine hundred. It was a bump she and Geoffrey had thought through, thought possible for an American of means who hadn't balked yet.

Nor did he balk now. I sniffled, blew my nose and nodded. She took it for assent. "Can you pay in advance?" Odd vonce?

I laughed, which led quickly to a sputter and a choke. I wondered if Colette viewed me as a child might view a fairy godfather. I'd stopped at the money exchange after seeing the three drunks in the street. They would be my paragon, I'd thought then. A fat wad pressed my hip: the rent we'd agreed upon, three months' worth in odd vonce. But it wasn't enough. Revelation was instant, and so was application. "I think I'm sick," I said.

"That is normal."

"I can't breathe," I said.

"It is very normal. It happens to everybody."

"I don't think I've breathed for a week."

"Of course you have. When I went to New York I wanted to leave every day for a month. I was sick as a dog. As a dog I tell you!"

She grew fervent with French consolation. "My head is packed with snot."

"What is not?"

"My throat is sore. It bleeds."

She whisked that away with a chin jut and a flap of the lips. The waiter came with cognacs. We sipped in silence. "I'm leaving in two days," she said. "For the island. For my art. Painting means everything to me. I've planned this for months."

"And I'm certain you'll make your trip. You're very resourceful."

She looked worried, then suspicious, as if I could be a poseur—as if I might fly the coop like the grackle I really was instead of paying up like the wealthy American I pretended to be. "Yes. Well. Could you pay now?"

"I'll see what I can come up with." The brandy was a heavily promoted brand but it recoiled and winced. I sipped it for the last time and said, "Now I have to sleep. I know you understand."

"Yes. It is normal. You will see. You know you must learn to give things a try. I have noticed that about you. You are very impatient. Very unsatisfied. You'll never get anywhere if you don't give things a chance. Your accent is getting much better."

She gained confidence, which the French will do if no argument follows a statement. I looked down on her then, not a happy view for me, seeing a middle-aged, disappointed, lower-middle-class woman with left wing justifications of class-transcendent greed, trying to teach me a lesson in life. In my appreciative smile, I felt better read, more worldly, kinder and gentler and tangibly more successful in several areas. Personal development for me had meant sacrificing comfort. I had been most willing to sacrifice personal comfort to lie down in a shit hole for three months, and now this French floozie wanted more.

She nearly nailed me in the act of superiority. So I dropped back, as an American man on the road, for whom *savoir faire* is best left to those who know it best. Tilting my nose so it could drip into the nasty cognac, I put my voice between my eyes and bid her, "Bone swar, sweetheart." She winced and at the rest of the truth winced again. "You and Geoffrey can find a new tenant. I think breaking our agreement works out well for me too."

"Oh, no! He can't!" He con't! "Geoffrey is…"

"Worthless?"

"Oh, no! I would never call him worthless."

"Why not?"

"Because he is…an actor. He's not…handy, you know. We cannot find another tenant. We have already made the place unavailable, just last night I was asked if I knew a place for rent for a few months, and I said no, I do not. Our place is taken."

"Who asked?"

"My friend Jim Haynes asked. He knows of your apartment. How well it is located and the view and the rent." I smiled at the rent that was known. "Oh, no, it is taken."

I nodded. "I must sleep now, Colette. We will talk in the morning."

"Talk of what? What have we to discuss?"

I shrugged. "We don't need to talk. You seem anxious."

"No. I am not. I'm anxious to leave for the island is all. I was ready to leave two weeks ago."

"But you had no tenant."

"Yes. Tomorrow we will talk. Can you go to your bank?"

"Of course. Anything you need and more if your needs increase."

I got up and left. Colette followed close by. Maybe she feared solitude in a restaurant so crowded. We walked fast with no talk and a scant good night in the courtyard.

Sleep came quickly with resolution. Waking was easy, confirming a jaded woman's assessment that a man with no patience is happiest on a day of change. The aches and pain were notably less, but the barbwire bog persisted. I dressed for travel and packed. I crossed the cobblestone courtyard to the wider, fewer, more civilized steps to Colette's apartment and knocked.

Busy and nervous, she also packed. Opening the door and turning away she said, "Come in." She went to the phone and dialed. "Geoffrey asked me to call him." She waited and then spoke quickly in French. She held out the phone, and I took it.

"Hello, Geoffrey."

"Hallo! You must be having a wonderful time there! Colette said the Armenian place was very good!"

"A little spendy I thought."

"Sorry about your cold. You know that's very normal."

"Yes. I've heard that somewhere. Still, it's difficult to accept. You understand."

"Give it a few days. You know the city is a wonderful place in summer. Blue sky, not so hot as in the south. The weather changes dramatically this time of year. Paris in summer is like a…a village on the Baltic or something. It has that empty, quaint feeling."

Geoffrey called it "the city," like New York, and I realized then that it is like New York. I nearly asked myself aloud what the hell am I doing in New York? Geoffrey said it wasn't so hot as in the south, as if he knew the south was where a more savvy man would go, because it was better. Geoffrey provided guidance: I would go south. Still, listening to this unfortunate man recite lines from his best role, I felt a strange warmth. With good manners in the midst of his greed and alongside his scavenging wife, he skirted confrontation. I did, too.

"Geoffrey. I'm leaving, you know."

Geoffrey knew. "Yes. Now look. I want somebody in there. Somebody reasonable."

"You want me to find you a tenant?"

"You must find a tenant if you want to leave. The place is yours."

"I don't speak French. I don't know the city. I have no phone. How can I find a tenant?"

"You speak very good French. Colette can help you." Colette packed in a hurry.

"Colette is leaving. Besides, it's not practical. And I don't feel a sense of obligation."

"Bloody Americans! We agreed!"

"You raised the rent. Unilaterally, as we say in America."

Geoffrey failed. "If you don't pay, we'll call the police."

Call the police? For a cash rental? Would they guard the border? These and other clever retorts were easily at hand. But Geoffrey was beat again. I gave him silence. He asked for Colette. I said yes and thought it best to hang up. But Colette in Paris on the phone with Geoffrey in London, sharing their desperation over fleecing a tourist for money seemed golden. "Colette. Geoffrey wants to speak with you." I stepped back.

She spoke briefly in French, hung up and dialed again. I caught odd phrases; *les gendarmes, allez vite, un voleur.* I split fearlessly; it was best.

At first I went slowly, since hurrying is a concession to guilt. Then I hurried, fitting in with the man who knew about luck and the dancing drunks who would die young and happy. She watched from her balcony as if in overview of life's unfairness, art and the island. She watched me, *le bon chance*, slipping from her grasp on fleet feet. Up, down and out and humping it to the Metro, I was on the road again, feeling better already.

XII

Leaving Paris

 Six blocks to the train station was too far for a wounded soldier behind enemy lines, but a hundred yards to the Metro could be made in a dash. Besides, the Metro was underground and crowded. I wore my hat and dark glasses, fitting in. Thoughts too, felt chaotic as Frenchies in a maze. Hattie was south. I could call or go or let it go. Leaving Paris in a hurry was the same as last time but sober, sans music and mystique. And last time didn't seem so hostile or overcrowded or buried in media chic. Cheap goods festooned the streets. Honkytonk commerce had its own momentum and resentment, flowing along the sidewalks. Colette and Geoffrey made sense in modern Paris, and I did too. The difference between them and me was mobility. I was leaving.

At the platform two black men on the far side scuffled like siblings, rough but playful, until a punch landed. The big one went about one-eighty, five ten, the smaller one three inches shorter and forty pounds lighter. But the smaller one had some moves he'd learned in amateur wrestling, and he looked precise, quick and clean, shooting inside. The big one swung again and missed, too slow. The smaller one got the take down and the break down and move to the side for the half nelson. But what could he do? Go for the pin? No, this was for keeps, city rules, underground, and mean as a little man ever was, he went for the two-handed head smash. But his vigor brought his weight too high over the big one, who slid out and back, freeing himself and gaining his stance, lowering, loading up for a launch with all his might, to drive the smaller man onto the tracks.

"Train!" I yelled, bringing many French glares my way in perplexity, as if to ask what nutty word is that, and why would the nutter yell it. So I reset and yelled in my best nasal/glottal rendition, "Treh!"

Ah! They seemed to get it, turning back to the action and the low rumble coming on, just prior to the rancid gust out the tunnel like that preceding a well-greased turd. Fearless, and hardly a man to be pushed around after successfully coming so far from North Africa, the smaller man one leapt gracefully off the platform to avoid the charge, landing on the tracks, just in time to see the folly of his bravado and, moreover, his imminent death. Sprinting back to the platform, he stumbled and sprawled. The distant clack rose to vibrant thunder, bringing onlookers to the fore, to see the action and scream bloody murder. Two people reached from the platform as the smaller man jerked up on adrenaline and grabbed their hands for the pull up and out. Light beamed out the tunnel and the roaring train drowned all else. The smaller man shook free for more fight, but the big one grabbed and held him, hugged and kissed him. The big one had seen the future and was saved. The smaller one struggled but weakened on the kiss. The train pulled up and humanity flushed itself, out and in.

I rode a few stops avoiding eye contact, except with those who insisted, to whom I explained, "*Tant pis*?" What can you do? I shrugged under a chin jut and puffed lips. They nodded in comprehension, and in two more stops I rejoined the endless flow.

A short while later I sat outside a café facing the station, holding the ticket in my pocket. Harsh symptoms seemed to fade on mere prospects for heading south, for a small town on the Med on the nine o'clock express—the night train. My nose went drip, drip, drip, and so did the low, dark clouds and then my eyes. Breathing matched the traffic, wheezing and sputtering. Glands throbbed in synch. Wet gained momentum from a drizzle to rain to downpour, briefly, and back to drizzle.

I watched and waited, blew my nose and drank tea. I got up to pee and sat again and waited, repeating as necessary, as the tired little arms slogged through the seconds, minutes and hours.

XIII

Transmigration

Waking from one dream to another, I sat up in the *clackety clack*, bearing south with no oxygen. Lung constraint had wakened me. I sat up to see the door and window shut and five other bodies breathing deep, snoring. Damp, clammy and dazed in the dark, I got up, bumped my way to the door, fumbled with the latch and answered, "It's a'right," when a gruff Italian voice challenged movement.

Two couples and a male cousin shared the same sleeper on their way home to Sicily. "Ah," I said when we met, "You are mafioso?"

They didn't laugh. The male cousin shook his head, produced a half carafe from somewhere and said, "Drink this." I drank.

Just south of the city, conditions for life degraded in the post-nuclear wasteland similar to just south of most cities. Industrial slum crept along the earth for miles. It was mostly Arab refugees living in the last phase before the next phase. In decomposition, Earth reclaims its heritage. And this was in the dark, lit only by twinkling lights, softening the grim truth but not enough. Countryside and trees were only another hour down the line on the express, and lungs soon opened on the rural reprieve, inhaling hungrily on original air. Glands shrank. Is Paris so filthy that a country human cannot adapt? I think it is. But who would buy postcards showing the deathly pallor? Who wants to spend all that time and money getting there and then admit it was a terrible mistake?

Waking to clean air felt like a rebirth with new confusion. Italians, like the French, don't like fresh air and shut everything tight, to make life more secure. The habit may derive from history, when winter brought The Reaper, who avoided warmth. But this was July.

Leaning on the open window in the corridor, I breathed easily in appreciation of life's basic exchange: in with the good and so on. With dry clothing from my bag, I hit the WC and stripped, cleaned and changed. Emerging in first light, I found the conductor in his service booth with train-pack coffee, hot, bitter and electric. The sun rose.

In no time it was midmorning and Genoa, with embraces from my new Sicilian friends. Italy felt like a new world with a new language and a different culture, not so haughty and more soulful but still crowded as a science fiction movie or Paris. A taxi driver said it was thick now because fifty-six million people have no place else to go. Soon I would join them with my toes in the sand and diving into waves. I would immerse and be healed.

But Italy had gone south as well. Genoa didn't thin out like it once did, down along the coast. Buildings got shorter and roads narrower, but density held firm. With no horizons, no rounding the bend or cresting the hill out of town and into the country, things thickened near the sea.

The driver was proud of the Hotel Continental; it so well reflected the area's emergence into modern tourism. I got a room with a shower and air conditioning and clean sheets and a view of the parking lot and the choked road. It was a hundred fifty a night—dollars, U.S.— but a steal next to Geoffrey and Colette. And the credit card currency conversion wouldn't cost nearly as much as another lunch with Colette.

The gift shop was good for swim skivvies and goggles, and the friendly clerk pressed to sell a gold chain, what every man on the Med needs, but I declined. In the lobby old, white men in starched white jackets drifted for tips. I didn't mind tipping if they did something, and being ignored felt nice.

A rock jetty fronted the hotel and over it stretched a cement slab for chaise lounges and umbrellas for robust Italians. Many bare breasts glistened with grease in the gender-neutral scene, and I dove in for further immersion. The chill surged, but in no time muscles stretched for a cleaner yonder. I made distance, feeling better all the time.

Along the bottom, about twenty feet down, something surged, pervasive and white, a pollutant perhaps, but it didn't move like fluid and was surely the wrong color for sewage. So I went for a look: toilet paper, Kotex, tampons, Coca Cola bottles and cans in Classic and New Coke, both Diet and Regular, though most of the labels hung on by a speck. Plastic bottles in layers and assorted trash and, oh, a few rubbers, sent me up and out like a Trident missile. I'd been with sharks less threatening. Past the bare-breasted persons with hardly a second glance I made my room for a disinfecting shower, wondering how fifty-six million people could shit in their own pool.

I calmed over a few beers in the lobby bar and switched to Campari, so the place could settle in with less bloat. I strolled down to chat with the man handling towels and seating by the water. "Is all the sea here polluted?"

He looked down at my hand for a tip, looked up and said, "No speak."

I spoke softly, "You want to fuck with me. *Capiche?* Fuck with me?

"Yes," he laughed. "I know."

"I don't think you do." At least I felt better, washed and breathing. The yellow haze over the Med ran to the horizon, so I walked up the hotel drive and up through old neighborhoods above town, into an area of stately homes and trees, past slow, friendly people. In an hour the houses thinned. In another hour, another village looked more promising but with no beach. Only big, smooth rocks fronted a shabby hotel, guarded by another old man in a white jacket, who said, *Buon giorno* and scanned downward for lire. He wanted twenty-two thousand, about twenty bucks. I asked what for, and his hands drifted over the sea at chest level, palms up like the Pope.

I told him the rocks looked greasy and swarming with flies, and these women were fat. He smiled and told me I could go there, just there, pointing to a cliff across the bay where people lounged on an outcropping and more people reclined on another ledge at the water's edge. He said the path would lead there.

The water looked cleaner at the ledge with less scuz than at the shabby hotel with the twenty-dollar fee. I shared that assessment with the two German girls sitting nearby on towels, waiting to see if I would invade their space. The pale, skinny one lit a smoke and looked away.

The husky one with more tattoos than a biker club said, "Yes. They clean it very much for two years. Only here…" She pointed to the shoreline debris collecting from waves and currents, wrappers mostly and Coke cans, with a few tampons and toilet paper flecks. "Only here it is bad. But you can swim past here very fast."

"Do you swim?"

"Yes. I swim."

"You wanna?

She lit a smoke and inhaled big. "You mean all the way?" The bay was a mile across.

"No. We swim halfway."

"Yes. I swim."

The two women were naked so I shucked my Speedos for parity. The big girl smiled with admiration or pity. "Last one in is a rotten egg," I said. She looked puzzled, but I was in. She was game and a good swimmer for a hundred yards, until her breathing labored. I stopped. She stopped. "We go back?"

"Yes. We go back." We went back. The anorexic one waited on the beach with a towel to enfold the husky one. Once properly hugged and dabbed dry, they spread the towels and relaxed with more smokes. The big one held her cigarette up vaguely in my direction and said, "This. Not good for my swim."

"No. Not good for my swim, too."

"Ah, you smoke?"

"More and more when I'm having fun." I copped a smoke and lit up and sat in the sand nearby.

A motor yacht plowed into shallow water by the ledge, too fast that close to shore. A hundred feet long, it threw a big wake and blew smoke when the show dog at the helm leaned on reverse to stop in time. The roar faded to whoops and giggles of a hundred gay men, naked and holding hands, carrying on like silly fellows on a wild lark. Gold and diamonds glittering here and there on tanned bodies made the scene slick and sparkling, like a fantasy fulfilled by design. A few at the stern swayed with the swell. A short, stocky man swelled with the sway, nearly parallel with the flagstaff. The wildly gay romp seemed in sheer defiance to society in general, and in specific regard to the Vatican, hardly an afternoon drive down the road. They made great show, giggling and shrieking, playfully sneaking up to plant the goods.

"They will not suck on each other," the husky girl said. "It is not allowed."

"Not in public anyway."

"Yes. Not in public."

The stocky man approached a tall, thin man, turned him around and spoke to him from the rear. The thin man giggled and bent over. The short one moved in for a thrust under the blue skies and yellow haze.

"It is worse on the other side," the husky woman said. She didn't mean flagrant sex in public. She meant pollution. "The Adriatic Sea. It is dead. Phosphates. Mostly from German manufacture and from soap. Nothing can live, except one species of algae."

I'd seen it on TV. Seeing it in person and swimming in it made the world smaller still. I doused my fag and asked the big one, "Would you and your friend join me in a bottle of wine?"

She smiled, turned to the pale one and spoke softly in German. The pale one muttered, and the big one turned back. "No. We will stay here. Thank you."

I sat a minute longer. Evening was a few hours off. Maybe I'd wait until dark to call Hattie. I had the number. I might not. I could decide later. Maybe I'd be strong.

The two women chatted about strolling into the village for drinks and soon rose and walked away. Such is life on the road, among strangers. Left to the dirty sand and iffy sea, I killed the smoke because it hurt more than it soothed. Better to savor the warm and dry, the freedom from sniffles, drips and swollen glands. I stood and wondered what and why and headed back to my room on the low road. I dressed and headed out again and made the village by happy hour, hot and tired. Ass to elbow in a celebration of overcrowding, people guzzled beer and wine and threw cans and butts into the harbor. At a market on the fringe I got bread and fruit and took the high road again, returning to the hotel by ten, weary to the point of depression.

Traffic jammed outside. The sun seemed stuck on the yellow brown horizon, crimson smoke framing the stillborn twilight. I shut the terrace doors, pulled the thick drapes, put the AC onto sweater weather and called Hattie. No answer. Good. I was weak.

Frustration eased with several beers and sound sleep to sunrise. Then came checkout and a taxi back to the station and a train north to Switzerland. Movement calms an anxious man. Italy, like France, fell away, behind the line, gone forever, discounted in a blink and a twitch. Clacking rails became a mantra that eased me again to sleep, saying somewhere else, somewhere else, somewhere else. I dreamed that the landfill above Beach Road overflowed and covered the earth.

XIV

Further Flight

 Waking up on a train in a daze and a sweat, packed in the body smell of others, can make a man wonder where he is and hope he's not. People endured, crammed into seats and aisles. Luggage and knapsacks equally dense overhead were those of college kids playing On the Road in Europe Broke, except for Dad's Visa to score the cash advance, as necessary. They aped Euro-cool, as seen everywhere, sucking their smokes to blot any breathable air remaining, until a sleeper dreamed of asphyxiation and woke; this is no dream. Eighty bucks for threadbare blue jeans, as if holes might show experience, or some shit. The kids reached for seasoning. But the road, like the world, had gentrified to packaged norms.

I grappled with the window but failed. I beat on it like a drowning man, submerged. I would have broken it, but it opened. I breathed. Others murmured about too much air or the nutty old guy. Marginally oxygenated, I settled back with yesterday's *Herald Tribune*. THREE

FOURTHS OF EUROPE BEACHES DIRTY WITH TRASH AND SEWAGE. A village in Liguria had reported toxic waste at six point four percent, bad enough, but the reporter exposed village stats as false; Liguria actually measured ninety percent toxicity. The reporter explained the diagnosis as a constant based on tampons, counted at the high water mark. From each tampon, sewage and toilet paper are accurately extrapolated, with menstruating women in fixed ratio to the general population. That is, shit and toilet paper emulsify, but tampons are stable, so to speak. I eased the paper down to ponder. I'd left Liguria that morning. Small world.

The man beside me said, "We have no feeling for the sea. For us, it interferes with agriculture. It is a toilet big enough for boats. It is a problem." He lit a smoke.

The woman facing me moved her knee. I moved mine. In a while she moved hers again. She lit a smoke. We stared. A mulatto mix with golden skin and curls to match, she glowed with an exotic blend of feminine youth in other-worldliness. Like Hattie but different, not so big and hearty but frail, weakened by smoking. She smiled, reading me, I thought, like Hattie, with assurance. I constrained a half smile and wry mirth; to think that a modern adventure, nay, a pilgrimage to the temple once known as open road would come down to pollution and hormonal engagement.

I finished the story in the *Herald Tribune*. Her knee brushed my own again. I looked out the window and scanned the paper. She moved again, surely seeking comfort. As the train pulled in, we rose. She smiled, reaching for her valise. I helped to lift it down and followed her to the exit. We got off, this young woman, the college kids and me. I held back briefly to take in the trees and cool air and with those things a sense of hope. Moving slowly with the crowd and through it, across the platform to a suitable opening, I felt reasonably confident that an invitation to coffee or tea would feel…reasonable. But as I cleared and said, "Pardon me," a man about my age stepped forward and embraced her. A black woman followed. They turned to me.

Oh, hello, I thought. I was just pursuing your daughter. "How far is Lake Geneva?"

"Oh!" the father said. "Not far. Only an hour from here!" I nodded on another wry smile moved on. She looked back with a toss of her curls and wistful eyes. Small world with growing gaps, or would that be a deepening abyss?

I sat in the station café with a coffee and a smoke, savoring the trees and slopes and the valley yet wondering: If each life is a story, and a story has characters, where are the other characters in my story?

I switched to beer as the day went hazy. I drank as the haze tinted yellow and thickened. She came back for a chat and a beer several times in my mind for a few hours, until clouds filled in, and I wobbled out for a new ticket, a compartment this time, for the ride to the lake. Dusk was difficult, fading in solitude, the end of a day transpired but hardly fully lived. Repress that thought, I thought; transit is necessary, if life or anything is to find a new setting.

The evening train up to the lake was also packed. A rangy fellow in deep contemplation crowded my compartment beside his sweet, young companion. Like a magpie in springtime, she chattered that she and her cousin, presumably the thoughtful guy, had decided on this adventure, and so far it was all they'd hoped for and more. She chortled over where they'd been, perhaps teasing me to wonder what they'd done.

She stopped short when the Tubbses and the Snoles from Swinerd,

North Carolina came in and sat. How did we know who and wherefrom? They said as much. I cringed as Noah must have done when the less savory species came aboard. Loud and stupid, they couldn't believe the gall of the porter on the last train, which was the wrong train. Why, that feller wanted sixty thousand dollars to tell them they'd made a mistake.

The patriarch Tubbs meant to say lire. "Hell, Ah told at guy, why, ere wadn't no way'n hell Ah'd payum sixty thousand dollars!"

The adventurous faction from Swinerd, went six, eight head of Tubbses and a similar count of Snoles, ventilating their gumption together. Two seats shy of enough seats, they shuffled like in musical chairs, knowing they could get it right. "Don't you know it was Wayne lost his ticket at that last stop? Had it in the wrong durn pocket is what. Ne'n Mary Ellen couldn't find the johnny. Ah swear to God! N'at fella wanted 'at cash. Why, Ah gave the man four thousand liras!"

An older woman sat beside me. She asked, "You speak English?" It felt like a compliment.

"Mm...." I shook my head. *"Pas beaucoup."*

"Oh. Well." She murmured as the elder Snole teed off on missing Monaco 'n all 'em nekked women. "You boys are all talk," the woman said. "Why, you wouldn't know what to do with it if it set right down in your lap."

The boys went mute, but rambled soon again about the good times ahead in Marsales, Lion and Paree. And Amsterdam, though it might be cold, but they did want to have a look-see at the whores. This is what the world came to, I thought, ruination and gridlock on the open road, the end of adventure as a pure pursuit, as something meant for the strong-hearted who can find it. The noble concept had been decocted to pap, served on a platter, a plastic one with a doily.

The thoughtful young man gave up his seat to an old woman, earning a round of niceties. He lit a smoke in the passageway and advised, "It's beautiful. Really beautiful. Amsterdam. And it's not so cold."

"We hard it was whald!"

Shoowee! Woo hoo!

"Yes. It is. But I just… I saw so many young people there…" He choked like a missionary, sensing rejection of Christ in the native population. "…destroying their lives!" He smiled and frowned in two twitches.

The Tubbses and Snoles shut their mouths wide open for some startled cogitation. It ended when the conductor came for passports, and mine was a U.S.A. With stink-eye aplenty, they seemed to ask, *So yo shit don't stank?*

The train clattered and rolled in pleasant syncopation that could not last with so many hillbillies on hand. I split for the corridor, for a stretch and some air. Nobody took my seat. The young man smoked another, looking intense, possibly disturbed, a potential suicide from anxiety depression, or a serial killer, or maybe he'd move to North Carolina and run for Senator, though he didn't seem cagey enough, and seemed a better candidate for stringing up by his rep tie. Or he might make it back to Amsterdam to destroy some of his life, like electroshock therapy but with hash. "They still sell hash in Amsterdam?" I asked.

"Yes. Everywhere."

"You didn't try it?" He harrumphed. "A long time ago, I lost ten days in Amsterdam, stoned." He smoked and looked out the window. I went back to my seat. The Swinerdians had doused the lights. The women read romance novels under seven-watt book lights. The men snored.

Everyone got off in Geneva, but Geneva was too big, so I got another train to Montreaux, where jazz is a tradition. I drank a few beers and arriving in Montreaux just after dark, I scored a gram of hash from another young man whose life seemed less severe. I found a small hotel and got thoroughly stoned on the hash, which happened to radiate excellence; so soft and warm, ambient and friendly, like a major missing player in my story. I thought I'd call Hattie to help populate the cast but lay down for a minute and fell asleep.

XV

When You Least Expect It

 Maybe I adapted. A smoke with a double espresso can make sense some mornings. The nicotine and caffeine got me going, out for a walk to stretch my legs, to go for the going and maybe to run into something new, something or other.

Because something was wrong, because a series of wrongs had stacked up—Hattie, the world, the trip, me. I didn't care if I cashed out and headed home, but I'd come so far, and it was such a pain in the ass getting here—here being a bigger-than-life ashtray called Europe—and such a pain in the ass being here, so much wasted time and money; I'd give it a few more days.

Knowing the downside before a trip would render adventure easy and meaningless—would make the bubble-headed kids correct, counting miles as experience. A bad trip would be avoidable, if a traveler knew the score up front, but the score remains mysterious—or at least it used to. I'd been wrong on this one, and I doubted things would change from north to south or east to west. The picture postcard lied. The still-life would remain overpopulated. Fast forward would reveal more of the same. Scandinavia seemed better, but the newspaper said North Sea fish and marine mammal kills at historic highs could no longer be blamed on naturally occurring bacteria. The kills sourced to human effluent and oil, both flow so freely into the North Sea, because smells are not so strident in the cold. A travel agent could advise that you simply must see it! Because you can't really smell it!

The future looked bleak, but then all thought is framed in mood, and moods tend to darken in the final minutes of play, down by too many points for a likely comeback. But isn't that the rub? Isn't that why they call it a comeback?

Two more smokes and another stiff coffee helped sort things out. The world seemed used up with people, cars and shit. A pilgrimage won't work anymore, in most places. The pilgrim will find tourism and tourists and culturally flavored gingerbread. The tourist will go home.

I'd come to this second café on a sidewalk rounding the lake, a hundred feet from thick traffic and separated by lush greenery, allowing the lake's serenity to serve as antidote to a road-weary soul. The lake looked and smelled clean, and though the yellow sky hung low, the café manager insisted, "Not pollution. No. Not pollution."

But it was. Switzerland's many valleys become wind tunnels for the exhaust of a hundred million cars. The lake was clear to the bottom as far out as the bottom was visible from the shore, no tampons or soda bottles, but carbon singed the air. The worst of it accumulated a few hundred feet up, and breathability at ground level was like ice cream over crap compared to Paris or the Med.

So I ditched my jacket in a mile and then my shirt and hiked three more to a sweat and fatigue that felt good. A lakeside bar with four stools and an awning looked inviting but closed. A woman stacked glasses in back. I went for shade and, with luck, a drink of water.

Her baggy blouse billowed over stretch pants with red chevrons below the knees. She worked over an old, steel sink, her hips and thighs showing considerable bulk but as much strength as padding, indicating youth or a life of work. I thought she'd hold up into the later rounds, when legs count most, as I pulled out a stool to take a break. She looked up and seemed surprised, like I'd interrupted a private thought. The place was empty but for us, and her face shone like sunrise on the lake. Full-bodied with red lips and good teeth, she led with a bosom of remarkable heft, yet it scoffed at gravity. Animate and warm, she welcomed, like a woman who loves her work, lighting up on a perfect stranger. A certain, nurturing love and *joie de vivre* shone as well. Maybe my depression made me more sensitive or receptive, but this light seemed bright at any hour. And I did want a nurse to sing a lullaby, as I rocked gently in her arms. She turned as if for a side view, with flourish.

She asked in French what I would like.

"*Une bouteille d'eau, s'il vous plait.*"

She seemed graceful in drink-prep, as much in pirouette as mechanical movement. Sweat beads perched on her brow, above her lip and on her cleavage. She dabbed all three with a tissue and looked up, glowing over this and that. Her black hair in its thick, wild radius highlighted her fair skin, smooth and hairless in contrast. Her translucent chemise covered her luscious self like a scrim on a play unfolding. What was the difference between this scene and the one on board the good ship Anal Penetration of only two days ago? I asked to be sure of myself in assessment of real life and right and wrong. The difference seemed obvious, between nuance and carnage, but that was my rationale, my value system. The difference was significant in that sense, but not so much in the scheme of things that veer in the same direction.

I had not savored the action on deck but enjoyed the show before me. Does subjective understanding make a man wrong. Of course it can, but it need not make a man bad. I too glowed, imagining the view from beneath her. Here was a woman a man could look up to. My ex-wife once stared sadly in the mirror, with pencils under her breasts. They hung there, squeezed in place between torso and breasts, no hands. She felt her youth had gone on this woeful milestone. I'd thought her too smart to be depressed over failing a test from *Cosmo*. I assured her that my nuts nearly hit the water, and jowls lead to wattles all too soon, because age happens to everyone, if they're lucky. So what? The ex-wife needed no derision or superior counseling. She closed the door.

"Je m'appelle Maria," the big woman said.

"Enchanté," I replied, eye to eye. She smiled with appreciation and comprehension on the transcendent plane. One day she would hold a pen and pencil set in place and maybe a blotter and small credenza and some office supplies too. But not today. Today a wisp of straw could nestle under the cornice, briefly, until drifting away. She accepted my heavy eyes as nature's way, from many years of men and their eyes, descending to her gravitational field. I did not feel weak and base but tolerated and welcome. She giggled and turned away.

Maria was anomalous in nature, hugely feminine to the point of caricature, a female figure of fantasy. She drew the stares of men as a black hole draws light. Serving an orange drink over ice, she watched me quaff as a concerned hen might watch a chick. Serving another to quench a deeper thirst, she rattled on.... I slowed her down. *"S'il vous plait, parlez plus doucement.”*

“Ah? Vous êtes Italien!” She was off to the races in Italian.

“No. Je suis Americain.”

“Non!”

“Mais oui.”

“Mais votre francais c’est très bien. C’est très, très bien!”

“Non. Je ne crois pas. Je parle française touristique!”

“Française touristique? Ah! Ah! Ah!”

She liked my joke.

It was chemistry.

It was on.

And it was strong. Conversing another hour in languages we didn’t share, we agreed by virtue of a pidgin miracle that a rendezvous after sundown would be good. *Après de soleil descendre* was my shot at that one. She lit up, red in the face at a bold proposal, and nodded like a piston. We went past chemistry to international currency. I would learn that for her it was another shot at a man who would love her first for her breasts and secondly forever. That man could be me. For me the bells tolled.

She turned around to work the cooler, perhaps to preclude surprises on the hind quarters, a precaution that seemed base and unnecessary but then practical and perhaps necessary too, experience and disappointment being as demanding as they are. And isn’t that a strong woman for you? Opening her stance to go deeper for the wine, she splayed like a butterfly fillet but came up quick and caught me looking, and she laughed and blushed, gaining what some women spend fortunes having surgically enhanced, which is beauty, in this case of the natural kind.

I didn’t care about the fat and felt a moment of growth, spiritual and otherwise. I'd never not cared about the fat. I didn't care about the dimples or wobbles. I wanted her naked, smothering me with tits, bouncing me off her bountiful self like a play toy. I wanted the works—and in profound transcendence of want, I saw the light. Oh, sure, it's an old, shopworn concept, most often applied to those who can't see it. But she also went beyond luscious curvature to goodness in being. In that light, came love. She said she was twenty-nine and looked nearly that young. She'd never been married and had no children but took care of her nephew. She wanted to marry someday, if the right man would... come along.

She said my French was good. I said I knew better. She said she only wished she spoke English like I spoke French. I told her if she did, it would sound like, I meet you with, sun descend, after. *"Oui!"* she said, *"Comme ça!"* She spoke seven languages, but I said it was eight, counting body language. I explained, and she laughed like a hyena.

Did she have a boyfriend? No. No time. "I find this difficult to believe, with prime exposure here by the lake and so many thirsty men passing by. And you do seem...frisky."

She looked puzzled but grateful. *"Merci."* She laid her hands on mine with voltage that came as no surprise; she was so big, with panache to match. A minute of silence seemed naturally sweet, unlike the void between those who share hormonal urges and no more. Dialogue seemed incidental; we simply held hands. She felt safe and warm. She leaned forward with a blissful smile. Careless fingers touched a nipple, and it rose behind the silk.

"My God!" she whispered.

"You do speak English."

She shrieked with laughter, pulling away, rationing, to better sustain my hunger. I tried to imagine tiring of so much woman, but of course I could not. I told her in failing French and slow English that France and Italy were different from what I'd expected. I'd learned that any gratification derived from my journey would be found elsewhere.

"Gra…tifi…cation?"

"Satisfaction. *Satisfait*."

"Ah!"

"Where now shall I search?" I asked rhetorically, leaning her way. She laughed, backing away and telling me it's good to stay naïve. Otherwise you will always be cynical and stay home.

I smiled in reflecting, having decided to go home only a while ago, and only a morning hike later feeling a warmth ooze over, as if perseverance had led to a rich reward. She poured wine. We drank. She poured again. We drank. I suggested that this may not be a good idea.

"*Porquois pas?*"

"Here we are with this feeling, and you know I'm half crazy to see you *a la carte* and touch you, but…."

Unable to follow, she shrugged. I continued, "But we can only talk on the surface. Maybe that's all we need for now, and I can tell you have insight to offer. But we can't delve into ideas because of our language barrier." *Nous ne parlerons pas les ideas* was the best I could do, which sounded something like, "We will not talk the ideas."

She shrugged again. Maybe. Maybe not. This is something to think about. She smiled sweetly, and I got the message; the volley had begun, idea and response. We drank, and she poured again, perhaps with a feeling of progress similar to that of the first cave woman who poured fermented juice for her cave man.

We conversed in the free exchange of nuance, innuendo, unsubtle hint and playful touch. Patrons arrived, subduing our flirtation. A man stepped up to the bar and downed a short glass of muscatel. After four or five he turned and said, "Nah!" He smiled with pleasure.

A family took a table and two couples arrived. Maria performed her dreamlike dance, catching my eyes on her way out, before and after taking orders, on her way back, prepping and serving. She tittered sprightly on pixie feet, carrying her tray high on her fingertips. I laughed. She took it for rapture, for intoxication with her and the wine, and I suppose it was. She recalled the hippo ballerinas in *Fantasia*. She must have seen it; she knew the choreography. But I bit my tongue on that note. It was unfair. She was not hippo-like in any way, except maybe ever so slightly in the hips. She was big, not simply big but with grace and delicate form, with the grandeur so vainly coveted by the French. Except in Maria it was real.

It must have been late morning or early afternoon when a tour group came down the lakefront walkway on their way to the tour boats just around the bend. Two and three abreast, they moved resolutely as a centipede speaking white noise.

Once they faded round the bend, Maria said she didn't like the tourists. I shrugged, fairly soused. A well-preserved woman in her late thirties and a *très chic* outfit with shoulder pads and a few pounds of jewelry hurried up the sidewalk on short steps, constrained in her tight dress and high heels. She registered sexually in spite of her pancake makeup, rouge, eyeliner, shadow, blush, mascara and lipstick. She showed good legs, excellent derriere and lovable curvature elsewhere. She was a test, because man is often weak for new women, and though weakness may lead to ruin, he will pursue. Yet upon this woman I stared, wondering where was my other woman, the one scheduled to care for me at sundown, from whom I strayed. Perhaps in my inebriation I saw Maria as the woman at home. Is that so unreasonable?

"Did a group come this way? A tour group? Are the tour boats this way? Do you speak English?" The heavily made-up woman was late and nervous, having a bad day and clutching her clipboard. She seemed annoyed with my altered consciousness. Maria shrugged. The woman didn't know what to do.

"*Ils sont là bas,*" I said. "*Les bateaux. Peut-êtres cent metres.*" The woman waved her arms in frustration.

"What? Where? This way?" She turned circles like Curly Joe and grew more distressed.

"Just there. Around the corner," I finally said.

"You speak English!" It was an accusation. I'd toyed with her. I hung my head. She tromped off. Maria laughed and chattered, something about the skinny tour bitch. She poured a victory round. We drank.

XVI

Uncritical Love

A man can lose track of time in summer, when late afternoon turns seamlessly to evening, so far north the sun hovers low from six to ten-thirty. Waking up from stone drunk, cheek to dirt, twigs pressed across the brow and sprinkled through the hair, what's left of it, drool wicking a snail trail, head pounding, eyes blinded, the question was, simply, Wha? Nnuuhh….

I sat up in pain. A giant form blotted the sun, at once a relief and a fright. Maria squatted with a wet rag and a little hairbrush. She wiped my face and shooed debris from my head, emitting tiny whimpers in her heavy breathing.

She leaned until my nose was nary an inch from her cleavage. I sniffed. She nurtured, as if holding a babe, pulling me into the firmament. I sniffed again, and there it was, flowers. I could have slept again, as she worked me over, cleaning, brushing, caressing my head, rubbing my shoulders, lifting me effortlessly to the vertical and infusing me with reasonable posture. She chattered that it was seven o'clock, time for our rendezvous. My head ached; it was so far from ready. But who is ever ready? Nobody came to mind, and quietly I went.

Her second job, in the bar up across the road, began at ten, so we only had three hours. She knew exactly where to go. Love prevailed.

She helped me up the grassy hill, rubbing where she knew I hurt. Maybe I became frailer, knowing she was there for the rub. She chattered, I couldn't tell what, as she eased me into her car, got in herself and headed out of town and up a mountain road.

Cool air and glacial mist were elixir to the muddled mind; I rode like a rag doll, waking up. To my immediate left was Maria, guardian angel, messenger of love, loving recipient of my need. I felt neither crass nor self-centered but only equal to her great gift of giving. Way up and pulling off the paved road, we wended along a fire break, through trees and boulders and a cooler, thicker mist and stopped. Falls gently rumbled into a small lagoon that spilled over its lower lip. We got out and watched in awe, realizing the moment our lives had converged upon. The falls beckoned with revival.

She walked around the car, lifted me out, unbuttoned my shirt and pants, pulled them free and tittered, gently touching the goose bumps rising. The beast slept, cowardly in the face of frigid immersion, oblivious to the warm reward. She didn't care, coming in to wrap her arms around me with a moan, putting her mouth on mine. She seemed hesitant, deliberately delicate, angelic in her soft contact. I sensed constraint, caution, perhaps, based on experience. The exchange was romantic, and yes, hearts fluttered in proximity to each other, yet our kiss unveiled a potential of unknown character. What's the difference between flowing water and a flood? Shivering, naked and pained,

I sensed her need heading my way in great waves. The beast ducked farther into cover. She reached with thumb and forefinger and a cackle that resounded through the forest.

In choreography for the ages, she toyed with her top button, teasing, taunting, torturing it to surrender. The second button, as if seeing and learning, gave up more easily. Button three fell away and four was good as gone, giving way to giddy excitement, rapid heartbeat and fear! What if they sagged? Or drooped, or disappointed in any way less than what had been imagined? But never mind is all a man can think, so far down the road he longed to take. Response rose in every bone but one. Shivering to beat the band and hypothermia, I hurried with the last two buttons. She tittered and grinned, confident as a debutante in spring, as I peeled one shoulder and the other, arriving at the great canvas and cable harness with its turnbuckles and clevis pins, swivels, shackles and clips. I feared the face of God but hurried. She seemed proud. That helped, and why wouldn't she be confident, with a harnesses in lace, embroidered flowers and flower scent in her cleavage? Well, she could be making the best of an unfortunate situation, but I pressed on, *et voilà!*

"My God," I assured her. I hit the treasure like Scrooge McDuck in the loot cellar, diving in, coming up for air, tongue trilling hill and dale and under the granite ledge where no pencil could stay. I skied uphill to front and center to encourage what the brisk air had missed, until I stopped. A resonant shudder in basso profundo, like the mating call of the humpback whale, rose from deep within. It warned of potential, of critical need, of survival of the species, herein unleashed. I eased up, grasped the objects of desire to warm my hands. She whimpered. The little soldier stirred in his bunker to peek at the ruckus outside, but kee-ryste, it was cold. What about a bed and sheets and room service?

She wiggled from her pants like a fish from a net and pulled me by the hands to the edge of the little lagoon. She let go and jumped in, shrieking again in delight. I followed, sensing sudden death by cardiac arrest. She came up easy as a polar bear, breathing casually, cooling off.

I fought free of the gripping cold. I sought relaxation as the best frame of mind to die in. In staccato breathing, purpling, I waded out. She played in the water while I trembled, neck deep and going down. She came to me, my nymphet, enfolding me with cushy warmth, her heat pouring into me as she huddled me to herself and up and out, to the car, where she wrapped me again in a fairly clean towel from the back seat.

Dried and dressed we descended again to lakeside Switzerland in summer. The air tingled, and so did we. No talk required, we eased under the soft blanket of sunbeams and evening haze.

Maria's flat circumscribed her life. Three floors up from the bar where she worked, it completed her daily orbit. She eased me gently onto her bed, fluffing pillows, stroking my head and moved to the kitchen, where a few minutes of soft sounds led to steaming potatoes and cabbage, hummus and pita with lemon and oily green olives. I thought it best to have sex before eating and then again after and wondered why she wanted to wait. But then everything smelled so good, and I would learn why soon enough: The golden interlude prior to biblical knowledge comes only once in a romance, and she wanted to stretch it out, to make it last, to give it depth and character in many facets, to have it for later.

She beckoned me to the table. We sat still, as if sharing a prayer of being and gratitude. She poured sparkling water and tea and observed in another silence. She smiled; all was well. We ate slowly, loving the moment and simple dishes. She chattered in French, something about the Arab influence there on the lake and how she loved Mediterranean cuisine.

"*Parles-tu Arabic?*" I asked.

The familiar form of French lit her up. My first use of it, casually over simple repast, opened her eyes wider, as she smiled and chattered in Arabic. I asked if she could teach me. She tried but only for a minute. "*Je suis tarde!*" She was late. She stripped, changed and left, saying I should eat more and rest and come down to the bar anytime before two, when she would be done, when the night would be ours.

I lay again in utter peace, savoring a day of life, wondering if I should fetch my kit from the hotel. I would rest first for an hour or two, watching the brilliant sun sizzle into the lake. I closed my eyes on the tick-tock clock on her dresser—ten o'clock—plenty of time. I woke in a minute, just past two in pitch dark, lost in space under two Jupiters.

The firmament moved, until the South Pole suffered sudden warmth, proving conflict in the absolute universe. Darkness descended in a dream of offshore drilling on a distant planet with unstable atmosphere and quirky terrain, leading to tremors and the earthquake. The little soldier bore on, seeking friendly life in that faraway place.

XVII

Describing the Intimate

Physical detail rarely enhances the picture in romance. Without love, only bodily function remains, in clinical profile or earthy jargon. Sperm to splooge, for example, or vagina to cootch, sexual intercourse to fucking, and so on, all of it mere matter and flesh flexing to discharge, in the race all species share, in folly for some but headlong for all, to dust. Some species get by on osmosis or cell division, but those primitive reproductions seem distant from romance. With love, bodily function becomes incidental, beyond the moment.

On the other hand, if personal contact is glossed discreetly, then love may look timid or equivocal or worse: average and mundane.

A book widely read that summer, poolside, on trains and in cafés, failed to capture the sweet social nuance of pursuit and loss of that control in physical contact. The back cover raved, "Marvelous…. Riveting…. A Joyous Read…. A Sizzling Page Turner."

The main character was honest, courageous and kind. He played hard and had sex with willing female characters of varying size, color, shape, height, accent and inclination. The main character said, "We spent the weekend wearing each other out." I imagined them stripping and waxing floors, vacuuming and shampooing carpets, washing windows and screens. I could not imagine sexual exchange for two days and nights, even as I watched Maria with tireless contentment. One female character left the story on a grand exit: "Is okay. Now I will eat you." *She dropped to her knees.*

With kneepads, I hoped. I've never seen a woman drop to her knees. I asked Hattie for a special favor on the edge of the bed once, with her on her knees.

"Why?" she asked.

"Something new," I said. She stooped to one knee, then the other.

"This won't work," she said.

"It will," I said. "I read about it." She bent awkwardly to make the angle. Then she stood and pushed me back on the bed. "This is how it works best. You should trust me on this one." She finished the puzzle quickly, announcing, "There you go. All done. Next."

Hattie was cruel in giving like that; and there was the cut across the grain. *She dropped to her knees*, on the other hand, was a different kind of cruel, too hard on the knees.

Sex with Maria was big and golden. She was to women what the Hope is to diamonds. Her physical being reflected ambient largesse, heart and soul included.

XVIII

Essence of Maria

 Maria lingers on a first glance that never ended. In soft light and scent, she endures. It happened late and again early. She pulled the shades, so it could happen midday. She cooed, finding her stride and long-haul rhythm.

Maria was pleasure bent. She leaned into love.

Hovering overhead on all fours fairly hid her broad backside and heavy thighs, presenting her fulsome self to advantage. I didn't mind the bulk. Maria felt like a milestone, a growth opportunity. I could not judge her, except to admire her breasts and spirit. The rest of her moved from extreme to conventional, what comes naturally with repetition and familiarity. She kept excellent white Chianti chilled in a bucket bedside, to keep me tipsy. Maybe she thought the buzz would blur her mass, taking it from fact to concept. And she moved weightlessly on top. Our communion in the universal tongue seemed like safe haven, secluded and secure, private, hospitable and snug, especially for a woman so big.

With nuance she could follow or lead. She could move mountains with her tongue. She poured wine, put the glass to my lips and said, "Do you like that?" It was a request. Every man hears it. Some listen. It was a rare phrase in English too, born as well from experience and need.

I never ate a big, fat woman. She wanted it. It was brief, slow with spooky effects, like walking into a dark room and having the door close. Who's in there? Well, of course Maria was in there, waiting, anticipating, salivating. Thighs enfolded ears. I looked up and over dimpled horizons, across the jungle to the plains. Wine eased the rational view, most of the fearful and the bailout. She'd timed me right. I was drunk. It was dark. I laughed. She tittered. I burrowed in. She moaned.

Hauntingly reminiscent of my first departure from home as a youth, it brought to mind that first job, out in the world, at a lakeside resort. Or maybe I used those scenes as substitute in the moment, as more assuring that spelunking a dark cavern. The waiters and waitresses stayed in a dormitory called Holiday House, where odd shifts at odd hours meant the party never ended. Only a busboy at seventeen, I got next to a college girl, a senior no less, who kissed with her tongue. Every day the kids went down at shift's end to The Ledge, a private spot on the lake only a foot above the water. We climbed the sheer cliff behind The Ledge to another ledge twenty feet up. Another twenty feet above that put the hardiest boys forty feet over the water. Everybody jumped the twenty-footer, and the guys went forty at least once, if they wanted second base. Years later, the girls would resent this machismo but still admire it, as they had loved it back then.

At forty feet on a toehold, I could only tremble so long, before the others would sense a choke. They got quiet. I could not step back for fear of social death, even as I knew real death waited below. I pictured the launch, the arc, the acceleration and impact. I knew I would die, but the die was cast; so be it. I would not be shamed on bowing out, or so I thought and thought, until Tom Hughes, a big, muscular boy with a drawl, climbed up and said, "Don't thank about it. Don't thank for one durn second. Jump. Just fuckin' jump." He'd jumped higher ledges in West Memphis, so he knew, so I jumped. I fell forever.

Years later, I jumped and fell again, massaging those inner thighs with my ears. Maria prayed, mostly in Italian. I expected *Ava Maria* but got only *Dios Mio*. The jungle thicket, dark and dewy, demanded courage and resolve, for social salvation and no time for fear or squeamish uncertainty.

Wending the acrid path seemed wrought with quicksand, asphyxiation, swamp things and utter love. I held on and set fear aside. Falling thirty-two feet per second squared from forty feet up, I laughed on impact with relief and, moreover, with the joy of survival in spite of the pain. Neither Tom Hughes nor my coed told me to cover my butt; water jammed in like a broomstick. I limped for a day, even while tongue wrestling on second base with my seasoned girlfriend.

Call it synchronous, a convergence of non-coincidental events that strive to make sense of the Universe: I savored those youthful times, as Maria jammed her thumb up my ass. Maybe she thought I'd like a thumb up my ass. I didn't. It didn't matter.

In polite terms, we exchanged pleasantries and proceeded to termination—no, not termination, though we seem to flail in life until we can't. Nor did we achieve fulfillment. Few people do. But we finished the bottle and slept, marking two huge steps toward peace. I woke in the morning with a nipple in my face, hugely compelling but unlovely. We mounted up again, more mechanically and hazy, and slept again, until she woke me again with another pleasantry, which should have seemed sweet in its giving essence, all one way. But depletion made her effort more demanding than lovely, until it was over. We got up, opened the shade, stretched and again wondered.

What came next was also on cue, because life seems all too often scripted with cues. Forever got all used up. Still loving as ever a person could be, she hit me, figuratively speaking, of course, square on the chin, as it were. She seemed bigger in proportion than only last night. Flitting about naked, she turned and shook like a woman who knows she is loved. I asked about the lakeside bar. Would she not be late? She said no, yesterday was her last day before vacation. We would have two weeks together, starting now. Were we lucky or what?

What? A healthy man wants to move with daylight, wants to press round the bend and proceed with adventure. The hormone battalions lay dead and wounded. Suffocating clouds gathered over the bright, new day. That's how it is.

XIX

Love Test

Two weeks isn't forever. Two weeks isn't forever. Two weeks isn't forever.

Maria made the bed, tidied the flat and began prepping for the stage that all the world had come to be. Swirling her hair in a high stack, she looked regal. She glowed. A few pounds of earrings, necklaces and bangles added weight, if not gravity. Still naked, she perched a hefty rhinestone butterfly on her left breast. I failed at ecstasy, so she put the butterfly away. She offered her breast, perhaps for a touch. She tittered. I looked at it objectively, indifferent, yet I rose in weakness. She saw it as strength. Bug-eyed, she shrieked. Look at that, after such a night! She spun away to her wardrobe promising *A plus tard, mon ami*. Later, my love. Harnessing herself with dispatch, she pulled a billowing satin dress from its hanger and threw into the air, glancing my way with a sparkle, catching its bottom hem and shimmying like a great marine creature who knows these waters well.

Situating her great self into place, she aligned the ruffles and billows, snugged her hips and adjusted the shoulder pads. Shoulder pads? She had a stance like Bronco Nigurski's without shoulder pads and looked formidable as a fullback ever did, but even more trussed, gussied, frilled and twilled. With a final spritz, she twirled in presentation of the public self. Like a small building with banners, she said, "Come. *Nous allons au Grand Hotel manger le petit déjeuner.*" We would brunch at the Grand Hotel.

Brunch at the Grand Hotel was a grand feed and a grand show of linen, crystal and subservience. It was five-star foo foo in tourist format, what non-dominant people fantasize as ultimate pleasure. The cream-based fare dominated my heart. Maria was proud, possibly redeemed. In her finery, she clung to me in two-day duds and shadow.

Who cared? If I could give this back to a bountiful giver, then more's the better. I went along. She scanned for friends and acquaintances. She waived. I was on display.

First came wine, then salads, then soup, wine, appetizer, brochette, fruit and cheese, baguette, wine, coffee and a short break before dessert. Marie chose for us from an eight-page dessert menu, and we soon faced great mounds of ice cream and sugar cookies, sugar sticks and whip cream clouds. Fruit-layered waves shored up bon-bon ledges and slowed the dark chocolate lava oozing down the slopes. Maria called the waiter back and spoke very fast Italian. He bowed and spun away and returned in a blink with chocolate sprinkles.

She smiled beatifically at life and death with a sugar coating.

Sensing my discomfort, she sat up with a pinky raised and began, angling sideways, eyeing me, spooning the creamy stuff daintily into her gob. I felt weak. I wanted no more, neither to careen the slopes or mix it up in the creamery. But regret was a weakness I'd long regretted, so I joined her, digging in.

She rhapsodized, "*Nous avons deux semains. C'est très bien, non?*" Two weeks. It's very good, yes?

"*Mm. C'est parfait.*" Mm. Perfect.

She had an idea for a little trip I might enjoy. Her local knowledge would be of great benefit, she said, and I would return the benefit to her with my company. What a sweet sentiment. She mentioned her fluency in the languages, after all, and she knew her way around. I could feel her lively spirit and freedom from moods, and it was good. She was very fat, and I was amazed once more, dipping into the goo.

We would go north through Brussels, to a little town just over the border in Holland, a seacoast burg she'd heard about for years and wanted to see. We could leave today or tomorrow, after a visit to an ailing friend who lived in a tiny studio with two others. It would be crowded, but she wanted me along. I sensed another display, but who cared?

But another night on Maria's trampoline seemed wearisome, and declining the hot buffet seemed somehow, rude, like I'd be disappointing my generous hostess. I was wrong to think that a woman needs it like a man, that a woman must squish to ditch the stuff, in order to relax like a man. A woman needs love like any sentient being will do. As a female of the human species, she often prefers long term, with security. I felt hopeless, seeing only challenge, and I felt painfully honest. Two weeks loomed like a wall with razor wire on top.

She sensed my fear, taking my hand gently, her hand warm and moist. "I will eat you," she said. "I will eat you very much." She practically cried, sinking in pathos, rendering us pathetic.

I smiled, kind of, appreciating the sentiment, hoping she spoke in the figurative sense. I mean, after all, she could eat. Still, she was sweet like a saint, playing to romance with practical imagination.

We walked the few blocks uphill behind the Grand Hotel to the cellblock of studios that served as housing for the wait help. Jane was a waitress, had been since arriving from London eight years ago. Her longtime friend Julian had been with her since he'd arrived three years ago. They weren't an item, not like Maria and I were an item. Julian was too depressed for romance. Now he faced a crisis with the biggest show of his life scheduled for that very afternoon at the biggest club on the lake, with producers and agents in the audience. The funk was on him like mold on cheese and he could not play. Julian was a pianist, when he wasn't depressed. He lay lifeless on the sofa, melted there, taking his smoke to the nub and practically chewing the butt.

"He's depressed," Jane said. Bright-eyed and effervescent, she hugged Maria and kissed her cheeks. Then she hugged and kissed me and whispered, "Don't you just love Maria?" It seemed like a trick question. I did love Maria, and in a blink wished I could love Maria as Jane did. She spoke fast French to Maria, who answered with a shimmy and an *oo la la*.

Jane turned to me. "He's a wonderful musician, really. Nobody plays like him. But he gets depressed and can hardly move. Move, Julian, so they can sit down." Julian rolled over and tucked his knees to make room.

We sat. Julian looked undead. "He rolled over on command," I said. "The truly depressed can't do anything. Catatonic." We waited. I wondered if Julian was once a thinker in Paris but didn't ask. Finally, I said, "Julian."

"It won't work," Jane said. "His mother and father are both psychoanalysts. They can't do anything for him."

"You mean they can't figure it out?"

"They say he's manic depressive. They gave him some pills, but I hid them. If he takes the pills he can't play. At least this way he might snap out of it. He's not like this all the time."

"What a relief," I said. Julian grunted. "Julian!" I yelled. He twitched. "If I can tell you one little thing to try, will you try it?"

Julian murmured, "Yes." This was a good sign.

"I need an ashtray. Can you hand me an ashtray."

He looked pained, but he sat up and reached for an ashtray. I reached for Jane's shoulder beside her neck and massaged it. She moaned. "Just as I thought. Jane loves you, and she has a terrible ache in her shoulder."

"I do, you know," Jane said.

"Julian. Will you rub Jane's shoulder for her?"

Julian winced. "That would make two things you want me to do."

"Rub the fucking shoulder!" He winced again and rubbed. "How do you feel now?" He shrugged. "See? You're doing something for someone else. You must give, Julian."

He rubbed weakly. Jane moved into it. "Give what," he weakly asked.

"Just give." He grunted. "You play the piano without asking yourself why you're playing. You give the music, like Jane here gives you a place to stay."

He smiled weakly. He loved Jane and rubbed her with more feeling, until he slumped and asked, "But why?"

"That's not part of it, Julian. Why doesn't matter. It never has. You may never know why. But you know how. And I promise: you can die as soon as you're done. Now stand up." I stood up, not threateningly but hovering, imposing. "Stand up, Julian." He grunted, so I pulled him up, and he stood there like a straw man with no spine. "Move your arms and fingers." He flopped things around. I spoke, nose to nose. "People all over the world are depressed, and I'll tell you why. It's because they take. Gimme, gimme, gimme. Here you are taking three seats while three people are standing up. Give. Give us your seats. Go give yourself a shower. Then we'll give your legs a stretch and walk down to the goddamn piano and give some music. That's all there is to it."

A smile twitched. "Just sit down and play?"

"You're a genius." Of course this little play made mockery of a failed being. Julian could relate to that too, and he turned sadly downward. "You're slipping, Julian. You're thinking. Don't think. Stop thinking. Every thought you ease up to, crush it with an act of giving."

Julian thought. Twitching in and out of a smile, he said, "I don't know if this will work."

"Nobody knows. But it's all we got. It's worth a try," I said. "We know nothing. Nothing is good. It's more than we knew before. This is progress. Give, Julian!"

"Nothing is good?"

"It's a good nothing, Julian! Not an empty nothing."

"But what if I get...."

"Give!"

Julian nodded, smiling freely now. "I'll try it. But...."

I whispered, "Give."

Troubled and confused, Julian shuffled to the bathroom, mumbling, "Give, Julian."

Jane loved the show and showed her appreciation with another

144

hug, this one without three kisses. This one went to the personal energy exchange popular among the spiritual crowd. Over her shoulder, as our auras comingled, I saw a photo on the wall by the bed, the only decoration in the place. Julian and Jane smiled for the camera, on a dock at the lake under blue sky, topless, he scrawny, sunburned and stooped. She beamed in the photo, looking at her disabled friend, infusing him with love and strength. What a lovely woman, I thought, as she infused me. Was that a pelvic thrust? Or just a random movement? Either way, she set the little wheels to turning in the head up top, pondering strategy to allow the fat one to hit the road, so Jane and I could continue our convergence. Harsh, perhaps, but also merciful in nature's indifferent way....

"Oh. Hi," Jane said, pulling back a quarter inch to say, "This is Horst."

"What?"

She nodded at the corner, where Horst sat. He'd slipped in or maybe was there all along, blending with the furniture. He slumped in a chair, the smoke and dust blending well with his natural haze. Salt and pepper hair on his head and face emphasized the mouth hole. Horst breathed through it without showing his teeth. His embouchure didn't sink below grade, indicating the presence of teeth. He smoked like a small factory on the Rhine. Spittle-flecked lips and narrow eyes made teeth incidental to the overall impression he made, which was shit bum, on the make for something to eat and a place to sleep. He stared, as if up and out from a sub-niche in the substrata, a niche that was mine only moments ago. Quick discourse between Maria and Jane was rife with *une problem*, but I would need another minute to fill in the blanks, including the biggest blank.

Horst shifted on the threadbare chair that matched the sofa and the unmade bed. Movement in the tiny abode was sideways by necessity, and confinement must have factored in Julian's depression. I already felt worse about the situation. This was life in a box, except for Jane. What did she see in a scurvy lump like that?

Horst attempted to climb out of his ashtray image with cornball macho—with a heavy gold chain and shirt open on chest hair like an Airedale's. Dingy and crummy as an industrial slum, his leathery skin and lumpy muscles showed time in the trench, not the gym. Horst had been around. He would die young and knew it and didn't give a fuck. Drunk again and lighting another smoke to go with another stale beer, he rested easy in a light sweat. Empties lined the windowsill, ash flecked. Wiping his chin with a furry arm, he belched. Jane beamed at his amazing skill.

He grunted on a half nod. Jane flitted about, seeking distraction, rearranging the mess, elaborating on *le problèm*. She was preggers, and the lucky fella was not a family-type guy.

Horst smoked. I shrugged. "Overpopulation is a terrible thing." Horst nodded. Jane and Maria shot stink eye. I covered. "They say the wrong people are having children. You could be the exception."

Horst grunted and asked, "Do you like to smoke some hash?"

I did. So I sat while Horst rolled a joint. Maria fidgeted, impatient with Horst and me. Jane gave the update. Her third abortion in three years was different from the first two. It never went away, the soul of it. It lingered, until it could slip back in, and here it is. "Here," she said, patting her tummy.

"When did it slip back in?"

Horst laughed. Jane blushed. Horst sprinkled hash into the tobacco and rolled deftly into a megaphone spliff. Lighting the fat end, he pumped an ember and passed it over. Anyone can take the mix, if lungs are properly pre-coated with tar and nicotine. I took it easy and still had a coughing fit. Horst laughed again. How bad a guy could he be?

Jane didn't know what to do. It was a mantra. Horst and I passed the joint, until she knew what to do but could not do it alone. Without Horst, she didn't know what to do.

Horst smoked and drank.

Jane murmured variations on uncertainty, until Maria put an arm around her and pulled her near. Horst smoked it to the nub, dropped it in an empty and leaned over to remove a shoe and sock. Clearing toe jams came next. He may have done the other foot but leaned back and shifted sideways instead to ease a bit of flatulence and pick the eczema from his elbows. We could only speculate that the satisfying interim had let him forget the other foot. He seemed cool in the clutch, ignoring impending parenthood with aplomb, but then life was a clutch. So what could he do but stay cool? And we were stoned. He explained in surly grumble that didn't want Jane to go away and didn't want to be a party of three. He loved having Jane around and surely wanted to fuck her again, frequently, starting soon. He just couldn't be bothered with the other. He nodded at me with a gruff smile. "Pretty good shit, yeah?"

I had to admit, "Fuckinay."

Jane's friends told her to abort, and she knew why. They loved her and looked out for her; she could hardly support herself much less a baby too, but still. Had she not proven that she could live within her means? "I've always got by, haven't I? I mean I've made more sometimes and less sometimes, but it's been enough, hasn't it? I don't want to be a burden. Maria isn't a rich one, you know." She laughed at youthful poverty. Maria answered in hard, fast French.

Horst raised an eyebrow. "My God, she's some fine big tits, isn't she?" He looked my way.

"Yes, she is," I said. "The biggest, I think. And the finest. You can't imagine." He leaned near, as if for detail.

Julian came out of the bathroom, spit-shined and grinning. "Give, Julian, give." He dropped his towel, handing an ashtray to Horst and rummaging for pants and a shirt. "Give, Julian, give."

Jane slumped on the couch, stuck there, as Julian had been stuck. "How far along?" I asked.

"Six weeks. I have four more weeks to decide. I don't know what to do." She looked down. Maria watched me, expectant, hopeful, like I would know what to do. Horst lit another smoke.

A long minute passed. Julian scatted a tune in the bathroom. Jane sighed, expressing her happiness over our visit. Maria smiled sadly. We waited dreamily. Maria and Jane turned to me. "I have no answers," I said. "Life is full of challenges. Jane is a lovely person. What do I know?"

"You know," Maria said. Jane smiled my way. Horst smoked.

"Horst. What do you want to do? Has anyone asked?"

Horst didn't hesitate, perfectly stuck between knowing and numbness. "I have nothing. I am content to have nothing."

"Jane wants the baby." Jane nodded. "This feels like a natural progression." They waited.

"*C'est facile*," Maria shrugged. Jane sat up. Horst smoked. Julian emerged, beaming, ready for Sunday school, in need of parental supervision.

"Oh, Julian!" Jane rose to him, and the odd plot thickened, the three-way love dashing whatever I could offer, though a unique scenario emerged in a blink, wherein Jane and Julian could find happiness ever after on Julian's steady income as a great pianist, and baby makes three. I did not share this thought; it seemed so uncertain, so unstable. Beyond that, Julian had adapted to despair. Horst loved himself best with his needs fulfilled. Jane loved Julian, who had everything a man could have, except for a thumper, which Horst could provide. I fancied sitting in for a set, as she was on him, smoothing his wet hair, smothering him with hope.

Maria fidgeted and said we must go.

Jane agreed; Julian had less than an hour to stretch and warm up. Blending his mantra, "Give, Julian give," with his scat, he moved in syncopated rhythm out the door, and down we followed, unlikely entourage to a newly live wire on his way to fame and fortune, on the verge of short circuit and disconnection.

Horst rose like a trash heap come to life. He shook off the funk of so many hours in a chair, drinking and smoking. He looked like a fighter in the later rounds, shaking off the beating and psyching up to throw a few more. Horst personified machismo but not as a pose. Horst had paid for the role. At least he was a friend and not a mugger—not a mugger in an alley at any rate. His demonstration of nothing to lose made the rest of us stronger. Jouncing doggedly into the great outdoors, he looked like walking wounded, ready to throw the upper cut. And he asked, "So. We are having a son?"

"You got one," I reminded all concerned. Julian was decrepit and not yet thirty. He smoked less vigorously than Horst but nearly as much. Beyond café paralysis, only music separated him from the bitter end. The music was his gift, and at the stage door everyone knew he would die young too, maybe during the matinee. But he was ready, assuring that "Hey, it's okay! Really, It's okay. It went away. I'm fine."

Yeah, and Germany was best known for its daycare centers. We pretended belief with a nod here, a thumbs up there. Maria whimpered, kissing him left, right, left, pressing her breasts for fortitude. He gave way. Jane slid in with another hug gift-wrapped in form and delivery and cosmic osmosis.

Meanwhile, back in this world, Horst said, "I am starving. Do you have money?" Jane said yes, we would go now for something to eat. She touched Julian's cheek, as he slipped through the door to other side.

Topside, on the terrace, the haze persisted but the sun shone through. We took a table in back to look authentic when we yelled for more. We ordered up, beer for me. Maria hesitated on scents from the kitchen but went along with a sigh. Jane couldn't eat, didn't feel so well, but a lemonade would be nice. Horst got the double schnitzel and the fried chicken dinner. Do poor people comprehend comparative values between a restaurant meal and a week's groceries? Or is lavish ordering a sweet revenge?

Relaxing in the sun, we listened to Julian warm up. A crowd drifted in and soon filled the place. "He really has quite a following," Jane said. "He's terrific. Wait till you hear."

People stood at our elbows and pushed from behind, seeming to love the density. Then came Horst's massive spread with steamed potatoes and house salad. He didn't mind the crowd. He dug in two-handed, engorging to kill the hunger. Crisply flecks on his cheeks and chest and the grease pooling on his chin showed yet again that Horst didn't give a shit.

Jane reached over to whisk the debris from his mouth with her lovely finger. He jerked away like an irritated child. "I love it when he looks happy," she said. Horst grunted, fanging a fat-dripping thigh, coming away with a mouthful in his mouth and another mouthful hanging out and the skin of it dangling beneath that. Moving like a snake, unhinged, he lurched in great gulps. Failing to engulf this game, he shoved the mass in with two fingers.

I turned to his surge and grind to ask, "You think your soccer team really is worth a fuck?" He turned red and worked his jaws, until everyone laughed.

"He's happy," Jane said.

Maria leaned close to tell me, "One time I fuck him, and he never comes back." She spoke in English. "He is no good. He fucks my good friend, and now she has the baby." Dishing scorn freely, she pegged Horst as a womanizing animal. I looked down to avoid association and Horst, who had other bones to chew, beginning with the end of a leg bone, crushing it in his molars.

The announcer introduced Julian Hamilton, who began playing on utterance of his name, sliding into a melody of mystical fusion between jazz and classic. Suddenly alive, he shut them up. Silence prevailed, except for elegant music and gristle grinding.

Soon, even Horst stopped in mid-chew to listen. The music informed on life, that it was often inverted, that Julian was a virtuoso with no body, that he should be big and strong, and Horst should be frail and meek. Maria should be Jane. Jane should be Maria. I should be somewhere else.

Julian played three hours to a standing ovation and at the end looked ready for the end. Horst got drunk or stayed drunk. Jane loved his happiness. Maria rushed us out with the crowd, but I held back for a final hug. I told Jane we might never see each other again, but you never know, and if the occasion ever arose….

"I know," she said.

A long day stretched toward evening and reached far north up the highway, toward the little coastal town Maria had heard about for years but never had a chance to visit. We pulled into a small hotel in a little Belgian town along the way, under trees so big and lush they blotted out the stars. I spoke only English. "Tell me, Maria. What do we know about this place?"

We shared a distinct feeling then, that I was biding time, pulling her leg, putting her on, that the end was nigh.

XX

Saxuality in Repose

 Leaving Paris at night, sloppy drunk and late for a train, on a wobble and a spin, a man sees space turn in on itself. The maze flip-flops, French yack bouncing off the walls and down the tubes. Hex tiles and monotone slur like brie and melt like a dream.

Arrogant signs say this way and that and point to nowhere, until three new tubes appear. They look empty, with new signs. Fucking frogs, a foreigner might think. Feet accelerate through the goo to catch a train on time or get left behind forever. Momentum jogs alongside, a slapstick mime reminding a train chaser of what's been lost in the world of grace to the world of hurry.

Soon a stride is sweetly timed in the vortex like flotsam in a swirl. But wait. What's this? It's a man with no legs on a filthy rug with a battered sax, playing in the key of Metro, missing a note here and there but with such feeling and tone. I ask, *"Où est le train de Gare de l'Est?"* He plays on, one-handed, waving the other at the sign overhead that points straight ahead and says, Gare de l'Est. I reach deep and come up to play percussion, coins dropping into his dented tin bowl, the big coins at ten francs each, which seems fair value for a clear spring in a hopeless bog.

For years, I heard the music and wished to hear it again. I wanted to be drunk again in Paris again, until recollection and two bottles revealed that drunk was where I wanted to be. Paris was simply a good place to be drunk; it's so dirty, hostile and crowded. You can't go back. Still, you make the trip.

The going gets you down like it did on the first go-round, but you forget. Maria in harsh light was a compulsive eater compensating for loneliness. I was the perfect entrée.

She declined to speak, which is bad for a date but good for easing the strains. She let me be.

She sensed desire in our little room but not the desire she'd hoped for. I wanted away, like Horst, never mind his dirt and bad manners; I understood. Away is what many men want. I wanted away while listening to the melody in my memory until way past dark. I heard it in a chair, staring out the window, until the music went away.

Maria slept. She didn't stir when I slid in beside her softly as a single note.

Chaos would be more acceptable in the morning.

XXI

The Last Room in Vlissingen

We went the wrong way somewhere in Belgium for an hour and turned back to Rosendaal to get the right road to Vlissingen, the port town at the end of the line. Maria had fingered it for years on her map and said it seemed good, and she'd heard it was good, with the sea and beach and salt air.

Two nights of Maria seemed like a small lifetime. She'd drained my tubes, chafed my nub and put my mind on asceticism. The days were worse. Daylight was harsh to my love, with no shadows, and the fat rolling like ocean swells. Dimpled and stretched, she could make any man's eyes bulge, stretching her tongue to please. Yet she'd worn me out, leaving no chance for cream sauce. Her mass and sweat repulsed me, and more hair in her armpits than Larry had on his head didn't help. I squirmed, slipping away.

Maria still shone but her great, lovely bosom became lazy flab. These harsh perceptions hit us on a midday rest stop off a side road on a blanket on the ground near her car. This was vacation, time to relax and enjoy. But nature was cruel. I tried making light of our adventure together but sensed failure.

We reached Vlissingen in late afternoon, hot and sweaty again and facing another grim truth. On Saturday millions of Dutch and Germans storm the beaches. The little town swarmed thicker than flies on road kill. We found no room at the inn. Maria looked ill from heat and the heavy burden. I parked her in a café on the beach and strolled up to look farther.

I found a pension in semi-bleak mode and knocked. A tall, gaunt man in a bathrobe opened the door, looked me up and down and said, "I have nothing at the moment."

I returned the up and down and said, "I must have a room. I have no place to stay."

He smiled into a death's head and gave me another up and down. "Wait." He made a call on the phone behind the door. He spoke Dutch then covered the mouthpiece and leaned my way. "You are very lucky. I have found for you the last room in Vlissingen. It has a *douche*, but the *toilette* is...is..."

"Down the hall."

"Yes. The *toilette* is down the hall. I do not know if it is good. But if you have no choice..."

"I feel lucky." And sometimes saying it makes it so. He slouched, waiting for a real answer. "I'll take it." Uncovering the mouthpiece, he rattled confirmation. "I'll piss in the shower."

"What?"

"Nothing. Is it set?"

He rattled more, rang off and said, "You must hurry." After copious directions, he offered a skeletal hand to shake and said, "Come back here. I will have something."

"Yes. My wife and I would like that." He stood straight, backed inside and closed the door. I went for Maria.

Forlornly fanning herself over iced tea in the crowded café, she waited. People pushed and shoved to the water's edge and the other way to the curb. Even in a crowd, she looked self-conscious, perhaps feeling more so. She was so big, and I was not.

The directions were bad and Maria got worse, approaching apoplexy, as we crept through traffic seeking streets that weren't there, reaching dead-ends. She closed her eyes and nodded off. The little car shrank and felt like the caboose of a circus train. She was the fat lady. I was the thin man, roustabout and driver.

But the real circus had only begun on the main canal in front of the Garuda Hotel, our last room at last. We parked three blocks down and walked past many fun rides with four speakers each, shrieking, crackling disco, bells and buzzers. I yelled at my romantic interest to stay put, while I went aloft to secure the rigging.

The Garuda was opposite a kiddie fun ride with little cars on a track. Sirens screamed to liven things up, and a recorded carnival woman howled in Flemish. My ears hurt. I felt them for blood, as a Japanese man inside beckoned me up four flights to a room over the chaos. "What time do they stop?" I yelled.

"What?"

"What time?" I pointed to my watch, pointed outside and slit my throat with a forefinger."

"Oh! The music! It is not funny for you?"

"No! It is not funny for me! It is sad for me!"

He looked at his watch and yelled, "Twelve o'clock! At the very latest half past!" He smiled and pumped his head.

The room was old and cheap. Dark and stuffy with flaking wall paper, rickety furniture, no lamps, a mushy bed and a window over the noise for eighty bucks. "Is okay you don't like, because I have no room more. No room more everybody! You leave is okay too. You go five hundred kilometers is no room more."

"I love this room. I love the shit smell and the shit feel of it. I especially love the noise."

"What?"

"I'll take it!"

"You pay now!" I counted out the guilders. He snatched them and hurried off. I went for Maria.

She looked beat and confused. We slogged up, and she sank into the bed. I sat beside her and put a hand on her but had nothing to say. I went to close the window, but it was stuck open, so I laughed and yelled, "We're here for a reason!"

"What is it?"

"I don't know yet!"

She looked hopeful, rising to close the musty curtain and engulf me like an amoeba on a speck.

"No, no!" I yelled. "Not now! I can't!" Nor could I ever again. We couldn't stay. We couldn't leave. We went to the streets and wandered the shabby seaport to midnight, when fatigue drowned the noise. We returned. I fell on the bed in my clothes and slept.

I woke a minute later with Maria beside me yelling that she had to peepee but didn't know where to go. I pointed at the door and yelled that it was down the hall. She went but came back, yelling that it was locked.

I yelled that she should peepee in the shower or the sink. What would she have done on her own?

She sensed a game, a change of mood and playful distraction there in Hotel Hell. She romped and shrieked, delighted with prospects for revenge, as if she would be the first to piss in the sink. I doused the light. She hoisted her skirt and eased her ass into it. I closed my eyes as she tittered, until the masonry fractured on a seven point oh, fragments crashing to the floor. Nobody heard.

I woke at three in silence. She lay beside me naked. A gang of vandals came down the street yelling, kicking cans and beating pipes on fences. She stirred and sat up. I closed my eyes and breathed slowly. She rolled to me for a touch. I grunted and rolled away. The cease-fire outside finally took hold.

We slept late. I cracked an eye to see if the coast was clear. It wasn't. She watched me, propped on a pillow. I faked sleep and rolled over. She rubbed my back. I moved into it, her strong hands easing the knots. She moved down to my ass and around to my thighs on a certain agenda. But morning communion was not to be. Throwing the cover back, I bolted for the shower, where I also brushed my teeth.

Disappointed but resigned, we shared a bleak breakfast of white bread, butter and instant coffee. She called it a good deal, because it came with the room. I nodded, rehearsing the rationale for our parting. The truth was simple, but the noise cranked on cue, so we only laughed. I took her hand and said we were there for the same reason we met and traveled together. And now we would part for the same reason. I didn't know what the reason was, but....

"I know," she said, sad but stoic, and I loved her all over again, for seeing the reasonable light. I told her we would talk soon. She said nothing, with a half smirk that said yeah, yeah, yeah. I told her I'd be back in Switzerland in two months. She smiled and nodded. One more march back to her car in a fit and a sweat with the bag and baggage of our stuff and our selves, and it was down to a hug and a peck.

She pulled slowly from the curb and my heart went with her. I watched her go two blocks and turn. I cleared the pavement, clicking my heels for a brand new day and life everlasting. I felt base and mean and well adapted to the world. Maybe it was only the world of men and not the world of love, but I had loved her, and I would challenge nature no further. Maria had guided me here, to this first step on the journey of my redemption or resolution—or ruin—with no direction or plan. This step felt better than the last, like jumping off a cliff again, maybe, falling free.

On the way back to Hotel Hell for my bag, Hattie intervened. I imagined her on the train south, looking out the window. Did she realize what we had, the fun and mobility and cash to support both? Did she gain perspective on seeing old friends? Did she wait for my call?

I had the number, so she must have wanted me to call. So I called.

XXII

Growing Pains

The morning grew old and burned down to ash, and from the ash rose a great, feathered anxiety. She'd left the place in the south of France, so the number was worthless. She'd gone to Italy but nobody knew when or why or with whom, though a fellow did show up just before she left. He may have been Italian and had mentioned a family visit in the beautiful hills. She'd left another number that surely was for me.

I wanted her on, saying she missed me too. I imagined her heartfelt report, that the Italian Alps were beautiful, and she'd met some nice people, but she wanted the old buckaroo back for some radical fun. We could hit the coast of Spain and ferry across to North Africa and smoke hash and make the scene.

The forwarding number was a dud. They spoke no English. I could call back in two hours, when someone would speak English. They thought Hattie was a city to the west of Florence. I didn't laugh and wished for Maria, to translate.

Far north in the seaside dump called Vlissingen, satanic disco and dervish funk howled. The carnival woman screeched her laughter and taunt. Two hours passed on instant coffee that tasted like dirt, and the Japanese manager wanted to know: one more night, maybe? He nodded vigorously. "You pay now."

"Go away." I dialed again. Hattie answered. Relief came in a huge wave breaking clean.

"God, I've missed you." she said.

"You have?"

"Of course. I have so much to tell you."

"How much could it be?"

"Oh, you know. It seems like so long. I met all these people, and this place is so beautiful. I've never seen anything like it."

"Maybe we should get together for a drink and talk it over." The connection welded into place, yet the next instant brought on another wave, a close out.

"Claudio's family has lived here over five hundred years. Just about everybody here is his cousin."

"Do they have high foreheads? Did you count their fingers?"

She covered the phone and asked someone to count fingers. She giggled, as if a few might be missing just now. My own fingers itched for something to choke, as pain rose in my chest and clutched my throat. "Is nine enough?" She giggled again. Could she toy with me so cruelly?

"I only called to say hey."

"Hey," she giggled. But it wasn't funny. She felt awkward, on the spot, which pointed to the real issue: Claudio's missing finger.

"I'll call again. Okay?"

"Wait. Where are you?"

"Holland. A little town on the coast."

"I love Holland."

"Who wouldn't, with the tulips and wooden shoes? Hans Brinker is here, you know."

"I don't know him."

"Oh. Well, you think you'll be staying there in Italy?"

"I don't know."

"What do you feel?"

"I don't know."

"Is it a new feeling?"

"Yes."

"Can you describe it?"

"You can probably describe it better."

Touché. I loved it when she moved inside, shutting me up like few people could. "Listen. I'm experimenting. That's all. Haven't you ever done that? I don't know what I'm doing. I miss you. I want to see you."

"You're a kick in the ass. You want me to come down there and save you from a guinea kidnapper?"

She laughed normally now. "That would be fun."

"I don't even know where you are."

"I was kidding. I'm not kidnapped. I'm just having fun. I got so bored where I was, I thought I'd go crazy. You know. I just need a little time. A little more time."

"Time for what? What kind of experimentation?

"You got a one-track mind. I think you must give yourself quite a bit of pain with it."

She pegged me: sexually obsessive, jealous and neurotic, her tone suggesting easy dismissal of my concerns. "I think there's something wrong with me. I miss you so much. You're the only person I ever really talked to."

"That sounds equivocal," I said. She hesitated. I suspected non-comprehension. "Ambivalent. Wishy washy."

"I love you. Don't analyze. Don't dissect. Okay? He has a sexual problem."

Whammo! But if Hattie taught nothing else, she taught me quick recovery. "Mm. That's tough. I can see where a girl would feel challenged. How tough is it?"

"Stop it. He's a good guy. I want a little more time."

I laughed but shouldn't have. "Then you want to come back, so we can talk, and I can get it up?"

"I don't think so," she said. "I'm just having fun. I'm only twenty-two, you know. Besides, we weren't exactly getting along."

"So what? Should I call back in three hours?"

"Give me a week. How's that?"

"Terrific. I won't have any trouble at all with a week. I'm sure I won't think a thing of it."

"Well, you shouldn't. Holland is fun. Especially Amsterdam."

"Is this guy standing there?"

"Not right here. But don't worry. He knows."

"He knows what?"

"He knows I love you."

"Jesus Christ, Hattie."

She laughed again. "Nobody ever called me that."

"I gotta go. I'll call you in a week. I'll be in Amsterdam. But how will you find me if you need to?"

"Relax. It's only a week. Hey. You met anyone?"

"Yeah, I did." My turn to twist the knife. "I met a fat lady. It's been interesting. She wants babies. I never hung out with a fat girl before. She's very nice. We have some strange fun; she's so fat. But I don't know. I don't want to hurt her. She's so giving."

"But you always hurt someone. You have to, or you're stuck. You know. You stay in a bad place just to save some pain, and you end up hurting yourself."

"When did you get so smart?"

"Call me in a week. Okay?"

"You like hanging out there with numb nuts, because you think it'll hurt him if you leave?"

"Call me in a week. Okay? And please wear a rubber. Will you promise me?"

"You want to stay there instead of coming up to Amsterdam for some fun?"

"Call me."

"And room service…." But she'd hung up.

XXIII

Fire and Ice

 The battered phone with ear grease in the holes seemed a perfect totem for my mood and the death noise outside. The manager came again with more pidgin greed. "You pay now."

The scales were balanced on Hattie and me. I'd spent days and nights immersed. With breasts and thighs abounding, I could get it up, at least at the beginning. Yet I feared a net loss on the Italian front. I held the phone, imagining her resourcefulness.

"You pay now." The little fellow had his hand out.

"Go fish."

"Yes. Yes. Fish. Dinner seven-thirty. Fish."

The noise peaked outside. I shagged my bags and walked down two blocks to avoid complications on discovery of the broken sink. I opened my bags in an alcove and sorted them down to one. Around the corner in an alley a woman peeled potatoes. I gave her my own bag of peelings.

She knew it was hot and stashed it quick and grabbed the next spud like I'd never stood there.

Slogging to nowhere with a heavy heart, I felt relief in movement. Mental residue condensed on the walls of the vessel and rolled, pooling on the bottom, growing stagnant and evaporating. The shoulder strap hurt. Sweat poured. Discomfort served to distract from the more difficult reality.

In a few miles, I stopped and looked back at the fading din and chaos. I wanted a taxi, and there it was. Perhaps my luck was changing. Sliding in, I asked with difficulty for the train station.

The driver turned, confused.

"Station of the trains."

"You want to go to the train station?"

"Yes. Very good."

He shrugged. "Voila." He pointed. We were there. I smiled idiotically but felt victorious, riding the ride of no ride in the taxi of no taxi. It was a start. The driver spoke quickly about the fare. I gave him another stupid grin and got out. Next stop: Amsterdam.

The crush and clack lasted three hours or five. A thousand bodies pressed in and about, many with Sherpa Brand knapsacks for the very best in roughing it across Europe. Most smoked, staring cross-eyed at the embers of their meaning. The day slogged onward, and pulling into the soot-black city after so many hours and miles, bodies and smokes, time turned its trick. I was still a week away.

Amsterdam hadn't changed in twenty years, except that back then it was brothers and sisters in denim and leather, and now it was merely thousands teeming in the streets. A boy with hollow eyes lay propped against a station wall, downed by life. His head lolled on a rubber neck as his hands searched his pockets for paper and tobacco. He rolled tobacco and hash, watching the magic dirt crumble magically. He lit up and drew deep and smiled.

I stared. His vessel got emptied long ago. Then it melted. Now his mug steeped with warm, dark goo.

A tug on the shoulder brought me back, and I turned to another boy of the street, pulling on my bag like it was his. It wasn't his, so I jerked it free, stepped forward and turned. Eye to eye, we saw each other. "Fuck you," he said casually, on his way. He looked back, flashing a knife, in case I wanted to tango. And he carried a shirt pulled from the slit in my bag. What a town.

I hurried on. The voice on the public address system admonished: *Don't put your bags down. Don't stand still. Don't talk to strangers. Keep moving. Watch your bags. Beware pickpockets…* Dirt and desperation thinned outside, where thousands more squatted on the flagstones to pull on their dream smokes. This was it. We'd won.

The canals flow between the streets around the center, Dam Square. Flow may be a stretch. They freeze in winter, thick enough for Hans Brinker. But this was summer, with spirulina frosting and beer-can sprinkles.

Distance from the center seemed to ease the tension. I stopped at an alley café for a coffee and pastry and watched two guys at the next table, stoking their pipe. I asked if that stuff was…available nearby. They laughed. One nodded yonder at Club Ballou, a small door under a neon dancing bear who smoked a megaphone spliff. I finished up and headed over.

Club Ballou was a ten by twelve with a percolator, four booths, a counter with two stools and an Arab woman to work it. I whispered, "Do you have hashish?"

"What?"

"Do you have hashish?"

"Hashish? You want hashish? Good. Here." She reached under the counter for a plastic box with file cards and labels: Pakistan, Zero-Zero, Spoetnik, Libanon, Premiera, Kashmere, Manali, Maroc-Super, Turks, Caramello, Thai, Skunk, Jamaica, Columbia, Hanoi and Transkei.

I asked, "What's the difference?"

"What you mean, difference?"

"Say, Maroc. Is different from…Kashmere?"

She pulled the files for M and K and offered a smell of each. One smelled like shit and dirt. The other like shit and dirt with sugar, or like incense and glue and opium.

"That's it? They smell different?"

"No, no. Maroc heavy. Heavy. Very nice. Kashmere is…"

"Light?"

"No, not light but… You feel wool from Kashmere?"

"Soft?"

"Yes. Soft. And thick."

"I like Kashmere."

"Yes. Is very good."

Like the wool, it was twice the price. I warmed to prospects for a top-drawer high. I deserved it. The riffraff did not. Even so, it was only twenty-five guilders for a gram, hardly twelve bucks, not that a gram was much to go on, I thought, going two to the pipe store for a little clay chillum with a screen for two guilders more.

In another minute, I was back at the alley café with another coffee, hold the pastry, pinching a fourth of my gram. What the hell, I could get more. The same fellows watched me, as I smoked fervently, as if to catch up, getting high.

But the high kept rising after the fuel burned out. And there I was, orbital and still rising. The fellows laughed, so I took things out of gear and coasted to leveling. Or was it gearing out of leveling and coasting to the take?

Softness thickened, as represented. No question: This Kashmere was the sippin' whiskey of hash. And a vintage this smooth was easy for a man of seasoning. It didn't get in the way like the marijuana could, nor did it impede coherence, dialogue or movement. An experienced person could smoke this stuff all day. It was so light. And good. I ordered one more coffee for the road, loving the world in its softness. And I stepped out, on my way again, watching my feet in amazement.

The afternoon stretched endlessly with the sun half down, and it was already seven. Walking felt like a cure, so I followed my nose, turning here and there for a reason or no reason, and in five blocks or twelve, I looked up to a street sign: *Herrengraat Strasse.* I was here, twenty years ago with my brothers and sisters, when the two big clubs, Fantasia and Paradisio were in full swing, and the student hotel called Herrengraat Strasse 88 was at the same address.

Coming in on the four hundred block, I headed down to the past, beginning with a sit down and reload for a new launch, up and ho. Hi ho! What a town. Years ago, I got the boot at H 88 when my eyes rolled too up. What a town.

Recollecting, way high on Kashmere hash, I strolled into the past. I'd paid three days in advance back then, but they passed like no time at all, and on the fourth night, dark and late and terribly buzzed, I had no bunk. Eminently practical to suit the times, I crawled under one and slept to the middle of the night, when a bouncer poked me with a broomstick. He pulled me out and up and along to the door and showed me the street, this street. Darker and colder in the wee hours way back then, I sat on the stoop for five more hours to daylight, sensing the boogiemen, cruising. They passed, apparently unaware that we were all brothers and sisters.

Decades later I wondered where the kids had got to and turned into a drab hotel. I wanted to check in, stash my slashed bag and know I'd have a bed through the night. The woman at the counter was a looker by design, accustomed to stoned guys staring, practiced at mild annoyance. She pushed two forms and said breakfast was seven to nine.

The third-floor walk-up over the street was nestled among the treetops with a bed, a nightstand and a coffee maker. And a bathroom with a shower. Hotel Hell and Maria felt far away and long ago. Slanting sunlight and cool air with no noise save the little pipe softly hissing and the leaves gently rustling felt like snug harbor. Blasting deeper into space, I wished the world the very best and nearly gave in to a lie down, a brief one.

But I knew better, and the prime fillet of a beautiful new day in a Kashmere cloud waited just below. Down and out and down farther toward 88, I stopped in front of a bar to listen. Was that Creedence? Indeed, and in a blink, a Heine draft went down to quench my care and woe. The barkeep was right there with another, so I sat and drank for one more tune, singing like Ringo. *No, no, no, no, I can't drink it no more…*

The bartender laughed and left with the faucet running and the sink filling, until it overflowed to the floor. I reached and turned it off. He swore on his way back and drew another round, on the house, as a good turn deserves. And another and so on, until, quaffed with exuberance over luck, his with me and mine with it and one thing and another. "Aw, fuck it," I finally allowed, which earned a nod here and there. Farewell to that little oasis was also sentimental, considering what we'd been through and the fucking mess somebody nearly had to clean up, not that anybody would have noticed if it wasn't cleaned up, but still. I said I'd be back and sat there like a bump until feet found footing and moved through the door and out and down to a brand-new town come to life. Things were waking up, not exactly like sunrise but with a new brightness and more people out and about.

The dirty buildings and trash-strewn streets and shit-green canals seemed eventful in twilight. Invitation glittered. Unshaved and glad for the nubs, I felt fitting, not so much at home but headed there. This place didn't shave either. Along with fresh bowls lit up and wafting everywhere came the scent of gentle anarchy. Was this a new revolution, or a vestige of the old guard? On a bench by a canal, I stoked again for the spirit of the thing, for perspective on my march to the past.

Two blocks farther and under construction were the ruins of H 88. *Verboten Toegang.* The foyer was open but the door inside was boarded shut. Barbed wire blocked the ventilators and seemed an appropriate memorial to the war dead and walking wounded. I didn't linger but stooped for a Dutch dime on the ground, heads up, which put a stupid grin on my face. To think, twenty laps around the sun to find the far side of a coin. Luck had changed, maybe.

Next door was a long, narrow bar off the street. A sign out front showed Woody Woodpecker smoking a megaphone joint. Smoke came out of his ears. The place was a hallway with a bar and stools. I ordered an American sandwich, once the bartender explained it was cheese and tomato. He served it with a shrug and said he had no kitchen, and it's good.

I put my magic coin with a few more on the counter for another Heine and asked about H 88. The bartender said yes, it got closed after so many years of infestation, filth, junkies and crime.

I told him I was there back in the day, and it was a time, a time it was. Yes, he used to work there. He turned away to load a tape, Creedence, *Bad Moon Rising.* He drew another round for us, like we were vets from the same engagement. I stoked the pipe to further demonstrate everything that was still everything.

"You Americans," he said. "You smoke that shit straight. Unbelievable." I passed the pipe and was duly impressed by the billowing cloud he pumped at will. Squinting quizzically he asked, "Kashmere?"

"Fuckinay," I confirmed. He smoked more until we were socked in. "Hey," I called. "Are you the motherfucker who got me with a broomstick and kicked me out in the middle of the night?"

"I think so," he said, and we laughed till we nearly cried. He said no shit, it must have been him, he'd poked so many under the bunks. He turned around. I thought he would next show me the broom. But he turned back with a hand-carved wooden box and said, "Try this." From the box he pulled a glass vial with a glass stopper with a dauber on the end. He dabbed a globule of tar into the pipe.

"Opium?"

"Not exactly. This won't lay you down. Not right away."

"How long do we have?"

He shrugged. "Easy two or three hours."

Plenty of time, I thought, especially in light of the six days remaining once this day got done. I lit the pipe and pulled it up to smoke signals and asked at the top, "What is this stuff, exactly?"

"Kind of a hash oil." It was smooth, no chokers, so I pulled until the goo flared, then passed it quickly in the old spirit. We hurried in deference to life and goo, both burning quickly, and we revered efficiency; waste not, lest ye be unwasted.

He impressed on intake and handed the pipe over. But twenty years hadn't left me stupid, or not that stupid. I took it slowly, just a bit and counted down. "Ten. Nine. Eight. Seven…" And there we were, heads pinned to backrests, faces drawn under heavy Gs and liftoff. I stashed my pipe, laid a few bills on the counter, grinned over a nod that spanned the decades, and was on my way.

"Flipside, brother," he said on the same grin. This was the flipside, brother, and the next flip would be the last side. We both knew it and shared a laugh, as the air filled with confetti, with all the images and thoughts that didn't mean shit.

Outside, the cool night air drew me in and lengthened my stride. I dropped into gear and went to cruising speed, where the place and night cohered to second nature. In a brief loss of contact with Houston control, I knew I would never find my hotel, until I remembered: Turn around, stupid. I laughed again for such a merry night on such a difficult day.

I kept to the main street, though some blocks were long and unlit. The walkway, bounded by buildings on one side and a canal on the other, required the straight and narrow, until an arched bridge led to a neighborhood with a warm vibration, so I crossed to the light.

Reality warped and crested as the quasi-hallucino-vibragrid tingled and turned faces in windows to purple and yellow wax, slumping onto molds. It was the neighborhood of the women with two smiles, the "whores of Amsterdam." Whore is not a nice word, but the whores of Amsterdam seemed immutable and immune to modern nicety.

They sat in their windows more lewdly than twenty years ago, because twenty years of whoring can jade the best of them. Then again, competition gets keen in any time passing. They weren't a tourist attraction back then, when the street flowed with sailors instead of rubberneckers from Moline and the odd novelty fuck.

I met an older whore back then, forty or so, who competed with the younger with, "Blowjob? Would you like for me to give you a blowjob?" She looked like my old English teacher, who I never liked, not even for a fantasy, so I picked a tender young beauty with bruises on her chest. I didn't see the bruises until she showed me. She wanted more money for showing her breasts, so I told her I was a student, and she sighed over a free feel. They were bruised from feeling, so I pressed them to my cheek.

It was me and Bumpy Oliver on the pilgrimage phase of the revolution that summer. Bumpy's real name was Lewis, but he talked slow enough to sound stupid, and kids are mean, so we called him Bumpy. We met at a frat party, both new to college and invited to meet the brothers, who bought us beer and served a drink they called Purple Passion, though it seemed more desperate than passionate. Grape juice and grain alcohol in a garbage can went down with gusto. Some of the new boys swilled it in the spirit of something or other and fell down. Some puked.

I had a beer. Bumpy leaned on a wall, a certain non-match for these brothers; he sounded so inadequate. He lit a joint and offered it, my first. I tried it as he drawled, "You know, the *Moody Blues* say thinking is the best way to travel, but most people would still rather take the bus."

Soon we giggled like hyenas over this and the brothers, making me unmatchable too. We became friends and adventured in Europe together. But that first night at the frat party, Bumpy was a farm boy come to college with a pocketful of joints, home grown to perfection, with humility. "Ain't nothing but a fuckin' weed is all it is." He let a few other boys try it too, as he recalled the family farm.

Some of the boys laughed. Some puked purple. Some looked worried. We weren't invited back.

Three years later, historically stoned in Amsterdam, we applied our college education to date for maximum return on investment. It was Bumpy's idea that we should jack off by a canal to get our money's worth. I doubted I could jack off by a canal. Bumpy agreed that it would be easier with some magazines and flashlights. But maybe not, with one hand for the magazine and one hand to wank and what? You want to hold the flashlight in your mouth?

So we walked and drank and smoked some more and theorized as college boys do.

I stopped at a bench, alone and far away and much farther along. I stoked the pipe so meaning could catch up, and I wondered what I would know in twenty more years.

We salvaged that night long ago when the working girls went to bed except for two, who really liked us. Bumpy got the old lady because he'd had her for English too and afterward said she was nicer now, and a blowjob was better than a C-.

Mine came on a whimper and a squirm and, "Come on, come on." We pumped the jam like sailors in a flooding bilge until, "Time's up." She pulled away and went manual, tweaking a sperm sample neat as the nurse of your dreams.

Bumpy and I stumbled back to H 88 for a nightcap.

Twenty years later I contemplated commercial real estate sales in Denver, closing slowly on a slur and drawl. I wondered if he was happy and walked into the night. Was I happy? Or anyone?

I laughed again. At least I was out and about, thinking it over, open to the world at large with total loss of bearing, floating free, such as it was. I would have gone back the way I came, but that seemed too far, and a simple diagonal seemed efficient.

Into the valley, I walked past the point of return, because the night boys of modern times approached, and retreat would invite the chase. Was I paranoid? Too much stimulant can bring it on. Or maybe the stimulant allow clarity in its simplest form. Staggering my way, arms swinging too high, legs bowed, this troublesome threesome trucked for trouble.

Decades of thinking arrived to present tense and a moment of letting go. One boy kicked a trashcan and laughed at the clang and clatter. The other two woofed and grunted, as if threatening the other cans. One threw a sidekick as seen on TV. They howled and kicked garbage down the street, speaking dominance in silly swagger from forty yards and closing.

Well, of course I was too drunk and stoned to deal with this, which I had learned to do; not deal with, that is. So I chose not to. I would simply pass with a friendly hello. Why not?

The question was rhetorical and possibly mandatory as well. I strode their way with sociable intention in mind, as I felt it flow from the core outward, through fingertips—"it" being the stuff of thought, of reflection and analysis, of comparison and what if. The outward flow emptied the vessel.

XXIV

East Meets West

 My wrestling coach once called me a scrapper in the mind with no goods to back it up. He meant I was a punk. We both went five-eight, but he went two-twenty while I wobbled in at one-oh-three. He had a stupid grin all the time. I didn't like him calling me a punk.

"Now here's what I want you to do," he said, laying a forty-pound arm on my eighteen-ounce shoulders. "You get some weights, a hundred pounds or so, and you lift every day."

The wrestling squad showed sparse talent in the lighter classes, and I was the best of the twirps. But I pointed out that if I bulked up, I'd gain weight. "You lift. We'll worry later about too much muscle." I liked the sound of too much muscle. I wanted some of that. I wanted the girls to sigh and the guys in awe. So I blew twenty bucks on barbells. Twenty bucks was real money then, but I put it together, because I wanted to win.

I lifted nights to the radio for two years and gained thirty pounds up from skinny to thin. Taller than most, I could still beat the muscle guys with my legs. I watched opposing coaches whisper caution to their boys: avoid the legs. They'll wrap you up out of nowhere. At sixteen and nauseated, I was Spiderman, long legged, spinning my web. I pondered Pythonian, because spiders don't really crush their prey like big constrictors do. Coach shook his head and walked away. I won most of the time but hated the fear grinding inside before every match.

"Never mind," Coach said. "The more scared you get, the less scared you'll be. Scared is what this stuff is good for. Use it up, and you won't be scared anymore for the rest of your life. Smile."

Heady stuff for a kid like me, but Spiderman gave it a go. The fear was a given, prerequisite to all other moves. When I lost, Coach showed me where I lost. When I won, he showed me where the other guy lost. He thought winning was natural, also a given until thrown away, easy as losing the fear. He died young of a brain tumor. I missed him terribly. Spiderman grew up and gained thirty-five pounds.

I led with a smile for years when people asked what I did for a living. I twisted a few strands for anyone who thought they might rub two nickels and come up with fifteen cents quicker than me.

Still a bit of a scrapper, I'd gained a bit of back-up. But a person who lives on wits knows the world as something other than the best possible place. It's only the most practical.

At forty, things change. The end comes into view. I tried a soft touch where impact would once have been. I didn't need a shrink. I needed a new coach to redirect as necessary.

When I found a place reminiscent of the high school wrestling room, others there laughed short and called me amazing, so full of piss and vinegar. I liked the recognition. But they shook their heads and called me a long shot, and gave me a chance.

I got harped on, yelled at and whispered to: drop the fight and relax. But I was relaxed. No, you're not. Do nothing.

I couldn't play mind games. Why couldn't they say what was up? I got tired and tired of it and especially tired of watching the old guys go threw through the throws with no umph, no give, no nothing—until I felt the other nothing. I remembered the first time getting high, when doors opened to places as yet unimagined. I joined in to feel the mush change into flow, in some cases into an irrepressible current, into the mush of no mush. My teacher saw and called me by name after three years of not seeing me. He said we have only one opponent in life. He was seventy-two and invited my attack.

A student obeys, so I did. He touched me, and I flew. I came up grinning, "Do that again." He laughed, walking away.

I took a few more years getting out of my own way. It's easy in meditation but difficult in movement for a scrapper with the goods. I longed for dominance. My teacher said I was wrong, lacking calmness and love. Not to worry, things would change in ten or thirty years. "Meditate. Don't think. Smile."

But I *did* meditate, I said. "Not enough!" In a few more years of thoughts trickling like water through fingers, the vessel could empty, still and silent. The smile went to the eyes, as necessary.

Like on the night three boys walked my way in Amsterdam, yelping like hyenas, feisty, on the prowl, ready to prey. I smiled for myself as well; boy oh boy, am I fucked up. But think of the good; does not the stimuli help filter the more tedious brain functions, like logic, odds, consequence and fear? Beyond the good, conditions cleared as the night twinkled with stars.

Closing in, the woof and growl ceased. They pressed. I stayed on course, neither squaring nor slowing but holding pace and looking past them. An aggressor stepped out and lunged, making contact at shoulder height.

I let him feel nothing in a basic move, based on faith. Clearing my path and his, getting out of his way and my own way, or some esoteric shit you never really get right but only approximate, as someone yells, "No, no, no! Not like that!" But doing it wrong a thousand times and a few thousand more, even lumpy nothing comes as a big surprise. I mustered what hospitality I could on short notice and helped him along, moving from the hips, out of his line, stepping alongside, one step back, kind of like Jorge D'Agusto joining Juanita in a samba. I could have kissed him but didn't want to. And my smile got twisted with so much giving at hand. Rare and memorable and packed as ever a moment was, with Sensei looking the other way, as Coach grinned stupidly, calling for the one-armed pancake and assuring that I had the goods to deliver. Coach didn't mention the soft touch, and I never got that part too well and wouldn't get it at crunch time, with a nitwit trying to kill me or worse, throw me into the green scum. So instinct ruled again in the next moment, with my dance partner and me, and in the next moment, it was only me. He went. He splashed.

I knew he'd want to try that again, but he'd be awhile getting out, because the water is a ways below. Which was for the best because his close friend came next, so I turned with a greeting, though with more reaction than a man of development likes to show. Well, we can only do our best, which was good enough, because the second guy veered off. Maybe my step was off.

Maybe I smiled too much, no matter, because the last of the pack was craziest of all. He stood back with a grin, affirming sincerity in the heart and knife. He held back to measure or assess or calibrate as best he could, or something. He didn't want to look foolish and surely didn't want to fail. He twitched. I didn't want to look anxious and tried my best to flow past empty to all the way full, or something. We played our parts, they seeking dominance, me to do or die. By then the second guy got his nerve back and came in with hands low, which tilted him slightly forward. I poured some mush, and he stopped short again but too late. No stopping allowed, not for him or me or the stellar bodies, and maybe not for some of the goods too, because you never get rid of the body until you-know-when. For now, we had time to keep and orbits to make. Ally oop and up, and the green scum soaked another. What an arc. What an entry.

I took years learning a few simple moves with minimal scrapping. The first guy might have sensed something other than dominance and submission. Up from the canal now by way of a ladder nearby, he hung off, covered in scuz and, for all we knew, viral contaminants. He came in slowly, and I didn't want to touch him, but then the third guy with the knife closed from the other side. I thought of Curly Joe—*Oh, I get it, a squeeze play!* I did not slap my forehead or do the Curly shuffle.

I laughed short, as if to further fend the fear but failed. It came home on a sphincter flex and triple time in the chest, the last curtain coming down, illusion over, Big D coming on. The scene warranted review and belaboring but not just yet. Instinct reigns, or death is at hand, and a distant voice from the dojo reminded: *If somebody comes at you with a knife, and you're afraid of getting stabbed, you'll die.*

Well, in fact, you must die in the moment, first in the head and then in the heart. Give it up and fill it up with death foregone. Now let's see who dances last. With fear as an old familiar, he becomes tedious, and more easily dismissed. With luck, death becomes a nuisance, also dismissed. Big D can shrink in perspective; it's only a matter of time anyway, and time doesn't matter when you're dead.

Okay, where were we? Yes, let's see who's got what. Do or die time, get flowing time, and don't think for a minute it doesn't help to be all fucked up.

The next moment brought Sensei, with transcendence, pain and follow-through, looking away and honing in. Peace begins with acceptance. Death may come, and the knife may be taken. It's a matter of training—muscle memory to a point but more a matter of no mind—and, of course, etiquette.

So this maniac came in slashing with his friend blocking my exit. I could not quite accept moving into a knife attack with smiling eyes, with so much mush and love and heavy shit clouding my brain, when I thought I was gonna die. I could have jumped into the canal, but a bloodletting seemed more reasonable. I didn't exactly present a forearm, but he splayed it at will. I set aside my niggling concerns for depth, severed tendons and so on, or rather those concerns scattered before the maniac coming in for the kill.

I never could relax like a model student, but profuse bleeding had a perverse, calming effect. The blood got me out of my head, so to speak. Down south, in the abdomen, I went to protocol, bringing the Universe in by half and again half and half again. Sounds removed and impractical; never mind, and it happens in fractional time. It's not mental but driven in the brain and heart and abdomen. It's frightening in its removal from logic, its dependence on faith, and it must conjoin with movement.

It displaced further fear and scenes of life passing before my eyes. So I brought it in again to half, half, half presenting a clear and easy target.

RSVP came right on time, until a wisp of a turn that felt reasonably correct, though it too gave up its gush of muscular insistence, as the distant voice yelled no! Easing up to flow out and forth and so on, reaching alongside the lunging arm, behind the blade, I led us farther out and gently down. We bowed together, as a duet, and I led my partner on around for an eye-to-eye.

How do you do?

The do-si-do came next on a step back in a sweep and a stretch, turning my partner's hand askew. Sensei called this move an act of love but said never mind, in the street. Break the bone, he said. But stay gentle. This mélange of images and messages in recollection sounds like a jumble, yet the bits fit neatly into the flow.

My friend went to his knees and then prone, where he flopped as necessary but wouldn't release the knife. So I twisted the wrist, until the hand opened and the knife fell out. I had nothing to feel good about, except finally getting it right, kind of.

I'm not a bad ass and, like most people, take a punch best when drunk. Stories about fights tend to be base and proud. But this wasn't a fight. It was ugly. Karmic resolution hovered on the periphery, as if debts needed settling. Who knew? Because I did feel good with the rest of the twist, even knowing my new friend was only human, emotional, sensitive, vulnerable and weak. I pondered that phrase, briefly: *only human?* I wanted to maim him, not so much for who he was but for what he'd become and, moreover, for what made the world an iffy place. Maim him, hell; I wanted to kill him, but that gets complicated.

I should have kicked the knife, but I doubted my grip and blood makes everything slick as snot, so I only heaved the wrist around the bend, past anatomical limits to the snap. The knife lay on the ground. The friend feinted a lunge, as if to grab it. He must have learned something though, because he hesitated on my next smile, which had to be more effective with so much blood showing. Then again, all those metatarsals crunching like celery was a special effect all its own. The follow-up is a finesse move that made me laugh, looking like Cowboy Bob Ellis's step-over toe-hold. I stepped over the shoulder, which froze the friend, because the next snap sounded louder, more like a broomstick than celery.

Adrenaline clears quite a bit of liquor and residue, but quite a bit remained. With blood flowing, I sensed imminent loss of consciousness. I had to wrap things up while I could. The other guy was hanging out, more like Frosty the Snowman than a feisty boy, but the threat remained. He feinted and ducked, so I dropped the broken bones and stepped toward him, done with fear for the moment. The friend wouldn't budge, so I tried a new smile and sang to him, "Wrist bone connected to de… shoulder bone. Shoulder bone connected to de…head bone. Head bone connected to de…"

I stepped toward him. He took off. The other guy in the canal swam to the far side, and the guy on the ground moaned.

What a vacation. Where was I? I asked the clear and starry night and got peace and quiet for an answer. And something about love, as I shuffled off, asking the guy on the ground, "Is this the way to Buffalo?"

XXV

Around the Clubhouse Turn

A custom of Dutch hotels in the economy bracket (two-star) is the tea and coffee amenity. It adds mere pfennigs to overhead with a teapot, two cups with saucers, some handy packets of instant coffee, some tea bags and more packets of sugar and powdered milk. It seems so paltry but offers the utmost in convenience on a morning after a binge and a knife fight last night, when a hangover threatens life itself, and the old resilience is long gone, and your insides are leaking to the outside.

I needed a drink but couldn't very well run out to the liquor store. Coffee helped, though I feared melting the wound open from the inside, after taking hours to congeal. I sipped left-handed because my right arm was stiff. I couldn't meditate all the way to recovery, but it seemed the thing to do for a few minutes anyway. Stabbed twice and badly shaken, I hurt in the head and buzzed with nasty questions. My moves were sloppy, my injuries severe, and I shuddered at the replay. So I eased up to another little bowl. The stuff is so amazing, so efficient with minimal fog. And it was, in its soft and gentle way, the hair of the dog that bit me.

The nurse said, "Don't worry." Coldly concise, she relieved my anxiety. The cut went deep but missed tendons, so the arm should heal in due time, with antiseptic, stitches and a bandage. The stomach gash wasn't so deep, but I trembled for what might have been, because setting fear aside got all used up. I reviewed the moves, presenting, pivoting, following and leading.

"He tried to kill me," I mumbled.

Emptying my bloody pants pockets, the nurse scorned my little chillum and baby Ziploc. "You know it is very easy to avoid this kind of trouble in Amsterdam." It was the middle of the night. I was drunk, stoned and half-dead from a knife fight and a long walk to the only cab in town and the bumpy ride to the hospital and a lecture, once again, on getting things right.

"Amsterdam or anywhere," I said.

"Especially for someone like you."

"Why me?"

"You have nice things. Why go to bad places?"

"I made a mistake. A series of mistakes." She smiled. Maybe she expected an argument. She didn't mind my staring while she undressed me and dressed my wounds. Mid-forties but showing strain, her beauty had outlived her warmth. I assessed my own lingering attributes and thought myself far more cordial, to say the least. Her tidy composure and silky blonde hair in a bun suggested further constraint. She seemed a caregiver by choice and aptitude. "Do you make house calls?"

She laughed. "It is very expensive."

"I'm rich." She was Christine. I felt the planets spin. She did me up in an hour and told me to wait. She came back with pain pills and antibiotics. "Do you work every night?" I asked.

"No. It changes."

"Well, I…. I'd…."

"We have the man who cut you." I sat up straighter. "Do you want the police?"

"Don't you want the police? I mean, yes. We want the police. He tried to kill me."

"You must come back to identify him. Tomorrow, maybe."

"Back here?"

"Yes. He'll be here a few days. You broke his wrist and his right arm and dislocated his shoulder. He may lose some use of that arm."

"What a relief. I mean, I thought I broke his shoulder."

"You don't seem like a violent man."

"I don't think I am. I just got lucky." She laughed scornfully, then called a cab and helped me dress, asking if one o'clock tomorrow would be all right.

"I don't feel so good."

"You won't for a few days."

"Great."

"One o'clock?"

"What's at one o'clock?"

"To identify the man who stabbed you." She waited.

"One o'clock. See you then." She turned and left. I watched her walk away as dispassionately as she administered her care. I wanted to lie down for a few days.

Beat, stabbed, half-bled, filthy and forlorn, I blamed Hattie, and I wondered. Was she sleeping? Or laughing? Well, I'd killed three days already and nearly killed myself. Or was it only two days? Or one?

Sleep was fitfully painful. The hash helped more than the pills, but it was still a bloody mess. Bathing took an hour with a wet rag. I was back at the hospital on time, asking for Christine, but she was home until tonight. They showed me the knife guy, severely drugged and in a cast from his right hand to his shoulder, with a metal brace from his collarbone to his wrist. He looked like a sculpture: Mugger Down. A Dutch cop asked if this was my assailant. I said yes, no doubt about it, he and two of his equally vicious friends. The cop looked me over and said yes, he knew the friends. He asked if they were injured. I said, "Only their pride, as far as I know." He nodded and left.

The suspect's good hand was chained to the bed. I leaned close to his barely open eyes and said, "Hello again." He flinched, fitting in to the world of his making, only human.

I didn't feel so good. The hospital was two miles from the hotel, so I walked slowly and planned to stop for a cappuccino and a Spoetnik to wile away a few hours and give peace a chance. What a town. A place around the corner had a story sign in three frames. The first was a pirate-hippie with curly ringlets, a long nose, a cleft chin and handlebar mustache. His very long tongue was wrapped around a fat joint. The second was a cloud of smoke over the man's face. In the cloud were the words Wham! Shit! In the third frame, only a neck remained, gooey and dripping, just after the explosion.

I like getting high but never considered total annihilation, like this, as if destruction of self would improve daily conditions. The fourth frame was the door, leading to a study in soot and grit with furniture and patrons to match. In this morgue of souls, the stiffs sat upright, in chairs. I couldn't stay but needed to sit for a minute between rounds.

A block farther down, the street was cleared but the sidewalks were crowded because two street mimes had set up their show. In leotards, swim caps and ratty, bogus goggles and fins, they faced each other from opposite ends of their makeshift stage. One lay prone on the sidewalk and frog kicked while the other pranced down the block. His fins flapped awkwardly. The crowd tittered. I wondered when the talent might show. Maybe the swim fins were meant to be funny. What else could it be? These guys had no skill. The prancing one passed a hat for charity. But they'd made a travesty of the old and noble form of man imitating fish.

A few blocks down was a better café, larger with many tables and a big front window filigreed with flowers and misty swirls of a smoky dream. A man's face ghosted behind the flowery mists and swirls, fleshy with heavy eyes under thick brows and dense smoke. Over all, a spider web veil blended with smoky wisps from the man's mouth. Beside him in the haze, with clear dark eyes and posh red lips, a young woman suggested wet as part of the dream.

I went in to see her from the other side and to have another little bowl. The matching scene inside was achieved with matching layers of paint. Service, like the artwork, was impeccable. An easy murmur got the cappuccino coming along with the other, and in no time the man in the window was me.

A guy out front on a stool played acoustic guitar, and harmony came on a buzz and caffeine and artwork, until another fog rolled in. Sadly, Kashmere became Booneville when stoned went to the gills. Spin cycle kicked in on pain pills, caffeine and life gone awry. Eyeballs rolled like boats with no keels. And a day far away in a time for healing and perspective became bleak. What could I see, dilated to the point of ocular disparity? Nothing was the short answer, not in dynamic form but the other. Never mind; let it be, and so it was, giving time a chance to work its magic, there in the heart of being as an artificially induced pastime.

A titter rippled the dreamy café when a man entered, wearing a three-piece suit with a flashy necktie and glittering stickpin. His smooth gait and debonair coif set him apart as a man of means, a visitor from the other Amsterdam, where commerce and culture occurred, and people met for cocktails to talk of world events, people who owned furniture. His clear-eyed resolve indicated no morning bowl for him, and none after lunch too. People laughed, as if hallucinating on what he'd brought to bear.

In two days I'd eaten a tomato sandwich, and that was last night, fairly early. Yet I sat, stuck, wondering what kept the denim and leather going on hash, day and night for years since I last sat here. Back then, we sat on the sidewalk at the American Express office, smoking our pipes, as cops stepped over our legs. The streets were less crowded, the kids twenty or so, and brotherhood was a frame of mind. The revolution was us, and Amsterdam was R&R for the troops. Bumpy Oliver and I got past the junkies at Paradisio, who sold rawhide bits as hash from North Africa for only two bucks. No thanks; we got matchboxes of kif for three bucks and got fluffed, fine and golden.

Paradisio was a gymnasium, low lit with mattresses on the floor and many huge speakers on the walls, so a traveler could lie back and groove to the Stones, Cream or the Moody Blues. The heavy downbeat matched the collective pulse, or maybe it was all white noise to match the collective coma. Bumpy and I smoked to giggles and couldn't talk when a fat chick with no underpants stood and straddled Bumpy and shook her booty in sniffing distance, until he sang along, "Who'll stop the rai-ain?" It was big, fat and dimpled and wobbly. I yelled that he was dead if she cut the cheese, but he couldn't hear, but he knew, and we laughed till we cried. Those were the days.

How long did they last, over the years? I drifted coast to coast other and out to the tropics. Was it going on then too. Even this smoky room was going on, as if smoke was time, passing.

Hash was illegal in most places because entertainment becomes innate, no purchase required. Pharmaceutical control required a prescription, and with doctors, lawyers and bud companies making money, who would cared? Hash became good, like cars, cigarettes, television and the rest.

But it doesn't work. Hash precludes endeavor on the material plane. A buzz needs no tangible goods. Concepts are revisited, resorted and aligned.

I worked in a match factory at eighteen, where shifts changed on a whistle. I got a dollar ninety-eight an hour and spent six months' of it before the first shift ended. But three days in I got whacked on another potential, death in life. The factory, its pipes, machinery and fumes, produced book matches, so smokers could see the name of a bar or get a diploma at home or write a phone number down.

I assisted Frank on the rewinder. Frank could not make sentences after thirty-four years on the rewinder, or maybe it only took a few days. He chanted a mantra while four rolls hummed—fifty-pound, hundred-foot rolls of uncut matchbook covers. "Thirty-four years," he called. "Thirty-four years. Quack. Quack, quack." A roll could jump the hub and tear down the aisle and knock a man down or break his leg. Or he could grab it and lose a finger. Frank had six left, but he'd saved hundreds of rolls and saved his section from loss, qualifying his section mates for the bonus and a better life.

"Thirty-four years," Frank called. "Working like a duck. Quack."

"Hey, fuck you, Frank!"

"Quack! Quack, quack!"

"Hey, Frank, go fuck yourself, you dumb fuck!" They loved him but hated the potential he presented.

"Thirty-four years."

Frank was my boss. He advised, "Thirty-four years."

I watched him and tried to help.

At lunch, one of the guys told me Frank liked me and wanted to keep me for his assistant, and that hadn't happened before. Some said Frank was richer than a Jew, because he never spent a dime except for coffee, milk and potatoes, even at lunch, alone by the rewinder. He lived alone in a third floor studio and only went out for work and socks. The guys said I should be his friend, because he had fifty grand stashed in his room, because he cashed his check every week and never bought nothing.

What, he puts the cash in the socks?

No. He jacks off in the socks and throws them out the window. He always buys the same kind, so odd sox match. Walk under his window near seven, and you risk the wet lump.

All the guys laughed, heading back to their stations, yawning and complaining about no pussy from their wives and no money from their jobs. But what could they do? Many were fifteen-year men or twenty, all junior to Frank, who came off lunch with new steam, four rolls at full speed, quacking, until somebody yelled, "Will you shut the fuck up?"

Frank quacked lowly for a while but gained volume. "Working like a duck! Quack. Quack, quack!"

I lasted the week and took home sixty bucks and spent it on retreads and a fill-up. I hit the road thinking of Frank. He was on the rewinder for the Korean War and on the day I was born, for Hiroshima and Nagasaki and back to Pearl Harbor. He was there on the day the first deuce coupe rolled off the assembly line.

He couldn't be there still. He had to die as all do. Outside went gray and dark. How could anyone show up every day for thirty-four years? His brain was a duck pond. People in offices have it better. Don't they? Escapees are rare, heroes rarer still.

Frank was an exception, not a hero but an escapee, easing out on a light beam, past reason and maybe past pain to get by on a quack, in peace, more or less. He'd crank it to redline, as four rolls rewound, hub to hub, friction strip rumbling bass vibrato like the word, Om.

I hadn't thought of him in years, but he popped up in Amsterdam a few decades after the fact, like a spirit in the smoke. If he'd walked in, I wouldn't have bought him a drink because he didn't drink. I wouldn't have made small talk because he couldn't. I'd have stoked him a bowl and lit it with a whole book of matches and sat back and watched him spread his wings and quack. To him, I looked up. "Quack. Quack, quack!"

XXVI

Dogs and Cats Together

 It's going on now, if not with Frank at the rewinder, then with a billion other quackers. I stoked the bowl for the old duck and the odd ducks, pulled time into lungs, billowing like a tempest and thinning into thin air.

A gypsy family entered behind their patriarch, an obese man with chipped teeth clamped on a soggy cigar. Waddling obtusely, he looked like he didn't give a fuck, like he'd gnawed many bones and would gnaw you too. Maybe he ate the nieces and nephews who refused to smoke—in they came to light up. He chewed, stepping aside while the youth moved tables and chairs for the gathering. He coughed into a rag.

Settling onto two chairs was a push and a squeeze. Hitting the stogie, he blew smoke on the next three breaths and nodded, so the others could sit. Fourteen of them sat and smoked like a calliope on fire. Exhaling with gusto in apparent family tradition, they chattered warmly.

I stood, mustered what equilibrium and bearing remained and

shuffled through the cloud. I smiled for the Hungarian family, staring together in wonder. Who stabbed the American? I didn't mind and needed to make the door for air and a new place to sit.

A Chinese place around the corner looked packed with tourists, but energy waned. A guy in the door led the way to a corner table, because a solitary man might prefer privacy, especially if he's limping and…is that blood?

Tepid tea and puffed rice were not good, and leaving gained clarity on slimy shrimp. A solitary person tends to question the self more often, to ponder loss and, in this case, violence and slime. Do signs bear meaning?

Never mind. I hung slime over the edge, onto the cheese cloth, and left. The Chinese guy called out, *"Quang chuck mau fung! Hau luk fu ching ca ching!"* Or some shit.

"It's slimy. The shrimps is slimy." But he insisted on ching ca ching, "You eat it. On the house." An exit with conviction felt good but shakey.

Out in the street on a hot flash and weak knees, I thought the conflict was not in me but came to me. Did I attract conflict? I thought not, even as the world had gone hostile. Could I have cleared the knife by moving less? Less would be easier, and maybe less was lacking, and so was strength, which could be a change for the better, less feisty and all that. But I felt bad, growing weaker. I would walk no streets tonight, but a shabby hotel room would compound the bleak reality I'd come to. Pondering options, I scanned the block for a decent sandwich, knowing where sundown would lead to, where a man most often goes, sometimes limping.

Hobbling on, I remembered a cat who couldn't quit. I loved him, and he loved me, even when he lost the playful spirit and peace of mind, when he gave up home and comfort, walking away from scientifically enhanced cat food, a three-tier scratching post, cushy nap space on the bed, a cat door and many rounds of chase the string. He gave it up to fill the greater need. As kindred spirits, Pete and I shared a focus, though his drive seemed terminal, while mine was merely compulsive.

He came home looking like he'd tried to hump the pickle slicer. Ears chewed, face gnashed, punch drunk, beaten and dazed. He oozed yellow goo, cat whiz and tar. He whimpered when touched and again when fed and again when lifted to the sink, where he sat for a warm bath. He slept on my chest wrapped in a towel and heating pad.

His drive was irrational. He chased it to the point of self-destruction, hard-wired with the fatal chip. He came home from the vet shaved and wrapped and draining from surgical tubing. An hour home, he wanted out. He wasn't allowed out, so he howled. He pissed on the couch and tore the screen. How could he be so driven? I could at least savor the day after, especially with no hangover. Pete was conflicted, making friends easily, the toms among them agreeing on plenty to go around. So why fight?

The draw was not rational but innate and irresistible. He would not be kept from it, even if it cost him his life.

Pete came home the last time punctured and cut with broken teeth and claws. Matted with tar and cat squirt, he got the bath and cried. He got another ride to the vet, who shaved and cut off the dangling ear, then spliced half the nose back on. After fixing the third eyelid and plucking shrapnel from the hide, the vet said, "This is it."

Pete understood and became a kitten again for a day and a half, until the call came again. I let him out, and never saw him again. He didn't look back.

Sexual drive did not dominate me, I thought. The lure was honest and clean: social contact, another being with whom to share thoughts. Did I seek fleshy contact with Christine to compensate something or other? I thought not. Christine was beautiful and my age, and easy to imagine in exquisite sharing.

If she declined, I'd relax with my handy tea service and heating coil. At least I'd get tired enough, and the night was clear. The streets felt gentler with shadows over the soot, with soft lights shimmering from the canals, just like in Paris, when Hattie opened her arms and said, "This is the city. Anything can happen."

I watched the zigzag bricks passing below. Maybe Pete got what he needed. I wasn't sure what I needed but doubted it was another woman.

A light shone in an alley, so I turned to it and sure enough, a stand-up bass thrummed a lovely riff before passing it to the keyboard for four bars more. Tenor sax came up the middle and soon converged on the head. This was right, so right, about-time right, right for another smoke, another drink and snug harbor for a wayward soul.

But the feeling available was a memory, gone in the making. The notes could be heard and the whiskey tasted, but not like before. It never is, and a new scene needs time to make a new memory. Or something lovely, I'm sure. But I couldn't stay because of the smoke, and I had a date with a nurse.

Outside again, the night tingled in relief. The smoky blue note faded, replaced with sheer, dumb exuberance. My old dog Junior would jump for joy after taking a dump, or when he had another bone to hide. What else is there?

XXVII

Christine the Nurse

People view recently divorced women as doubtful and in need of validation as women, but that's not fair. A woman divorced at thirty-six or forty-five sees potential with seasoning, but age can also bring anxiety. A woman suddenly free at halftime knows what she's missed. Divorce can be a catalyst in those old enough to know, young enough to want. Christine and I shared this understanding, but she sheltered in a shell.

Tall, slim and poised, she wanted a man with similar attributes. I persisted nonetheless. She moved gracefully and presented herself to advantage, leading with her hands. Long, smooth fingers and supple, fleshy palms seemed disproportionate, and her gold rings and diamonds seemed defiant to what had come to pass. But psychological sorting came after initial inventory. Her feet were clean, soft and supple with no dead skin and good nails, polished. Open-toe shoes with wedge heels enhanced her calves, and shapely thighs rounded to a shapely ass that seemed concise, though flexed in constraint of life itself.

These observations came early to a man on his back with his pants down. Humorless, dour, unsmiling, she seemed Belgian. Her divorce four years ago lingered in every breath. Beyond fatigue and intolerance, she seemed depressed.

She'd been alone ten years now, counting the loneliness that set in six years before the crash. She wallowed in it, counting and recounting it. She clung to it and wrapped herself in it. But these things also came later. That night, she was busy on the ward and could not go out. No, it was impossible, and a man can't press too much. "Ah. Well. Thank you again. For helping me."

But as I turned to leave, she said, "We could go for a bite. I'm famished. I have a break in a few minutes." She sighed on a half smile. Much later, in a sheer lace bra and matching panties, she purred. Why would sensuality be hidden as a secret self ? Christine had suffered constraint, jaded by force, shaken by rejection. She viewed social prospects as hazardous, prickly as a march through the brambles. I sensed her self-imposed barrier as defense, in preservation of self. Who could stand another defeat like the former husband had delivered? He had to be a dick, or she'd had no warmth ever and had been cold and distant through her marriage. I doubted her frigidity, Belgian roots notwithstanding, yet I doubted my doubts as well—until she pivoted on an invitation, indicating appetite. A woman has to eat and enjoy life.

That first night brought me back. I waited an hour, wondering if the wait was part of her craft. She didn't want to be easy and succeeded in demonstrating that. An hour was not easy. It was a pain in the ass, three minutes shy of a walkout. Or eight minutes.

With meek apology, she led the way. I was catching on, I thought, that she regretted this test and felt worse that I'd passed. Further tests would make us feel worse yet—would question cost/benefit on pursuit of horizontal sharing. That's what it came to: a DMZ of intimate contact, though the high walls remained topped with barbed wire.

Beyond chitchat, we ventured to needs and hungers. At a Chinese place, I didn't mention slimy shrimp but followed her through an over-lit room to a glass-top table, where we read the menu like students in study hall. She ordered this. I got that. We agreed on tea and shared a sigh. Let the games begin.

She'd been divorced four years but it felt like ten. She sought my eyes. I said solitude had been a comfort for me. Even with the children, time slowed for her. Oh, yes, she had three children. She sat up, showing her flat stomach, to state her devotion; the children meant the world to her. She needed more. "I have endured," she said. "I can, but, well, you know. Loneliness is…never mind." The former husband was also Belgian.

A well-known professor, Harry Fizzule, or something, had raised many eyebrows with his work in Para-French psychiatry relative to root canal in sub-set data without regard to gender, or something. Still at the University in Brussels, he'd remarried the same year as the divorce, to his assistant of ten years. The puzzle pieced together. Christine had been his assistant too, back when she began as a nurse.

It was a résumé of depression anxiety. I called for a beer. She looked puzzled, like I'd called for heroine and some surgical tubing for the tie-off. "She's twenty-seven," she said. "Don't you think that's how it is with men? They get to middle age and want young girls."

"Not all men."

She cradled her chin on her beautiful hands, forlorn, struggling up current, nearly gasping, "They're gone now. I had no choice, really. I can't keep them from him. I should be able to keep them from her, though. She has nothing good to give them, nothing to teach them. I don't just say this. She's very simpleminded, you know. I don't like her around them."

She looked down, to commune with her ice cubes.

"Doesn't custody usually go to the mother?"

"It's not custody. I have custody. They left this week, for a month. I have vacation time, but I don't want to go anywhere. I mean, no place sounds good to me. And what am I to do? Go alone?"

I drank my beer. Europe is shit in summer with the heat and pollution, overpopulation and traffic. "I want you," I said.

She flashed red.

"No, no. Please. That came out wrong," I said.

"Yes, it did."

"Yes. I just meant that we're about the same age, and…"

"It's very evident what you want."

"Sorry. I knew it showed. It must. I didn't realize it was so hurtful."

She blushed again and changed course. "I tune pianos. I love it. It's the only work I ever loved. I don't know why. It seems foolish. Well, not foolish, but it's impractical."

"And that's why you're a nurse? For the practicality?"

"There aren't that many pianos to tune. There are, but not for me. Nobody knows about me. I'm very good, you know." I drank.

Dinner was served. She watched me look under my steamed broccoli. "I don't eat much before checking it out from both sides." She blushed again. Touché. I smiled. "This looks good." I ate. "Mm. I haven't eaten in days."

"Days?"

"Well, hours."

"Do you exaggerate often like that?"

"No. Never." She didn't laugh. She glanced glumly down at her miserable fucking meal on a sad night in a rotten life with a chronic liar. I got another beer and ate my broccoli. She dabbed at her soup and floating wontons, belly up. "Besides tuning pianos, do you have any fun?"

"Fun?"

"Recreation. Exhilaration. Idle laughter."

"No. No, no."

"Do you want to have some fun?"

"I couldn't say. I think fun is for children."

"Did you have fun as a child?"

"Yes. But look, you don't need to talk to me this way."

"Sorry. Just trying to pull you out."

"Please don't."

"No, no. My mistake." In awkward silence, I finished my bamboo shoots and water chestnuts and followed with tea. I felt better but over-drugged and sleep-deprived and stabbed and challenged. "You know, Nurse Christine. I wonder if…." She leaned in, attentive and patient. "Would you…call a taxi for me. I…I feel very weak."

"I can see that." She felt my forehead. "Where is your hotel?" I told her, and she laughed. "You're staying there?"

"It's no good?"

"It's not what I'd imagine."

"What would you imagine?"

"Look. You can stay at my place for a couple of days. The children are gone, and I'm afraid you need looking after."

"Do you think I'm critical?" I took her hand.

"I think you're a sick man."

The offer was sudden and unnatural. Take a stranger into her home? But a private nurse in my time of need felt good, in spite of her depression. I said I didn't want to impose but did not say I hoped for sexual congress. I paid the tab as she mumbled about the way it is with Americans needing help and called a cab. She helped me along. Outside, she gave me a key and told the cabby her address. I should sleep on the sofa. Linens and blanket in the hall closet. She would see me in the morning.

The ride was bumpy with many turns. Either she needed a man who would leave town soon, or she was a nurse with plenty to give. Fetching my things came first. I stuffed it all and headed out to the taxi, nauseated and confused. I must have passed out until the cabby turned with a grunt. I came to with a groan and felt wrong inside. I paid too much and dragged myself up and in.

Softly lit furnishings were plush, overstuffed and mildly child-abused. The lampshades matched and the pictures hung in pairs, landscapes, portraits or little birds. The hutch reflected orderly sensibility spanning decades.

I could see Christine in an overstuffed chair surrounded by mementos of a sadly mistaken past. I found the sheets and blanket covered the couch. If I bled to death, I would spare the sofa. I lay down into purgatory.

I woke a long time later to the white light of the long tunnel, until the furnishings delineated. She lounged in a chair facing me, crossing her lovely legs with a sigh. I rolled toward her. "What time is it?"

"Two." The light was a dim bulb in the kitchen.

"Not so bad," I said. "You got off early. Was it a slow night for mayhem?"

She laughed short and sighed again. She thought something over and slouched. "My life must change," she said.

I sat up in the fog and pain. "Yes. Change is good."

"I think you have smoked too much hash."

"Mm. I think you're right."

She sat up and reached for the tasteful end table, where she opened the drawer and found her kit. Loading her little pipe, she eased into another context. "For me, it is only to unwind."

"It's okay."

"I know it's okay." She smoked it with small vengeance, only a few hits. She put it away. "John Kline is coming here. If I can find him, somehow…."

"Who is John Kline?"

She got up and walked to her stereo and played a piano selection, modern with classic overtone. She sat back down.

"You want to tune his piano?"

"I met him once. He told me he would give me a try. You know they always need tuners when they travel."

"When is he coming?"

"I'm not certain. In a few weeks."

Her voice trailed. I floated as well, but my fog was thick with no questions. The parlor practically tingled in uniquely European non-silence, as if time passing was history in the making. The scene felt like wax in lifelike perfection. The tick-tock clock timed our stillness, stifling speech until the tick and tock matched the air around us. I sat up in pain, in need of a piss. "I think I need some water. And a few aspirin."

"There, by the bath," she said. I got up, sleepy and pained, my baggy drawers showing my stiffy—hey, I had to pee.

"My God," she said.

I smiled sheepishly, covering with my hand. She looked away. "I miss them so much. I would kill myself if anything happened to them." Presto. It went away.

I leaned on the sofa for balance. "Sounds easy," I said. "We get the schedule, get tickets and go see the guy."

"No. I cannot. It is impossible."

I closed the bathroom door for a momentous piss that took me from desperation to acceptance in two minutes flat. Must have been the tea. She knocked on the door to advise Tylenol, not aspirin that thins blood. It was in the cabinet. I took some, splashed my face, rinsed my mouth, stomach in, chest out, and felt ready to continue my date.

In the living room we smoked another little pipe. I crawled back under cover as she huddled into her own. Shaking her head in the thick of it, she reaffirmed, "It is impossible."

"Very few things are impossible. You must know that."

"You Americans. You think you can do anything."

"I don't think I can do anything. I think you can meet John Kline. I think I could meet him tomorrow, if it was that important to me. As it is, I can wait. I can meet him when he gets here. I can introduce him to you, if you want to meet him."

"How can you do this?"

"Magic."

"Just as I thought."

"All you think is negative. I can meet anybody I want to meet. John Kline meets people every day. I can be one of those people."

"I already told you, you don't need to talk to me that way."

I lay back, closed my eyes and wondered why I'd given up my sanctuary. Oh, yeah, it was the nursing aspect and a greater-than-zero chance on sweetmeats. "How am I doing?"

"At what?"

I laughed. Depressed but alert, all funked out with no place to go, she strained in the braces. I felt reciprocal in helping her and moreover at home on an overstuffed sofa on the far side of Earth. Sleep came easily in a parlor for the wax museum going tick…tock…tick…tock…tick…. The fog thickened, floating the corpse in the airless calm. A dream of icicles became too real, too cold, and I woke again as her cold fingers laced my forehead. She looked askance and said, "You're doing well. You don't have a fever. You did have before."

She sat beside me for a while with one hand on my arm, the other on my opposite shoulder. Could she feel something? I had hope with no expectation but could not remain numb to her numbness. Never mind, in a while, as I drifted again, surfacing briefly to ask, "Why did you bring me here?"

She felt my forehead again, this time with single, brief caress.

XXVIII

Glacial Movement

"Do you want to leave?" she asked.

"No. Not now. I'm only curious."

"What is there for you to be curious about? You are sick. You need help. You need a friend who can assist you."

"It was a stupid question," I said. She smiled, her first of the evening. She stood and walked away. "Are you off tomorrow?"

"Off?"

"Do you work tomorrow?"

"No. My holiday starts tomorrow."

"Maybe I could take you somewhere."

"Where would you take me?"

"Anywhere. Anywhere you want to go."

She thought it over until her head broke inertia and wagged, pendulous as time passing. "I don't think so." And she faded into the depth, down the hall.

Sleep was fitful. I regretted being there and asking the wrong questions, being myself and crowding in. I regretted my carnal drive, losing grace in the face of grace. What a simpler world it would be without hormones, a world of give and take freely accepted. That's naïve. Missionaries don't fuck, or don't admit it, and look at the damage they cause. Then again, she could emit dynamic light, given a chance. How soundly we would sleep then.

Then again, I'd sigh afterward, moan and snore, which could churn her bitterness and fear of base need in the male of the species.

She seemed stuck, failing to climb out of her rut and refusing to try again. She lived in a tradition of depression, in which life is a painful affair. I shared the same depression, as many people do. At least I knew the antidote: little piston in perfect cylinder, rendering tolerable existence for the moment. Then I could head south to meet Hattie, my love.

Christine stacked up delectably, whether she gave in to us or not. Leaving her was predictable for both, I thought, and I wanted to help her in my humble way. I wanted to be with her and then be somewhere else, someplace happier. Sleep came and went on questions of giving and need.

Waking was neither refreshing nor rested. Coffee and muffins wafted from the kitchen. A towel folded on the sofa was a gentle lead. Into the shower and out got things going. The kitchen table was set with china and silver, and a sheer robe outlined another eye opener. She moved deliberately, leaning and pouring in happy resolve. "Good morning," she said.

"Good morning." I tried not to stare.

"Did you sleep well?"

"Like a rock. And you?"

"Yes. I did." She sat down and bade me sit. I sat. She offered coffee, cream, muffins and jams.

"Thank you."

"You're welcome." We ate silently, perhaps ruminating on other food for thought.

"How do you feel?"

"Better, I think. My stomach is not healed."

"I'll look at it."

"Thank you." We ate. "What will you do today, your first day of vacation?"

She laughed. "Errands. I have so many."

I nodded, uncertain what I would do today or what she expected of me.

"You should rest today. Try to stay still. The wound on your stomach is in a difficult place. It should heal more quickly if you stay still."

"Still and calm."

"Yes. Still and calm. You might get restless. I can't help that."

Oh, but you can. "Can I come with you?"

"For errands?"

"For a while, yes."

"Why must you come with me?"

"You're right. I mustn't."

"Yes. It's all right. For a while. I'm going first to the flea market. I love it there. I haven't been in ages. After that I think you would prefer keeping still."

"All right. The flea market."

"We will leave in twenty minutes?"

213

"That sounds like an excellent idea," I said.

She laughed again. The ice cracked. We finished. We cleared.

She wasn't accustomed to a man in the kitchen. The former husband was cerebral and helpless, best suited for reading another book. I imagined him tweeded with elbow patches and a pipe, like Yves Montand, starring in a classic tale about a genius in the suburbs tolerating his wife's simple mind while she cleans up.

"Thank you," she said.

"Thank *you*," I corrected. She paused, calving in glacial chunks. I felt the wave and insisted on finishing up in the kitchen. Sensitivity in a man couldn't have been all she needed. Yet she changed like a woman too long without help in her tastefully appointed breakfast nook. She seemed to love the offer but ordered me into the parlor first.

"Come. Your wound." She sat me on a chair and checked my arm, redressing it. Off with my pants, she had another go at the cut wending playfully toward what I wanted to show her. She didn't blink. Objective, clinical and beyond my fantasy, she kept the morning casual and charmed with small kindness. I was good to go with nary a thrill or a chill, except when she caught me looking down her robe. We blushed, but the lovely view felt integral to the healing process.

"Christine." I called her by name. "Do you think, since this is the first day of your holiday, a little buzz might be in order?"

"If you want to smoke hash, then you should."

I did, because an equal and opposite low seemed ubiquitously abundant. I fueled and fired the pipe, took my dose and offered it.

"Thank you."

"You're welcome," I said. Stoned again, we dressed for an outing. Her formality became laughable with the drug. I wanted to call her Miss but feared she'd miss the humor. She watched me. I smiled. She looked away.

And there we were, swirled like chips in batter, ready for an hour at 350° to melt the bittersweet between us. She had Spacecakes, only a quarter ounce left. She didn't know where it came from but suspected North Africa and Asia. We glowed and drifted, animate and spontaneous, the brains between us melting as well. She walked well in a stylish dress that promoted her sensual side, as if by design.

She saw me watching and looked away, perhaps resigned to the discomfort required of the courting process. Not that I was courting, but I did want to mate and thought she did too, maybe soon. I eased in with an arm around her waist. "You must be a good dancer," I said.

She snickered defensively. "I don't want to dance."

"I don't either," I said with a shrug.

"You are a strange man," she said.

I stepped aside. "I'm not strange." Her half smile warmed, I think, to show she meant no harm. "You must mean unique," I said. "Unusual can be an attraction. Not strange."

"I see stranger men than you every night. Bigger. Dirtier. Stronger. You could call them unique too."

"I don't think so," I said, easing back alongside.

Maybe we were getting somewhere. Her chilling propriety and clinical marriage had taken a toll, and she waited beneath the surface to rise and breathe.

"Come," I said, steering us into a café. "Let me buy you a coffee." We sat, shifted and glanced, what stoned people do on a Saturday, out and about. The seats were dust free, and so were the forearm radii on the table. She shared these observations.

An Arab teen served us. "You like hashish. All is very good. Very cheap. You buy yes what kind?" He presented the hash menu.

I pointed to the first selection, Holy Shit, and gave the nod. "And two cappuccinos." He left at a trot. Christine remained deadpan as a mannequin. He came back with coffees and Holy Shit. I loaded, lit and tasted the acrid sweetness of an opium lace, acceptable with a cappuccino back and well balanced with sugar, two lumps. "You might like this," I said.

She tried a short one and tweaked her nose. "It will make you sleep," she said.

Sleep is good for depressed people, I didn't say. I sipped. "Mm. This will keep you awake." She sipped slowly, drifting, like a toy on low batteries. We sat.

"How long is your holiday?"

"I have one month."

"I have an idea. I can take you somewhere." We'd already reviewed this idea and came up empty.

But she said, "I have two tickets to Greece…" She stopped short, like a flushed quail, looking up at two barrels. Two tickets abroad seemed as unlikely as her invitation home. The exchange moved us as defibrillation flops a body.

"Greece would be excellent," I said. "You take me."

"No. I already said no. I don't want to. It is impossible."

"Why impossible?"

"You are impossible."

Well, if I wasn't impossible where would either one of us get to? Stuck in Lodi again is where. I took her hand. "Christine. When I first came to the hospital, what did you think?"

"I thought you were bloody. Seriously injured. I learned that it was not so serious."

"What did you think when I came back to the hospital?"

"I thought you looked very tired. I did not think your bandage needed changing."

She sounded professional, like a witness in cross-ex. I tried again. "Why did you come with me to dinner?"

"I was hungry."

"You hardly ate."

She looked down. "That happens to me sometimes."

"Did you think anything else?"

"What kind of thing?"

"Any man-woman kind of thing?"

"Oh, no."

"Oh, no?"

"Why should I?"

"Because you're a woman, and I'm a man, and here we are."

"No. Men have tried to do this over the years. Just like you. But it is not possible."

"It is not possible because you won't let it be possible."

"Whatever you like." And so she sat, still-life with sadness cast in stone. We smoked, sipped and sat. I longed for the exit; she was too far gone, down, no spark. Her spirit of giving seemed one-dimensional.

I smiled. "Shall we?"

She looked up uncertainly, no longer trusting her strange lodger. I stood, and she said, "Yes."

So the gray, drab morning stretched to noon, pleasantly cushioned, marginally balanced. We walked. I stole glances, imagining where her legs could lead to, speculating more stoneworks.

She brightened at the flea market, recalling a few bargains from last year. It was rags mostly, with glitter and without. She browsed. I drifted. In an hour. she glimmered once, like a cold engine on a single sputter. "I know a place for lunch. Are you hungry?"

"Yes. I am hungry. Are you hungry?"

"Yes. I am. I am very hungry." It was our first exchange since Holy Shit.

XXIX

Amino Acids and Electrons

Lunch was a cold medley, also smoked. She gained momentum over what used to be, replaying, sorting out, not exactly letting go, but opening up. I lent an ear to her struggle. Her face had no expression short of beauty. She formed words in a lovely way that skirted her lost love but couldn't hide it. She'd been a lovely person with love still to share, but what a nut.

She spoke of Brussels, scene of the crime, and another place not too far away, Bruges, a theme park packed with tourists, ass to elbow, shuffling through the ruins, soaking up history and Coca-Cola. The place is old but suburban, converted to family fun.

She recalled old times. The divorce had been a death in the family and a mortal wound. She'd held the marriage sacred. I listened to a life that, to me, sounded miserable for all concerned. She described the professor as opposite to the poseurs of rampant thinking. Unlike the coffee-breath, nicotine-jag, baggy-shirt ultra-chic, the prof was a real thinker, validated in degrees. Tall and stately, he could stare with aplomb, especially at the wall, where his many degrees hung. He'd earned his tweeds and patches the old fashioned way, thinking, smoking his pipe. Unlike his distant cousins hiding in cafés, he was licensed to think, his thoughts qualifying for ink on paper. In time, anything drifting between his ears became currency for those who paid attention. She described him as attractive to young women in need of intellectual stimulation.

I said, "He sounds like a cardboard cutout, without daring, without do." I thought it would make her feel better. She smiled sadly and said, "We were stable. He made me happy."

"To a point," I added, testing her limits of tolerance. She said she loved family life and raising her children. The gap between mommy and the professor grew over the years, aging and disengaging, until he found the Fountain of Youth and traded in on a newer model.

She murmured something about devastation, as if his behavior was rare as monkeys taking wing out her stone-cold ass—I did not say it. She'd taken it personally, as if his craving was as an act of betrayal. I still had no response. Of course it was, and he was, but that is what some men do. She left me nothing to say. I could have speculated that he outgrew theme parks, station wagons and clutter. But that wouldn't help. He finally told her he wanted what he'd never had but couldn't say what that was.

"I asked him, 'What is it that you want?' He didn't know. I would have given him anything. Anything. I told him I would give him anything, if he could say what he wanted. He didn't know."

She looked glum. The professor chose to roll the bones on a fool's wager. I could have explained to her the nature of professors and fervent co-eds. I could have pressed the case for sexual crisis and dilemma, leading to happily ever after for some and devastation for another.

But…nah. I wouldn't have minded meeting him for a drink, actually, to get his views on Christine, to watch him watch waitresses. But he didn't matter, and he'd damaged Christine, breaching his oath of loyalty and letting her down with a bang.

Listen to me. I think the marriage bored her too, one more parlor object in need of dusting now and then. But she'd considered divorce no more than cleaning her house with a meat cleaver. Now a great sadness had settled on her and taken root. Her marriage was over but wouldn't go away, giving rise to doubt.

I would not explain a man's flight with a new woman "twenty years younger with breasts like casaba melons." It happens. Could he have kept a co-ed discreetly? Who cared? Nor could I challenge Christine's assertion that the new woman was "a slut with questionable hygiene."

Animate in indictment and sad in her eulogy, she felt her life had been thrown away, its matched furnishings and outings in the station wagon cast off like rubbish. She sat straight with a brief sparkle in her eyes that captured a seasoned beauty I doubted she had twenty years ago. She'd run herself around the emotional block and only now considered a life left to live. A day ago, she was only beautiful, defeated and aging, instead of sorting memories, dusting and re-shelving. She seemed hopeless, suffocated by self, doomed to win her loser's gambit.

She went deeper. I listened. She needed the purge just as I needed disinfectant and fresh bandages. Any comment would have stopped the flow, so I let her ramble, nodding, wondering why she clung to such boring detail, stridently repressing the truth, that the prof was a dud. I didn't fault him for the coed but for the stilted, stifling life he'd stuck them in.

Maybe we were peas in a pod, she and I, staring, nodding.

But she was done and caught me nodding at the smoky air. "What?" she said. "What have you remembered?"

"I only realized that we are similar."

She shook her head. "No, we are not."

"I meant that our situations are similar."

"Your wife left you?"

"Not my wife. My girlfriend."

"You are too old for girlfriends. You should have a wife."

"You're old enough to know better."

"Why did she leave?"

I shrugged. "Look at me?"

"Not that bad."

"Thank you. She was young. She is young."

She laughed the scornful laugh. "Do you love her?"

"I don't know."

She laughed again, derisively. "Men only say that to protect themselves. If she comes back, then you can love her. If she doesn't come back, you don't have to. Is that not so?"

I wanted to ask her the same question to prove my point of similarity. But it was too obvious and would have hurt her, and it still didn't matter if she loved her husband or not or would admit either one. I was already in dangerous territory, about to win the point but lose the patient. "Yes," I said. "That is so. I'm playing it safe."

We nibbled our lunch and had some water for the clarity. I didn't think I was attached to Hattie. She watched me thinking, until I asked, "Why do you think we met?"

"People meet every day. They can't help it. Can they?"

We ate silently in the impasse. We seemed to have reached an impasse, unable to help other further, across our stabbed and tormented wastelands, our dispirited tundra.

"Do you think she'll come back?" she asked.

Too quickly I said, "No." I lied. I knew Hattie would be back, but I wanted to ease the way for Christine, to grant her the peace of mind she needed, so she could open her mind and heart to the hot surprise, so she could see we were in this together. And I wanted her to see my resignation and perhaps take some for herself.

But she went back to the wax museum; do not pass go, back to the good old days that should have lasted forever. She hesitated. She smiled. She remembered. "Sometimes we would…." But the words played out and faded away. I finished my last cracker.

"Please don't stop," I said. "Not now."

But she settled into silence. Oh, well.

I dabbed my napkin and said, "Family life isn't easy for someone like me. You know, the simple pleasures of watching the children grow up, relaxing with a full belly and a fire in the hearth and all that." I had her attention, admitting that I would never enter the lost kingdom and preferred life in the wild. "It's not bad for a night or two, comfort and security and routine, but it's not for me."

"I would be surprised as well for you," she said.

"And I will be surprised for you."

"I will not remarry. I will not."

"You don't have to," I said. "Nobody has to. Nobody said anything about marriage. You can have a boyfriend. You can have a string of boyfriends." She blushed. I'd gone too far, but she showed a pulse. I covered and hoped for the best. "I'll be surprised to see what indulgence

223

you allow yourself. You're too young to be old, and fun is waiting to be had. You should know that and choose what you want to do. The world is still an okay place, and most people are still happy at least once a day."

Maybe she understood. She looked into my eyes, as her own eyes welled up. Maybe we'd need some liquor or more hash or another cappuccino. But we were easing in. I could feel it and felt guilty as well for my giddy anticipation.

But it's always one step forward and two in reverse in a campaign like this. Campaign? Well, yes, to be truthful, but a campaign like this does not preclude love, or should not preclude love, which is why many people take comfort in referring to the sweet exchange as making love. I wanted to in a big way, whether in spite of her depression or because of it seemed incidental, though it would be more fun if she could cheer up. She regressed instead on the next sigh, remembering how perfect it was, before it wasn't. "We had a Volvo." She smiled sadly.

Serene as Mother Teresa after saving a slum, she said, "It is rare in Brussels, you know." She meant the Volvo. She and the professor and the children had been unique. I listened over hill and dale as she warmed up and tittered down that road. Recollection was her opiate, and she was all strung out.

We cruised the byways of perfection lost, and soon dead-ended in the old, familiar swamp. "I think men are so weak for young girls, especially at that age, don't you?" She answered for me. "Oh, yes. You do. Your girlfriend is also what? Seventeen?"

I shrugged. I could have picked my nose.

She stared off. "I don't know why we separated," she said. "I think about it, and I can't know why. Can anyone?" She knew why but waited for my answer.

I filled the bowl, lit up and pumped a cloud. "You have values he didn't share," I said.

"Yes. That's part of it."

"That may be a bigger part of it than you realize."

"Yes. But he was weak too. How could he throw everything away for that? He was weak. Men are so weak. Look at you. Trying to take me away. You would get me to someplace like Greece and see a young girl with bigger breasts and off you'd go."

She had a point. I wanted to swear denial, and I honestly hoped her proficiency in the sack would make it so. But a man's doubt is palpable as a breeze, when a woman understands testosterone. Men are weak, some weaker than most. I believed sexual relations with Christine would lead to another go and another, as necessary or tolerated. That's the romantic delusion for the male of the species.

She and I knew the score. *C'est la vie* for me. *Sacre Coeur* for her. She seemed nervous, defenses fatigued. I sensed the red zone, the twenty yards remaining to the end zone. A waitress with a splendid rack watched from nearby. Did they work together, tag-teaming with accusation and proof, to flush me from my lair of innocence, testing my sincerity.

"Your ex-husband may have been a normal fellow, but from what you tell me, it sounds like he was bored." I treaded softly. "What about chemistry? You think people spend time together just because one of them has big tits—I mean, breasts?" She stared in disbelief. The splendid rack honed in—could she sense a threesome? "You deny the possibility of loving more than one person in a lifetime."

Her eyes puffed, lips twitching. Bingo. We waited, move to her. She would make it, or the play was off. Worn out from too much baseline volley—I switched to tennis to give her a chance—I moved ahead, not exactly rushing the net but prying us from tedium. She had given in her good and nursely way, and so did I. I stood. She followed. Was that her move? Crazy woman. Were we on? Did she just brush against my thigh?

But it all came down to the age old question: Who gives a shit? I hit the wall on the cumulative toll of wounds, hash, depression, the campaign and its intimations of commitment. I was done, tossing the racquet and throwing in the towel, and there we were, strolling down the street without talking, with no common interests or objectives— until a breeze came up, soft as a whisper, warm as summer. We glanced south together, at its origin, and her fingers found mine. Hands swung and so moved like a pendulum, off dead center and ever so slightly farther the other way. Fingers entwined and in no time worked their way into a lovely communion. Just so, we would swing farther this way and that, until finding our limits in need and appetite. I recall that exchange and hope she does too, for my benefit. In simple touch, we began exhilarating phase of our liaison. That's how love used to be. And personal pleasantry is the best measure of love.

Her hands felt rough, despise their elegant form. Calloused palms suggested too many dishes washed, too much vacuum cleaning and laundry out the ass. Yet holding hands changed everything. She'd initiated. I surged in response but knew the score. It called for conservative play, in spite of her need. I feared overheating.

I felt like the man for the job. Easing up to nature and honesty, we sought kindness and contact and found it available in each other. We strolled back down the boulevard in pleasant reverie.

The afternoon played on, conceding to the script we would play out. She softened but clung to instability with intermittent tension. She stopped and stared. She remained wary, apprehensive. I was the castor oil, and she knew it, but oh, the stuff was so distasteful. She missed so much, denying herself friendship with a natural man. She'd worn me out, used me up and left me indifferent, almost. She'd purged some of what haunted her but couldn't fully ease into the swing of things, not like me.

My wounds were leaking so she parked me at a coffee bar near some shops she needed. She picked up an entertainment tabloid and gave it to me, telling me to sit. She'd be back in a few. Meanwhile, I could read about entertainers coming to Amsterdam. John Kline, pianist, would arrive on the weekend.

Why is it, that even when a thing seems on, the woman is content to put it off another hour or two? Did she not realize that we could be enjoying our first great relief this very minute, or that we could be resting up for another in no time? I saw her reflection in a window, as she stared obliquely from twenty yards out. I turned her way, and she turned away. She walked back. She tried a smile on for size and stretched it into place. It may have hurt but was a growth moment, only recently impossible.

I excused myself as gray skies closed in. She scanned her list. I sat in pain and fatigue, surely looking less hazardous, as she smiled and said it was time to go home. She'd had enough, and I needed fresh bandages. We shuffled off to chez Christine through the hazy day. When I limped, she put her arm around my waist and made me smile. I loved her.

At home she unwrapped me slowly, admiring my pain threshold and relaxing like a nurse at work. After new bandages came tea on the sofa and a moment of mutual composure.

XXX

The Hotel Christine

Christine's perfect life had been left in ruins. She got stuck, browsing the rubble. My remedy was physical, though she was mental. Her perfect picture had chipped and faded, but she couldn't look away. I thought I could help. I thought we could get way out of town, much farther than Greece. Once past prelims, we could cruise. I would cherish our communion. Long term, short term; it wouldn't matter, once the other term was set aside. Curtains fall to rise again, perhaps on an act of love. If love seemed one-dimensional for me, the act could still be fun, which should be lovely on any account.

Comparison to Hattie was easy. Hattie was too young and far away. Christine was mature and elegant. She suited me. I lay on the couch. She watched. She smiled. It's just that easy for a woman: one little smile and Big Dick Johnson bangs the bar like a bum at a wine tasting.

I smiled back with a shrug. She tensed and began again on what her children were made to suffer and that heartless woman. I closed my eyes. DJ faded on hearing that dose o' woe. I feared she was merely an ache looking for an ear to pour into. I couldn't leave and had nowhere to go at any rate.

She rambled. I stewed. I didn't love her or myself. She toyed with me. I tuned her out, nodding on cue. At least she relaxed, droning into her marital problems and the problematic marriage of the professor and his new wife. "He comes to me for consolation! Can you believe that?" She couldn't believe it.

I rolled over, causing a bandage to pull. She leaned in to fix it, close enough for scent and a moment: chemical analysis. We were a match but blocked. I'd seen the quick embrace in movies. But what if? And a stab wound precluded quickness. She leaned back and stared, until I said, "Christine."

She stared still, taking me in. I breathed deep and closed my eyes. "Do you want to sleep in my bed?" She asked, clinically as a nurse offering an upgrade.

"Where would you sleep?" I asked, because in the end they break you down to dumb questions.

"In my bed."

"Hm. I am feeling tired."

She stood up. "That's funny. You don't look tired." She walked casually from the parlor to the bedroom. Hallelujah, I thought, dragging my sorry carcass behind, remembering Pete, thinking I would call it off as Pete should have done, to share some frustration and preserve my strength. But the male of the species, any species, will move in if he can, loaded for bear.

She stripped like a prisoner prior to a search, as if doubting her allure, leaned on a jamb by the bathroom. The professor was a dunce. I could not remember such attraction at close range. The drab afternoon rose to a hefty pulse.

Down to filigree and translucence, she stared, shifting awkwardly. I stared back and would still be staring, if she hadn't taken my hand for another lead. "Poor little one," she said. She meant me.

We lay down, two war-wounded, seeking renewal—or compensation, reassurance, vindication and the rest. Nature took its course, as it can, given balance. We made magic. At least I thought we did. At least I did.

Basic friction was methodical, at a matronly pace. She needed no cartwheels or headstands but only a gentle transit across the tundra of her making. Eye to eye, I smiled. She blushed. What a woman. In and out seemed eternal, no end in sight, until she twitched and chirped, embarrassed and sadly amazed. I trotted easily to the oasis, where we rested.

Resurgence derived soon enough from her pure and tireless beauty and tolerance. The night was young. Hormones and memories mingled with intermittent flares. By sunrise, the smoke had cleared on a changing world. We snoozed, had tea, smoked hash, ate and rested and rode again, maybe stocking up for the harsh season ahead. I considered a life in Amsterdam, lounging around Christine's, staying high and fucking. It couldn't last, but I fantasized, as she sought new levels of nursing. The professor went from dunce to failure. But there must be more to life than sex, and I determined to sort that out in a week or so. We moved into day three, or four.

Just as a marathon presents phases, so our experiment changed. Christine went from release to deep release, her body flexing as a single muscle, holding on until letting go, taking what she needed, killing what ailed her, seeking retribution, leaning into the kinks, chasing lost time, coming up gasping, "I've never done that!" The professor went to brain dead.

We made up for lost time but went too fast, outpacing our headlights. Feverish as game on the run, she looked ready at last for something more, for life sustained, as if cleaning her house with a meat cleaver might be effecting. I sat up to the thought of a cleaver swinging. Had I missed something?

"What?"

"Nothing," I assured, falling in again.

I couldn't match her vindictive spirit or pace, though I tried; he was such a jerk. But limitations on my side were only physical. I savored access to the most lovely vortices, also physical and beyond that, mental and emotional. She couldn't hide the mental, but that part too melted like an iceberg.

Soon enough, she flipped, in typical iceberg fashion, wailing on pressure too long constrained, pent up and released. She inhabited a body repossessed, until I missed the good old days of two days ago, when it was only Christine and I having a nice screw.

I too was getting my fill of compensation and self-defense, shoring up against difficult imagery of the one I loved, spread eagle for another. I repressed Hattie by replacing her, in the flesh.

I watched Christine in spasm and wanted to tell Hattie about her, this beautiful nurse with excellent hash and a grown-up house and incredible appetite. I watched Christine on top in a grimace, loping for the summit. I would tell Hattie about the sadness too, but not the shadowy trick, by which a lovelorn man changes a woman he loves to another woman he also loves. Chaos is part of nature, and a man has few regrets in such lovely conditions.

We lay silent in the eye of the storm. Did she wonder what might come next? She rolled away with finality, as if we'd scratched the itch, and the task was done.

An afternoon wore on to shades of gray. Christine and I had met the flesh and needed space and air, soon. I lay there, watching her lovely back. She sat on the edge. The big clock ticked away, timing our love. She turned with a forlorn smile as if to speak but said nothing. She lay back down, and we dozed. We woke to life beyond sex. The grays had blended to a single hue.

"John Kline will be here Friday," I said. "We can find him if you want to." She said nothing. "Do you think John Kline would remember you?"

"No."

Did she think I would remember her? I didn't ask.

"Does John Kline have a tuner?"

"I don't know."

"How old is John Kline?"

"About our age."

"How would a tuner convince a pianist that she's the tuner for the job?"

"I would tune for him."

"What if he wanted more?"

"I would tune first, and see what more there is."

"What if John Kline patronizes you for sexual advantage?"

"Fuck him," she tittered, blushing deeper than shadow. We laughed. She'd made a joke, a sobering breakthrough.

I told her about my own showbiz runaround with a big-time movie producer who promised greatness in Hollywood, but it was a ruse. He only wanted down and dirty on a rear entry.

She rolled my way and stared anew. Maybe nobody had told her a story in a long time. "So, you do something other than walk on the beach and collect the rent. You write scripts for movies."

"No, I don't. That was a long time ago. I called this guy…"

"You have a problem with homosexuals?" she asked.

"No. Not unless they manipulate and come on like that. I have a problem with anyone wasting my time trying to fuck me."

"It is only natural for them, as you think it is natural for you."

"You think I'm a homosexual?"

"You wanted to fuck me."

"I didn't insist. I didn't represent it as necessary to your advancement in the world."

"Yes, you did. You think this way that you have is invisible?"

"But you brought me home."

"I did not bring you home. I opened my home to you. You are injured." She looked down. "You are relentless."

"But I didn't…"

"Yes, you did. I did too. Because, in a way, you are right. I mean, for now."

Of course, I was right—and happy she felt that way.

She asked, "If you met a homosexual who was injured, you would not try to help?"

"I would."

She smiled.

"Why are you smiling? You don't believe I'd help someone who couldn't meet my personal needs?"

"I think you could perhaps help someone without wanting to have sex. But help me. Tell me about sometime when you did."

"I helped an old lady across the street once. I carried her groceries to her car, too. She wanted to give me a blowjob, but I said no."

She laughed. What a relief. She pressed on. "I think you're highly sexual. I wonder what you'll do when you get old."

"How old?"

She laughed again. We were building a new mood.

"I was only telling you about showbiz. Sex is currency there, what you pay for what you get, maybe. I knew this guy was a homosexual. I didn't care, but he led me on. I made trips to LA and took assignments and wrote treatments, to show my stuff. That takes time and energy. And money. And heart."

"So you were strung along and then lost everything."

"Yeah. But I wasn't married to the guy. I didn't want to make a life with him. He wanted nothing but me, bending over."

"What if you could have made a life with him?" She sat up. "What if you wrote the script for a wonderful film? And he produced it. And people thought you were good. So you and he made another film, and so on. That would have made you happy?"

"Maybe. And it could have happened, if the guy was real. But he wasn't. He only wanted to pump for oil up my butt, while I pondered Hollywood greatness. He couldn't put a movie together, and I'm not a homosexual. So we broke up."

"But don't you see? Motivation is the same, sexual or otherwise."

"You think all motivation is material? What about love?"

She laughed harder now, threatening our new mood with old scorn. "Listen to you. Love is something people do in the suburbs. Isn't that what you think?"

"No. That's not what I think. I think love is part of sex, when the people involved get to know each other and share motivation."

She smiled. "I wouldn't have expected you so say that."

"There was a time when I wouldn't have said it."

We pondered love and motivation.

"I was naïve, until the guy's receptionist told me our guy was broke, looking for money and meanwhile fooling a bunch of guys like me. I thought he was jealous, the receptionist, but then he said, 'You seem like such a nice man. I can tell: you're sensitive.' The receptionist said he hadn't been paid in a month but stayed on because the producer wasn't a bad guy except for being crazy on the make. The entourage stayed on because the guy had been so big. I could hang out and be positioned when the greatness came back, because positioning is what people do in Hollywood. But screenwriting for pay was not an option, and he couldn't stand it anymore, the receptionist, seeing sweet guys strung along."

Christine smiled at the profile. "What did you do?"

"I went outside. Santa Monica, where teenage boys on the street sell ass. This street hag comes up to me and says, 'I'm a screenwriter. Out of work. You got a dollar?' I gave her two bucks and caught a bus to the airport. The end."

We lay there, resting, in need of a life to return to. The drab evening wore on. I said, "If you love something, you should give it a chance. John Kline can't use you unless you help."

"You've been so patient with me," she said.

I couldn't argue and wouldn't mention my motivation. "No more patient than you've been with me. You're not all that hard to take, once you relax."

"You mean once I take my clothes off?"

How indelicate, when I'd shaped a compliment around her difficulty. We pondered patience and time. With bones aching, I wanted air and new scenery.

"I love you," she said. "I am in love with you."

Oh, God. How could I tell her? We got our medicine, each from the other. A hormonal man persists. With depletion, he's weak. She, on the other hand, felt fulfilled, breathing freely at last on the far side. "You make me feel like no man ever has."

No surprise there, but the comparison was nebulous. She'd dilated her heart to receive what was missing. She took my silence as acceptance of her fervor.

"The way you push it in. So deep. I love that."

I caressed her. "I thought you were doing that."

"My husband could never do that. His thing was too little."

"Mm. That's the worst, a little thing."

"Yes." She stared up, like a corpse, eyes open.

"You know my thing is not all that big."

She reached for it. "It's bigger than his," and down she went, seeking the impossible dream.

"And the others?" I asked.

She looked up, surprised. "It's only you. And him." And she proceeded to resolution, nursing her fantasy, feeding her revenge.

I rose to the occasion, but a man senses impact on hard truth, coming on. In the next silence, I held Christine, as she needed to be held, as a special patient and nurse for the ages. I could have told her I loved her, but she'd know the lie in a day or so, when I left. We would remain chemically bonded and could meet again, sometime, maybe soon. But eternal love? Nah.

I would rue the day I left such a one. A wise man sets doubt aside to see if it leaves on its own accord. I pondered Greece and the naked beach and carte blanche on frequent liberation from our need. Imagery danced but came around to the ultimate question of days and life, color-coordinated and matching under gray skies in perfect neatness. I didn't set out to find a new life. I had a life. No sensible man wants to be in and out, here and gone, but I was on the road. We could be happy for now, because I'd go home in time, and she'd stay here.

Hattie could provoke, challenge and irritate, while Christine could only be herself, and a far better self it was. I pondered years of it. We would taper to three times a week, then once. We would die to the cadence of the tick-tock clock. "I'm not really patient," I said.

"Yes. You are much more patient than he was. Much more." She snuggled. I feared another go but not really, because it simply wouldn't go. The mere shape of her aroused a tiny pulse and cast new light on life in Amsterdam. She was more my age and more stable than the other. We could cure her bitterness and stiffness and my own, and the younger one was unpredictable.

Hattie wouldn't last, and that seemed a benefit. Yet I wanted to call for the volley, to tell her I could stay here forever or another week, as necessary. Was that it? Winning a point?

Christine pondered potential from her pillow more tastefully. Muddled in contemplation, we slept.

She woke me with another nursing, with a focus that felt critical and problematic, presenting what had seemed a happy challenge turned… unpleasant. Yet in the wee hours, life comes down to blurry darkness.

How bad could this be? Would I not recall Christine's need as a glittering dream in my life of experience?

Or would the moment fit the darkness, in which I felt conscripted to another invasion of Belgium? We moaned, accepting more and less in life, in pummeling the thing between us. We seemed amiss. She went pneumatic and cried.

XXXI

Time and Tide

 She eased up on the dawn of a new day. We got up to coffee, a little light piano, sparse talk, no hash, the tick-tock stillness and a new presence in the formal living room. A mussed sofa, used tumblers here and there, hash and pipes and bedding made a scene of debauchery, displacing the former life of tidy neatness. Purged of constraint, immersed in lust, she tried to make sense of the new order. We sat. We stared, as if content.

She'd turned a corner, revealing her private self, she thought, or maybe feared. Her furtive glance suggested that I was the man for the job, or maybe only hoped. She asked as much, making me proud of her boldness and sharing her need. She suspected the underside of maleness, what the professor had shown. A sexual romp had cured what ailed her, or got her back on course at any rate, even as she struggled with sorting and planning.

Hattie often chided my age and easy fatigue, as youth will do. This was better, wary and poised. I was a fool, longing for the young one, knowing the heart is a foolish hunter. Hattie had nothing on Christine, who seemed better in every way, and far more logical.

Christine could do better than me. She could choose. Men glanced her way. I'd persisted to momentary greatness for me, redemption for her. She felt at home with love again, so we might imagine a life based on courtesy and passion. Would that be so bad? Would it evolve?

The week passed on growing compatibility. She knew of plenty more men. I was only first, or the most insistent, and the way had seemed timely. The sexual part improved too, with rhythm and modulation and reasonable breaks. She read me. She seemed to sense the end of our time in fading frequency, my pleasant but dispassionate compliance. She'd tamed me. We shared a love based on courtesy and sex with something missing. We couldn't last.

By the weekend I felt punchy from wine, hash and sex. She wanted more of it, much more, loosened up for love. We went out, evenings, to small bistros off the beaten path. She took my arm and laughed often. We talked of former life and her amazement in the moment. She'd imagined such things, but not with herself in the starring role. I assured her that people enjoy such things every day. She blushed and confided that she'd never done it every day. "Not even on your honeymoon?"

She shook her head. "This is my honeymoon." She left me speechless and touched my hand. "No, it's not. It's better than my honeymoon." She wouldn't say her marital frequency, but I guessed Sundays and holidays, down to holidays, down to Labor Day and the Fourth of July. She smiled. "I took the medicine. Not so bad. I like it." She thought and asked, "Do you think I love it so much because of you?"

"I don't know."

"I'm sorry I made us wait," she said. "I didn't know either."

Later that night she rolled over and kissed my face. I pretended to be sleeping.

We rented a paddleboat and cruised the canals with hash and wine. We rode bicycles around the park and walked around town. I asked one morning what she wanted to do today. She wanted to have coffee and smoke hash and get back into bed for you-know-what. Then we would have breakfast and go out to play. "It's Saturday at Hotel Christine," she said.

She made me laugh, as I realized her vacation made for Saturday every day, and she used me for maximum return. I didn't mind. It was what I'd wanted, and she seemed blessed, on the flip side of youth, ready to face life beyond the parlor.

I no longer thought of leaving as an escape but rather felt curious to see things play out at the end of vacation time. I'd mentioned leaving, but it wasn't discussed. With improving relations and no talk of romance, I felt no pressure either way, and her indifference was like icing on cake, enticing but not too sweet.

So it was that every day was Saturday at Hotel Christine, until that certain Sunday. It began in the morning about ten, after four hours of sleep, much hash and wine. Up for a leak, I slew-footed down the low-lit hallway, trying to remember when I began groaning, and the hall mirror caught me, eye to eye.

"Look at you," it said.

Thinning hair matted flat, sprung sideways. Lines and bags, puffy skin and nasal crust from wine, smoke and soot. Squinting, I could see that time won't wait.

The mirror said: *No more youth. Love the simple pleasures. Nurses*

243

*know best. This woman gives more than you think or deserve or may
ever receive again. She's a catch of magnitude who will have you
happily ever after, even as the beast in the mirror grows old. She will go
anywhere with the aging satyr looking back at you. So?*

I pressed onward, down the hall for a possible record breaker that felt
like three minutes easy. A quick shower felt compulsory to clean residue
and refurbish color. Nobody looks as good as before, but cleaning and
grooming help with dignity, if not composure.

Back in the sack, Christine waited, her sleepy smile an invitation
for further revenge on the spirits too long haunting. I crawled in with
caution. We'd been twenty-four hours without. "Mm," she moaned.
"Come here, please." She pulled me aboard for an eye-opener with no
mood, no headache, no menstrual onset or worry for the children. We
could get an *au paire*, but not a young one. We could discuss logistics
later.

Slowly hosing this mysterious, elusive woman, undulating into the
oasis for another rest, I murmured, "Christine."

She said nothing for a while, until murmuring, "Yes."

"I'm going to make a phone call this morning."

"How does your phone call affect me?"

"I have to call Hattie."

"Hattie is your…girlfriend?"

"Yes. I'm scheduled to call her this morning."

"Then call her."

This was my cue for disclaimer, something like: *I'm staying here, if
I may.* Or the other: *I'm leaving. I need to be with her.* But the lines got
stuck. I wanted Christine for her wisdom to see herself and me, and for
what we shared.

She said, "Go. Make your call. Use the payphone on the corner. You can have privacy there." She stared like a corpse again, eyes open on affirmation of what men do.

I could have said I'd be right back, this will only take a minute, or I love you. But a messy bed in emotional undertow was best left unmade. So I said nothing, pulling on my pants and heading out and down to the corner, to the payphone.

XXXII

Hattie, My Love?

Life under blue skies and sunshine felt invigorating, not so much free of the bind, except for maybe a bit. I was smarter than the dog who dropped his bone in the creek, reaching for the younger, juicier bone reflected there. Or maybe I hadn't yet heard the splash.

A few bums smoked hash and shared a bottle in an alcove near the payphone, a scene for a postcard: Amsterdam, where youth can play out at any age.

I called to clarify. In a few minutes, I would be clear, with a beautiful nurse for company. Hattie lingered, her vigor and spirit still a tease and a taunt.

The filthy little earpiece sounded faint. "Hello."

"Seven days," I said.

"I know."

"It's been quite a week," I said.

"I know."

"What else do you know?"

"Not much."

"How's Pinocchio? Signs of life?"

"You don't want to know."

She sighed in disappointment or gratitude, either way okay. I felt free. "You're probably right," I said.

"Don't start," she said.

"No. I don't want to start."

"Are we on?"

"On what?" Could she play me so loosely?

She asked, "What do you think?"

"Where?"

"Where would you pick?"

I nearly said Amsterdam, which would have been fun, once upon a time. "Where would I pick?" I asked back. "Where would you pick? Wait. Let me guess. I think you'd pick Paris."

"You're so smart."

"And patient. Don't forget patient."

"Where are you?"

"Amsterdam."

"You went there without me? I wanted to go there!" She whined like a child, spoiled. I felt better, based on fact: She was a child, and we were off, as in not on. How could silly talk compare to what I'd just left? A reunion with Hattie would support continuing youth for her and dislocated adulthood for me—make that more stupidity for her and a burden for me.

She wound down on tiresome chatter of mundane events. I thought we shouldn't meet just yet and would likely meet again anyway, back home, and that would be nice. She came on with a plea to meet, yes, soon, in Paris. We should meet in Paris for more fun and adventure. "We missed so much," she said.

"Life is a compromise," I told her, so cool that I felt the chill.

"I miss you. That's all."

"I'm grateful. That's plenty."

"Do you miss me?"

"Isn't that one of those…questions? Don't worry about that stuff." I felt heady and reckless, getting even.

She matched my cool and got smarter. "The road does you good. I can't help it. I miss you."

"I couldn't help it either. Loneliness gets you down, until you find a friend."

"You could find a friend and still miss me. It's easy. Once you get rid of the sex edge, then it's fun to miss someone."

Oh, these kids today. "Okay. I missed you. I found a woman. It doesn't work out that simply for me." Her silence signaled a direct hit.

"What didn't work out?"

"Nothing. That's what makes it complicated. You know I never had Pinocchio's problem."

"No. You have the opposite problem."

"You never complained."

"Would it have helped?"

"Maybe not. Anyway, I'm sure it's a character defect and with luck will burden me to old age. At least I can help those in need from time to time. This woman is beautiful but mental because her husband left, and she hasn't been laid in over a year."

"How beautiful could she be?"

"Yes. She's most likely a troll, but I'm so horny. In any event I can't roll in the hay six days straight and think, Oh gee, that Hattie, what a swell kid. I sure do miss her, well, gee, maybe I'll see her next week. That's what doesn't work for me. I mean it didn't work for me. It's not so simple."

The next silence signaled direct hits on other key installations, heart and soul. What did she expect, diplomacy? Had she not varnished Pinocchio's dowel rod all week?

"Six days?"

She left me no choice but to follow up with infantry and storm the capital. "Does that seem like a long time?"

"Six days?"

"Hattie, you've been down south for weeks!"

"Not...fucking!"

"Who's keeping score? You just told me to find a woman. What did you have in mind, tiddlywinks?"

"Do you love her?"

"In my way."

"That means no." Score one for the anti-aircraft flak, but it was only a lucky hit. "Is she beautiful and smart?"

"Yes."

"Oh, God...."

"This isn't like you. Would you feel better if she was plain and dull?"

"Yes." Crying over the hung-over, bleary-eyed goat in the mirror, she allowed insight, that victory is illusory, and so is defeat. "I want to meet you. In Paris. I want to...."

"I don't know. I…."

"Tomorrow," she said. "Tomorrow afternoon. Hotel de la Paix. I'll make a reservation. Say around five."

"Why tomorrow?" I asked. Christine had another two weeks.

"Why not tomorrow?" She asked back. An early break would give Christine time to recover and adapt.

"What's wrong with you? You sound…off."

"Or maybe I'm on. I love you," she said. "I know that now."

"Can it wait? I have to pack and get a ticket and…all that." And farewell with Christine, in which parting would burn the bridge.

"That's why I said tomorrow. I may go today and wait."

"Relax. I'll see you tomorrow." Maybe I could tell Christine it was an errand, and I'd be back."

"I hug you."

"Yes. Same here. See you tomorrow."

"Okay," she said, like a child with a skinned knee, in a need of kiss to make it all better.

Christine needed no telling, and no words could help. She sat in a funk. I wanted to be straightforward but got stuck in the same confusion. She smiled lamely and helped gather my things. I told her I could leave now or tomorrow, that I was flying home to the U.S., alone. The lies came quick and easy, and that was good, to spare the pain and wrath.

She knew. She appreciated the truth. I could stay another night, though she'd be away for two days, so this would be farewell. She laughed.

I didn't think she'd had a phone call of her own but had planned a retreat to snug harbor, for perspective. Again, she'd gained strength. She would have taken hours to assess only a few days ago, but she'd learned to trust her instinct, herself....

So she'd called a very nice man who had, you know, shown an interest for quite some time....

What?

She didn't want anyone to think a sexual merry-go-round would be good to try, especially herself. "But I should do something. I let myself get so...dependent. I like this man. He's nicer than you, not as daring but much easier to, you know, spend time with. We may be well suited. Who's to know? And I would like a companion for a while. I don't think I could love him, but I want to let myself down with a little kindness. I know all men like those things you made me do. So why shouldn't a nice man get to try those things too?"

"I made you do?"

"I don't mind that you can't love me. You've been good to me. I daresay you're good for me. You've proven that."

"You took care of me, too."

She stepped close to assure that it wasn't the sex. It was getting things sorted. She hadn't talked things over with an adult in a long time, and I did say funny things now and then, and she felt grateful for that too.

"I'm leaving to tend my property," I said. "I'd like to come back. I'd like to stay...."

"It's your spirit," she said, blushing deeply, as if she'd said, *Thank you for killing my inhibition.* "Your spirit is strong. I should have felt it at the beginning. I have never known a man so focused on what he wants. You taught me something. I'm glad you won the battle. I won't forget your lesson."

"I never fought a battle. I wanted you for your beauty and your giving," I said. "You taught me a thing or two."

"Please. Now I know something of taking. That's what I need."

"I'm a bullshitter with finesse. That's all." I drew her near and caressed her.

She took my face in her hands. "Yes," she said. "You are full of the shit. But I feel better. I have pain in my heart, and strength. I'm better prepared to go on."

"Going on was never in doubt, was it?"

She nodded and grew tearful. "I didn't know what to do."

I matched her nod. "Now you do?"

"I really must go."

Go where? Our eyes implored, as loss in life unfolded, as Christine stepped back.

"Yes," I allowed. "Yes, go. We must."

XXXIII

Seven in One Blow

The long ride south matched the long haul north for grit, bad air and overpop, shading prospects for a better tomorrow, or a break-even tomorrow. This train was bound for new scenery, what a wayward man wants most. A destination lured me in. Anticipation can be elixir, and I thought of Paris in the best of times, with Hattie coming on. A little hash didn't hurt.

Nor did it help, when this reunion with Hattie lost meaning in the fog. We had fun, sharing a playful spirit, our needs well met, including those of her favorite stand-up comic, Dick Johnson. Yet, in spite of all, insight struck, like when Alec Guinness saw his error in The Bridge on the River Kwai and asked, as he fell on the plunger, "What have I done?" A generation younger than Christine, Hattie lacked classic beauty or classic anything. We were off, a mismatch, a nonstarter, though we began long ago.

Doubt grew on small provocation. I'd longed to be free of constraint all week, more or less, yet the week proved fulfilling—more so than any fantasy. Stoned again under blue skies, headed to rendezvous with a dazzling young woman, I wondered why. Hash undermines wits, but something else seemed amiss, and I sensed the miss was mine.

The sorting process got skewed. Hattie at thirty, a few years out but not so far away, could be screaming at the children to clean up this fucking mess. And someone better bring the groceries in from minivan before it overheats, because the engine is running so the air-conditioner can keep the ice cream from melting!

We could avoid the minivan scene with seating for seven. Hattie could hit thirty-five with a career, tracking to management, talking the talk in a power suit and heels and lip-gloss to highlight potential.

She could be fat by forty and love me more for staying. I'd be sixty but fit. We could play tennis or croquet, over drinks and a bit more hash.

The difference between Hattie and Christine, beyond their ages of twenty-two and forty-four, was that Christine had delineated, more or less rounding the clubhouse turn and into the stretch. An hour out, I looked back with regret.

Hattie would level out soon enough. She too would delineate to the person she would be, one way or another. We might have fun for a long time….

For no discernible reason, Randy Basset came to mind. He was so crazy for fun, it was no fun at all. As a social carnivore, Randy was on the prowl all the time. He had a problem of manners and etiquette, much different than me.

Randy came on like pup, disarming, whining, misunderstood and treated unfairly. The sad set up led to the bold move. Money and women were bread and wine for Randy, and for these, thy bounty, he gave thanks.

It had been years, but his half smile underscored resignation in life on that long ride south. A low brow/low rent fellow by design, Randy was often funny for the effort, like when he slumped on a barstool, gazing at his drink, his crystal ball. He shared his visions. We laughed. Randy sold timeshare—a piece o' Paradise for only fifteen grand. The piece was a file memo, showing name and address of a wife and man who agreed to pay maintenance fees forever. If eyeballs rolled, Randy cajoled, "The fuck! You own it! What are you gonna do? Not take care of it? Yer the king and queen!" He avoided the gold-nugget accessories common to timedogs, choosing the more natural approach to separating fools from their money.

Looking up from his drink one evening, Randy grinned and said, "I got this idea. I bet I can fuck seven different women on seven days in a row."

I laughed. "Who will you bet?"

"Maybe you'll bet me. It doesn't matter. If you don't make goals, you're just another fucking stiff."

"Okay."

He nodded. "A different one every day. It's like a…a dream."

"A wet dream."

"You wouldn't like it?"

"You want to have seven women, one a day?"

"I do. You wouldn't?"

"Depends. Do you have the same fantasy on timeshare? Selling seven weeks to seven suckers, one a day?"

"Yeah. But it's not the same." We drank. "You got no romance in timeshare." I laughed. "I make friends, but... I got this worked out with women I like."

"Anyone I know?"

"Sure. I gotta count Louise. That's fair." Louise, his second wife, was shrill. They shared no peace.

"Who else?"

"I been getting it regular, running threes and fours any week I want." Threes and fours could mean women or weeks of timeshare. Either could restore purpose. "Let's face it, you need both, but money is for rent and groceries, and pussy is something else."

Randy's timeshare "resort" was twenty-six so-so condos with brown carpet and cheap rattan, straw baskets stapled to the walls and tropical place mats. Across the road was the "fantastic ocean view." Most buyers had never known such elegance and respect.

Randy made a grand on each extraction and twice got to fuck the wife, after the husband passed out on the sofa. It was vacation time after all, and Randy brought the rum and commiserated with the wives, rubbing shoulders to ease the strain.

Signing documents in the morning was all business and good cheer. What could she do, blow the whistle? Randy's future looked solid on a thousand weeks of inventory.

Seducible married women were rare, but he scored better on singles who agreed to "a few minutes of your time to look at our program here at Paradise Villas." Closure was short odds from there. "You gotta get 'um drunk. And you gotta have attitude."

Simone with the heavenly rack was a looker with a twang, from Lawus Ayunjellus via Noo Yawk. Randy got her drunk and called her worthwhile.

"How did you suggest the…romance?"

"Attitude." He drank. "I rested my dick on her shoulder."

"You can get arrested for that."

Randy laughed, "I didn't. She sent me a postcard. She's coming back week after next."

"That's two?"

"Yeah. I had four already. I got that gal we use at the club." He meant the beach floozy on at the "resort," who didn't mind fucking the week's "top producer" for fifty bucks, because we're all in this together. Not all the timedogs pitched in. The women refused, but the guys kept it going with attitude, one more time.

"What if you're not high man in two weeks?"

"Fuck it. I'll give her fifty bucks."

"That won't count."

"Says who?"

"Who couldn't go out and buy seven women?" I felt cruel, throwing a flag on what he saw as a beautiful play.

He recovered nicely. "No sweat. She owes me. I'll set it up. You're right. No money. And no fatties."

"She's not fat?"

"No. She looks good. Couple six packs. Low light."

"That's three."

"That's six."

"Who are the other four?"

Randy loved a challenge. One was Malta, his irregular squeeze. They drank and talked. I allowed Malta. She was female.

Then came Marilyn the vamp, nipped, tucked and injected. Marilyn flaunted the goods with spike pumps, a deep reveal, eyeliner, lip-gloss, red claws, gemstones and sass to back it up. She'd carved a niche, chumming with the wife while hubbie ogled. She let Randy in and gave him free range, until the ultimatum: Leave that scrawny bitch, Louise, or get no more sweets.

Poor Randy. She wasn't the hot tamale of twenty years ago or forty. He would not leave Louise on a lark, unless... "I called her. Told her it was over, Louise and me, and we ought to get a drink. She said sure."

"Did you pencil her in?"

"Monday. I gotta get her early in the week, you know, while I'm fresh. Besides that, she catches on. She could ruin the whole thing."

"Monday night? You'll miss football."

"Nah! We'll watch at her place."

"Before or after?"

"Halftime. Orchestration is my specialty. You know that."

"Sorry. I forgot."

"It's amazing." Randy basked. The clerk at the liquor store down from the resort would be sixth on the hit parade. "We talk. She's thirty-two. Just got rid of her boyfriend. He's a bum. She's nice, said she'd get drunk with me."

"Wild card. If she's not in the bag, you can't count her."

"I never said this would be easy." He tallied on a bar napkin and grinned. "I got to fuck Diane today."

"Who is Diane?"

"From the escrow office. She's an exercise nut, forty-five or so. You could fit her ass in two hands." He held his palms up. "Nice rack. Little waist. Good legs. You ever notice how older women go for me? She's a cunt. But I'm down there today, and she asks if I got an hour. I said sure, and she says, 'My place?' It was strange, driving to her place, not talking, walking in, taking our clothes off and getting it on. She's not soft anywhere. Tits like flint. I lick a nipple and she stares at me. It was…off. I asked her, what the fuck?"

"Unusual question for a guy like you," I said.

"Yeah. She says, 'I'm horny.' I told her that's why God invented dildos. She says, 'That's why God invented you.' That's all she wanted, slow, medium, fast. Get dressed, go back to work. Three years I wanted her. It was terrible."

"It was disrespect and exploitation."

"I didn't even ask for a blowjob. Wasn't in the mood."

"Ah, well."

"Yeah."

We drank. "Gee, Randy. You're a sensitive guy after all." He shrugged. "You're not counting Diane, are you?"

"Yeah. It's a long shot. I'm gonna tell her I'm sensitive, and she hurt my feelings, so cold. I'm gonna tell her I want to fuck again, but nice."

"Ah, nice! You are a specialist."

"Orchestration and attitude."

"Man, a whole week of different women." I wished him well once again, as golden fields flew by, Dunkirk, Le Havre, Rouen. Steel spikes clicked like a metronome on distance closing and on me, closing on myself. Hattie and wine would uplift. I opened the window on a buffeting breeze. College kids sprawled everywhere looked free at last, sleeping or smoking, but I didn't care.

XXXIV

Transmigration

 Randy Basset said he could run threes and fours any time, but the audit showed iffy threes that counted his wife two Sundays in a row after football, before 60 Minutes. The sporadic squeeze was a sure shot Tuesday afternoons, when the wife got her hair and nails done, and the in-house slut was good for convenience whenever. "I'm telling you, she's a luxury. Much better than jogging. And it's good for sales." Potential changed on the odd fuck from escrow and a postcard from LA. Randy smelled victory.

Life had evolved, no longer a scramble of basic needs and liquor. This was sport! He beat back excuses for a living, to reach any summit with attitude. Seven scores on seven days felt like playoff action, and Randy was in it to win it. The liquor store clerk felt likely. Marilyn, the retread vamp, would seal the deal.

"What happens if you win?" He grinned, pleased with a winning question. "What next?" Squinting at the big picture, Randy saw himself on the lone prairie with his Marlborough Lights, a bottle of rum and some grateful snatch he'd rescued on the trail. I ventured, "How about fourteen? Two sevens make fourteen, but no repeats would be better. Don't you think?"

He plucked a fag for a butt light, for emphasis, and inhaled on life itself. With a headshake for his sorry friend, he said, "You're negative. Anybody ever tell you? What about a twenty-one? And what's wrong with a guy trying to up his game? You got a bad attitude, Harry." He called me Harry in critical moments. On another deep drag, he gathered his things. Downing his drink, he said, "Take a look at yourself. You better learn to enjoy life, Harry. This is it. You're gonna be dead a long time." And he left.

Randy was never easy company, with the liquor, the smokes, the resentment and greed. I'd provoked him, challenging his meager, petty drive. He'd anticipated a cheering section, like I'd stand by with fresh drinks and smokes as he fucked his way to the podium. Maybe I'd arrange a tickertape parade. I came up short.

He had a point, a small point in a small life. Sport, pussy and liquor summed it up for Randy. He wanted to score on the big board. Somebody told him he'd be dead a long time, and it sunk in.

I saw him on the weekend. No hard feelings. He grinned, bygones be gone, to his credit. "Are you taking vitamins?" No, but he'd cut back to a pack a day and jogged down the street to get in shape. I told him his weak link was Louise, the wife, who could deny him on any given Sunday.

He nodded. He knew. We were friends again. He loved commiseration and planning.

"So?"

He'd bought her a diamond, which wasn't like paying for it. It wasn't a real diamond, but it looked real and should do the trick. I agreed that a rhinestone for the wife is not the same as paying for a whore. He nodded, validated.

The next week, he ran neither a four nor a three, much less a seven. He scored one, a happy one, rather than the solitary one he feared. Coming up short, his claimed victory at the buzzer.

That is, Louise asked what he paid for the fake diamond, which did not do the trick. He said a grand, but she rifled his wallet and found the receipt for forty dollars. "Like forty bucks is nothing." At least he campaigned the wife on Sunday. She failed, leaving the whole week to recruit a substitute for the back end, so to speak, or rework the wife or something.

But odds shrank again on Monday. The in-house slut was contagious. He said he could use a rubber, but she declined. "Honey. It ain't nice." Never mind; she'd have a week to get well, six days anyway, five minimum.

The attractive woman from LA canceled her trip. Nothing remained but to score where possible and hope for a miracle.

Marilyn, the old fuck, ran into Louise on Wednesday and said too bad about the separation. Louise said take him, please, but don't believe him. He'd never walk out on half of everything. Touché. Marilyn canceled cocktails. Randy needed to get laid by mid-week, on principle.

His regular squeeze got a boyfriend and wasn't fucking around for a while. The workweek ended with the liquor store clerk threatening to call the cops, even before he had a chance to lay his dick on her shoulder.

In the end it was only flint-hard Diane from escrow who helped out, Saturday night. As the long shot to win, she said she'd wanted to fuck him too and held back, but he was the best fuck ever, and now they were on. "Every day she wants it, noon to one, and she got nice. God, what she does." He liked her and thought his campaign was a success. Life was good.

"Sounds like a romance." I laughed at his grim view. He took it as approval. And how were sales?

"Top producer this week." He felt his prime coming back.

Stunted wheat flowed by for miles and hours, breaking for a poor village or a crumbling shack. The world looked spent, gray and forlorn. I thought Randy wrong but missed him for a few miles, a few drinks and laughs. Two hours down, three to go.

The old woman who lived in a shoe with so many kids she didn't know what to do stood in a dirt road, still as tumbleweed at high noon. The kids stared at the train, the world, passing them by.

I headed to the club car, wondering if Randy could sell some timeshare to the old woman who lived in a shoe. "You like vacations. You need vacations." I could see him at his worksheet with his rum, proving the amazing sense of the thing.

A woman of a different cut leaned on the bar.

I ordered a beer. She turned my way. Randy whispered, Move, fool! I smiled. She walked away, leaving me to fan my dewlap alone. I felt warmly indifferent. Christine's gift would linger, but I hit the WC to check for strays, to stoke a bowl and sing for the fun of it, "Oh, no, they can't take this away from me."

Gare du Nord near *Le Bastille* is striking in grandeur and grit, its ashen, wayward crowd a stream of humanity in apparent chaos, on schedule. Lost and found, they come and go. Cosmopolitan elite mix with the bums and kids, some gazing in realization of how far they've come, others wondering where next.

A small hotel in Paris felt like a monument to sameness. Generations of work had maintained standards here, minimal but stable, along with shelter for the owner, his daughters who cleaned the rooms and his tired wife. Arterial sclerosis felt like a pulsate in this life of pâté, cheese and wine.

"Ah, tien!" the old man said happily, his faith renewed on my return. He seemed validated, his purpose proven. He didn't mind getting up from a table of rich, fatty foods and a quart of wine. The wife and daughters, alert and colorful but shy, affirmed the truth among them, that checking out at sixty would be better than seventy, if such food and drink could make a drab life happy.

I offered to come back after lunch."*Je reviendrai après le déjeuner.*" "*Non non! Pas du tout! Ce n'est rien!*" He lowered his sandwich, dabbed his chin, removed his bib and reached for the registration papers. His sandwich nearly throbbed, a meaty challenge with slaw between hunks of bread, dripping mayo. A bowl of fries sat beside a carafe of wine in pink. He filled in the blanks, remembering my name and nation.

Three daughters stole glances and tittered in a blush and light sweat. I wanted to drink pink wine with them. I wanted to sleep in the barn on a promise.

I got a room and sat on the floor. My wait would be a meditation of sorts, to open mind and heart on this new phase of learning and love. In a few hours the hotel, the streets and foul air were not so bad as they'd been. That's what love will do for an outlook, or was it solitude and fatigue that helped me along? I rose to the bed. Surely it was me, adapting to what had not changed. Randy was right, in his way, about dead a long time. I'd come to terms with a few things, or at any rate endured. I didn't care about time but could do with some peace of mind. I saw the value of well fed and pleasantly drunk. I felt good, better than in a long time. I felt arrived in Paris. Ah, attitude.

The sea change was not merely practical but a gift of omniscience, of knowing beyond logic. On instinct, I sensed contentment. I thought Hattie would not come. Where was she? Somewhere else, a shadow at dusk, a dream coming into form.

She arrived in a blush, pausing in the door to arc her voltage to my own, to mark the moment of fact. She closed the gap slowly, not hugging or touching but shrinking the space between us to naught. She breathed in my ear.

Eyelashes fluttered on my cheek and a sigh on my neck eased us in. Like dew at sunrise, we sparkled. A balm flowed over. "I want us to be married," she whispered.

What? Married? This was my fancy and my fear, as the words resounded in the hearts beating together. "You mean like Elm Street? With kids and a station wagon?"

"No. We'll live at your house."

I had dreamed of Hattie at sixty-five. She looked good but sounded the same, young, impetuous, uncertain. Not that a dream can be trusted. Nobody takes money home from a dream. But the essence of a thing has value, spendable, investment grade value. Is not love part of essence? What's the difference between twenty-two or sixty-five? A few lifetimes is what, so we drifted.

We'd met again in the Paris we set out for, in a frame of mind more available down the road. We'd arrived to where very little mattered and shared the small death, le petit mort, what the French feel most after sex, when a person can easily let go.

This was different, on a bigger scale, maybe Le Grandeur at last, in a cheap cubicle at dusk with traffic below and visions of my mate as an old woman. I laughed—I'd be eighty-five, so some vintage squish might be nice.

I never feared solitude. I feared the ball-and-chain. How can anyone be alone in a world of so many billions? Yet as my spirit yearned, she drew me home.

All this in a sweet embrace? Yes, logic came and went in a blink. Affirmation rang like Notre Dame. Questions melted like Camembert. "What about the hunger?" I asked. She smiled ruefully, as if the hunger would be our burden to share.

"Lean and hungry is best," she said.

"What about last week?"

She took my hand and sat me on the bed. "It was nothing. I was foolish. I know more now."

"In a week, because Claudio couldn't get it up?"

"He got it up. I want to tell you, so you know. He got it up like a champ. But he wasn't you. It was like you say, about scent and feel. We had no chemistry. He was a nice guy; that's all. He was in love, I think. He wasn't a pussy hound, not like you."

"He didn't want you to leave?"

"Of course not." We hung our heads.

"Must've been good for him, anyway."

"It wasn't sexual. He couldn't get it up for a year and didn't know why but kept trying and wouldn't give himself a break."

"What break did you give him?"

"Just what you taught me."

Oh, God.

She shrugged. "Let it go. He couldn't get it up. I said okay, so what. No big deal. I liked the guy. He was fun. In a few days, he let it go and got it up."

"Could you see a pulse in it?"

"Hey. We fucked. Okay?"

"Yeah, fine. No problem here. I'm curious. Here's a guy, a pet project, kind of, and you like him, and he can't get it up. So you're counseling, and it works. He gets it up, and you're happy for him and you fuck him like a good nurse… Why couldn't you love him? You felt an attraction."

"I'm attracted to more guys than you'd imagine. This one too. He was beautiful."

"So?"

"I lied."

"You did love him?"

"No. I could have loved him. But he couldn't keep it up. Where can you go with that?"

"Oh, great." I was up. "You figured out that you love me because I can keep it up."

"Don't sell yourself short."

"Right. I smell good. I keep it up. What else?"

"Chemistry. We have chemistry. That's most important. You know, we harmonize."

She had me there, and she moved in. "It's not like you didn't get laid. It's not like your eyes don't turn for every skirt. Every tight skirt anyway. At least my guy was real."

"Your guy was real?"

"What was she like?"

I laughed. "She couldn't get it up." Hattie wasn't amused. "Serious. Good-looking, divorced, a nurse, on vacation." I shrugged.

"Why didn't you love her?"

"I did, in my way. She was troubled, leaving us very little but the bone to gnaw on. Woof."

"Yeah. I know. But you're not like that. You could get women like that, but you don't. It was more. I know it was."

I could? I shrugged again. "I'm not sure what you know. Call it coincidence. We met, had dinner, got stoned and fucked. It does seem coincidental that she needed help too."

"Yeah, the world goes coincidental more often these days."

I loved when she talked like that, taking a simple idea to global context. What a girl. I mean woman.

She asked, "How did you meet?"

"In the hospital. She was my nurse."

"You were in the hospital?"

"Yeah. I got stabbed." I pulled my shirt up to show the wound. As she went to horrid concern, I told how skillfully I'd handled my assailant, profiling simple efficiency.

She nearly swooned, feeling the wound and kissing it. "God. I'm a sicko. This turns me on."

"You mean now?"

She disrobed quickly sans sensual tease but with confidence. She was twenty-two. She could arouse a man, impotent guinea to aging satyr. "Sure. Why not?" Nakedly candid in twelve seconds flat, she said. "We should get it out of the way so we can relax."

I sat on the bed. She stepped up, pulled my head to her stomach and held me. "I want it slow," she said.

"Okay. I'll try to get it right." I meandered like a slug in molasses. She whimpered and cried, tears of relief, I thought.

"Are we in love?" she asked.

"You tell me."

"I think you don't have it in you. We both know it, and I'm willing to have you anyway."

"You'll tire of me. I have it. In me. But I'll get old."

Tears became sobs, and joining the beast she saw in me, we strode for the finish. The dam burst in a deluge, receding forthwith to whimpers, high and dry. She said she would always come back to me. It sounded like faint assurance.

"You want to be married but still fuck around now and then?"

"Not if you…go slow and pay attention."

"Go slow and pay attention," I repeated, touching the nerve as she had done. I went slowly with Christine, with patience and love. I granted Hattie her *cum laude* in love. Self-esteem helped her connect, inside and out, and a minute more helped the bond.

Still as two stiffs, resting in peace, we envisioned life and what we could make of it.

XXXV

Wine Time

We woke up, got dressed and left the hotel in silence, stepping intimately into a Paris night.

She led down the Metro steps to a long tunnel and a platform, where we boarded and clackety-clacked, to another maze. "Some people spend part of life down here," I said.

"It's so easy," she said.

People hurried, heads bent, surviving. "Mole people," I said. She let it pass. "What would they think of my place?"

"Anything is possible here."

"Maybe not anything,"

"What do you want?"

"Clean air. Countryside."

"Why are you here? Look. The floor is a foot higher in the center. Flood control I'd bet." Around a curve came another long walk to a long flight up.

"Must get funky in a flood. Brings the rats out. Back-strokers, dog-paddlers. Frog-kickers."

She laughed, "You are a bumpkin."

"Rapids, falls." We slogged up and out to the city. Evening pace was less urgent, more social, drinking, smoking and talking things over yet again. We ducked in at random. I wanted wine. She went along.

A tall man came through in baggy pants, clinging T and curly locks in a swing and bounce to complete the vogue image.

"Salt o' the earth with a fashion flair," I said.

She smirked.

"Artifice, made-up in a mirror, a pose, compensatory."

She wagged her head. "Tanning lamp and a curling iron," I said. He paused to blink his big, dark eyes, to see what effect his little show might work. "Eye shadow and liner," I said. She looked him over. "What do you think?"

"He's a good looking guy all right."

"Self-conscious to the point of silly," I said. "Do you think he's impotent?"

"Why should I?"

I shrugged. "You've known a few." She stared at me. "Do you think your experience with impotence is unusual?"

"No."

"You think that many guys can't get it up?"

"How many?"

"You mean as a percentage of your experience?"

"It's not that high. I haven't been with so many men. Some went to the other extreme, you know." Touché. She drew blood at will but took my hand and asked. "Has anything changed?"

274

"I think so."

"What?"

"Life."

"Does life change like the next page of a script? Can you edit for clarity and flow?"

"Jesus," I said, wondering where and how. "I don't know. How do you see it playing out?"

"I don't know too, except for the age difference. You're scripted. I'm editing."

"Were you suggesting marriage right away?"

"Tonight? How could we?"

"They must have a Vegas-style wedding service in Paris."

She laughed. "There's a narrative I hadn't thought of." We ordered again, pondering life or eternity, whichever came first. "Tell me about yourself," she said.

"What don't you know?"

"Your childhood."

"Nothing left but a few pictures." I drank. "All I wanted was Saturday and summer. I hiked out with my dog. My mother put our lunch in a sack. I took my bow and arrow. I shot at a black snake once and missed. Still makes me shudder. I got good at targets though. It was all green then, never before seen by white people. Now it's gone."

"You were antisocial even then," she said.

"Not necessarily. Fewer people then. My problem came later, when population doubled."

"Your problem manifested later. It was there all along."

"Manifested?"

"I hate it when you do that," she said.

"Do what?"

"What was your dog's name?"

"Otto. He was me. Alter ego. He ran alongside on my paper route, afternoons and Sunday morning, up at four. We sold seeds and cards door-to-door. We walked to the bus. In the afternoon, he waited at the bus stop. We were inseparable, except for school. What a waste. What a fun guy. You would have loved him."

"A boy and his dog."

"That's a simplification."

"Simplification?"

"He was a complex personality. I told him things. He counseled me."

"What did he tell you?"

"What a kid needs to hear, that we have each other and more fun than we'll ever get to. And here's another day of it."

"Did you tell him you loved him?"

"I did, but didn't need to. Dogs get vibes."

"I have an idea!" She reached for my member and rubbed it, turning to find a waiter, waving with her free hand, sweeping a wineglass. It toppled, breaking, spilling onto my crotch.

XXXVI

Paris Arrival

Truth barged in, love narc with a warrant, yanking me up by the shirt. I woke in a sweat, heart pounding. That wasn't a wet dream in the traditional sense, but Paris is unique. Wine spilled on my crotch was tepid pecker juice. Hattie had turned with an idea.

Her idea was to vanish, poof and gone. I sat up in the dark. Was this scene scripted or edited?

Precipitation from a dream condensed like a temperature gradient on an ethereal plane—like fog on glass. We skivvies had gone cold. This wasn't living but could improve on a change.

She knew it wouldn't work and came to play it in a dream. We could have a bit of pain now or wait until later. Truth settled like sediment in the cave of my making. Otto died twenty-eight years ago but lingered with a pledge and a nudge. I got up for dry skivs. He made things work.

Ah, fuck. Some times shape up that way, like waking in a shitty little hotel room alone from a dream and love gone away. What a maestro I'd become, setting up a homecoming so lonely and far away. A few hours ago, the sun shone on something waiting up ahead. It might shine again tomorrow.

It was midnight or one, not time for more of a dream. So I splashed my face and got out, down the narrow stairs to the narrow street to night traffic, seekers smoking and talking.

At the first place down I took a table and looked up, pointing to a carafe of the cheap pink wine they swill by the quart. It came in jiff with a fresh glass, and I poured and drank as if putting out a fire. Thirst eased, moistened in a late rain. Limbs loosened, and I ordered another, until a stream flowed by the campfire. The first was good, the second better, not so much twang or recoil, and another nod was good for yet again.

I wanted removal. Wine was a ticket. This quantity required strength in thought, lest a downward spiral could spin, out of control. The waiter asked if I wanted another. He stared. I stared back. He left.

I would head home soon. I missed it. I felt drunk enough to leave Paris. But maybe not.

Fifi walked in and sat nearby. Ringlet curls framed her face and suited her figure, supple but not fat, in a short skirt. Her bright eyes flashed my way, sans the bitterness some women feel.

On scrutiny, she held up. French women don't mind a stare. She didn't smoke, and I wondered why not. I leaned across the empty table between us and said nothing, because I couldn't, because of the wine and other complexities of a momentous evening. *"Bonsoir, Monsieur,"* she said.

I felt my head shake and heard a string of words—"It was big circles, Otto and me. A sense of direction then, younger, and Otto, well, he was a dog after all. But I was good. Cover my eyes, turn me around. Roll me over. I'll get up and show you north. Not now. No, ma'am." I looked around for bearings and a grip on the fast forward life turns into. "I'm not so sure anymore."

"You are American," she said. "I do not speak so good English."

"Yes, you do."

"Slowly, please," she said.

"Yes, slowly."

"Why are you here?"

"I was stood up. How about you?"

"What is stood up?"

"My true love did not arrive. She wanted to marry me. She was young. Younger than you."

"And you are so old? I think you are not so old."

"You are kind," I said. She smiled. "I know where she is. She's in Italy with Pinocchio. He couldn't get it up. Then he couldn't keep it up."

"Very much is up with you."

"Yes. I think he promised her the villa. I don't know. Maybe he has a brother."

"You are sad?"

"Yes. Yes. Yes." I considered sadness as pink at room temperature and drank it down. "I am sad. Sad as I've ever been. Maybe not more than for Otto." She watched my eyes go puffy. I felt a tear roll.

She came to me and pulled my head to her bosom, a certain remedy. Sobs flowed, more like an aging drunk on another binge than a man of the world in personal crisis. She didn't judge but rocked and assured that I would find love. I thought I had, until she said, "My true love will arrive too. Here is Philippe." A skinny guy with thick glasses and a black pompadour stepped up, devoid of emotion, offering his hand.

"How do you do?"

"Ça va," I feebly responded, wiping my eyes and nose. "I am admiring Fifi from afar. Excuse *moi. Je suis* drunk."

"He is standing up," Fifi said.

"No, no." I stood up. "I've been stood up. My true love did not arrive." I wiped my face on a wobble and a sleeve.

"She will arrive," Philippe said. "In the meantime, we will catch you up. Is that correct? Catch you up?"

"You will catch up with me."

"Yes. It happens when we drink too much wine. And I am having thirst."

"Mm," I slumped back down. "You are a funny man, Philippe. I think you could be American."

"No, no. I am not that funny." He raised a finger and called in French with urgency. Two bottles arrived in short order, presumably the good stuff. Then came *hors d'oeuvres* out of the blue, hot and cold, sweet and sour, *avec les fromages et les baguettes*. Philippe served reasoning with repast. "It is good to drink when we have such sadness. It is good to eat when we drink so much. With friends is best."

So the night began and ended again. Wine drowns sorrow, but it lingers. Philippe set the pace. Fifi monitored the patient. They said nothing of my capacity for wine but kept up. Philippe nodded and said I drank well.

I said I drank poorly, evidenced by slurred speech and disconnection of body and mind. "Thoughts unravel and… The sadness."

Philippe said it does not matter, the slur or stumble or confusion. Only the drinking matters, to soak the depression—*le dépression*. Few

Americans understand that. "They say we have a problem in France. And we do, but we also have a…a…. What is the word?"

"Addiction."

"Ability. We have an ability that most Americans do not have. We can let everything fall away, *comme ça*."

"Yes. I know. Just look at this place." We laughed. "Le Grandeur!" I mocked him.

But he grinned and said, *"Oui! Tu comprends!"*

"Mes amis!" I saluted and drank to make my point or his or see his point and raise him another bottle.

"Juste!… Never mind," Philippe said.

I told them my mother made me wear baggy pants like Philippe's all through childhood, hand-me-downs from old uncles, pants that made me look like a refugee from a midget show. So my first piasters went over the counter for new pants with pegged legs, so tight they looked painted on. I had a big, wavy do like Philippe's but with more grease.

Philippe and Fifi watched and listened like I was matted and framed, and they would see meaning sooner or later. I got lost in the woods with my dog. "I don't know why I told you that. I forgot. But it was something, I think."

Philippe nodded, as if at a well delivered punch line. Topping us off, he said, "Excellent. Tell again."

I drank and shrugged. *"No màs.* You tell."

Philippe said once, as a boy, he went south to a little town on the coast, where a friend of his uncle's would take him sailing. I nodded for a good sailing story. Philippe said he had to peepee badly and couldn't wait for departure. So he went behind the harbor office, because France is a place of liberty, where grown men don't need four walls to make peepee.

Leaking his little lizard behind the office, he looked up to see a big man with a head like a giant onion watching from behind a bush. Little Philippe still had a way to go. The big man stepped out with his *trés grande coq* in hand, beating it madly, watching Philippe make peepee.

Philippe topped us off again and looked content. "And so?"

Fifi said, "I have heard this story. And so Philippe finish his peepee and go sailing."

Philippe grinned.

"Excellent story," I said.

Fifi said she worked in a dress shop, not a modern dress shop but for a woman who designed dresses in a very small shop in a narrow alley. Fifi was apprentice, a seamstress with her own designs. She sat up, showing one of her designs.

I topped us off and said, *"C'est formidable."*

She blushed and said, *"Tu est gentil, Monsieur."*

Philippe said Paris enjoyed decay, and that was good, because the spirit of decay co-exists with the spirit of freedom. "And equality and fraternity," I reminded.

He said yes, but it changed lately, because the spirit of decay had decayed. He could not explain this in English, but it was like, for example, the difference in pollution. "If you step in horseshit, you say, 'Ah, this is shit.' You say the same thing if you step in green chemical, but it is not the same. Horseshit cannot hurt you, really, but the green chemical can kill you into next year."

"Unless you eat the horseshit, or it contaminates your fruit juice. But I get your point. Nobody else sees this?"

"They do see. But money is decay."

I commiserated on greed and a world encrusted, and an adventurer facing crowds at every turn.

"Yes. You understand. We walk now. I know a place."

It was three or four. Most places were closed or closing, most locked and hosed down. We took alleys to other alleys. Philippe and Fifi felt like guides through an ashen forest after a fire. Philippe acknowledged night people who stood or lay in doorways. He gave them a look or a nod in unspoken French. We came to a dark and dirty place where people drank at tables or the bar or drank while dancing to a black salsa band. We drank and danced in dark corners and dim light, in the doorway and the hall.

We danced until no dance remained in us. We danced slow in a lean and stagger, until I sat to watch my mentors dance, hanging on to the hour and each other. How often could they pull out the stops and dance all night? How could Fifi design or sew tomorrow? How could Philippe study engineering? But the questions did not translate past my own pursuit and tomorrow.

We had arrived at the crossing, where tonight breaks on first light. Philippe bought a bottle and we left again, finding new vigor in sunrise and wine.

They would have taken me to my hotel, but I didn't know where it was and couldn't remember its name. So they took me home and gave me a sofa, a blanket and a pillow. We sat together for a minute to savor the stupor, apart from ourselves and our lives, until Philippe said, "Now you see, my friend, we have come to where we must live."

"Not so bad," I said, taking in the sparse Parisian flat. With windows at both ends, seventh floor and way back in the courtyard, it was breathable. Five strides from the kitchen to the bath and a WC with elbowroom made up for the low ceiling and centuries of sag. The chipped plaster and cracked glass, the low wattage, burnished grain and threadbare feel of the place seemed to fit. A person could sleep here, take a leak here, stretch out and sit for something to eat here. A man could live here, if he must.

"Not here," Philippe said. "Americanski. Here!" He clutched his heart with both hands. I pondered here, as he said, "A man from the United States comes to my school for the big speech, you know, engineers and the new world order and America. He speaks like we are fools. 'You have your whole lives ahead of you,' he says. I tell him it is not so. I tell him, 'Suddenly you are gasping for air. And it is over.'" Philippe grinned. "Could be today. So. It is here we must live. But, it is not so good that we are drunk all the time. So. Pay attention."

I waited, but Philippe was done. "I am paying, teacher."

Fifi said, "He means we are someplace else. We are drunk. He means this is our…ability. We have changed. Tomorrow we will wake up and maybe remember what we see here. That is why Philippe says to pay attention." Philippe nodded off and snored. Fifi roused him and led him away.

I lay down under a cover of spinning gratitude, dropped an arm off the sofa for contact with the floor. A body cast from lead sank deeper into the old French sofa, sank far beneath the cover as though taking root. The arm overboard gained weight too, like a limb of an Earl Izumi ironwood—Earl Izumi hung cinder blocks from ropes on ironwood limbs and left them for fifteen years, moving the ropes every year or three, until the normally straight trees and limbs looked like Uncle Wiggly, the ancient, decrepit rabbit who hobbled down the road bent nearly double with posture so warped, his crooked cane was three steps out front to support his horizontal upper half.

"This is bonsai," Earl said, and I smiled, as the cinder blocks gained weight, wrist, elbow, shoulder.

We sank to sweet dreams, where want, confusion, loss and love do not jumble but nestle, warm and still, until a dewdrop formed into a kiss, still and warm, familiar and just arrived from far away. Settling softly on my lips with happiness, here at last by magic in Philippe's and Fifi's flat, high up and way back in a Paris courtyard among the ironwoods, my true love had come.

"I was late," she whispered. "I told the old man I'm your wife. I waited in the room. You didn't come, so I went out. Now I've found you. I was late. My trip was delayed."

I dreamed of delay, of running in dream slag. "Delayed. Waylaid?"

"I quit smoking," she said.

"But you never smoked, really," I said.

"But I did. Now I don't. Don't you see?" she asked.

I wanted to see. "I hope I will, soon."

"I know you will. I wish I'd been here last night."

"Yes. It was fun. I was so out of it. I feel different now."

"I know. Philippe said you would feel different. I think Philippe will be best man, Fifi maid of honor. We'll honeymoon in Paris."

"You've met Fifi? And Philippe?" Light seeped in, glaring like a judge handing down a sentence: You must live. Another day is here.

Soft as a fairy godmother, Fifi said, "Philippe is gone. I must also go. Stay here until you feel well. Philippe will return after this noon. He will like to talk to you then, about what you saw. *Au revoir, mon ami.*"

Oui, au revoir.

Movement is slow and painful in a Paris flat, stark and compressed on a plaster-flecked and rickety morning. Walking recalls the Tin Man in summer rain, creaking his way back to another room in a little hotel on small hope. The old hotelkeeper nods sadly at my condition.

Bonjour Monsieur. Bonjour. Bonjour. Greetings effuse from him and the daughters. It changes to commiseration on hearing my pained and graveled voice ask if anyone came looking for me.

They shake their heads as one. *"Non. Non, non."*

"And no…calls?"

They shake again.

In the little room I lay again. A passing hour leads to standing again and packing for an exit.

A block down, a small transaction yields baggy blue pants, black shoes and white socks, exactly like the square threads Mother made me wear so many years ago. And a black T-shirt with long sleeves like Philippe's.

It isn't yet noon so there's plenty of time for an espresso and a smoke, for relaxing a while in new clothes that don't feel nearly as wrong as they once looked. Recovery is marginal but further along than an hour ago, and I sit, sipping, smoking, thinking things over like a French guy in a café.

About the Author

Robert Wintner has authored 15 novels, 3 memoirs, 3 story collections and 5 reef photo books. Whirlaway came out in 1994 and is presented here again, buffed and seasoned with the spices of life and love. Robert Wintner is the nom de plume of Snorkel Bob, Hawaii's biggest reef outfitter. He lives on Maui with his wife Anita, Cookie the dog, Rocky, Yoyo, Inez, Buck, Tootsie, and Coco the cats, and Elizabeth the chicken.